DUAL NATURE

ELIZABETH KNIGHT

CREATIVE WONDER PUBLISHING

Knight, Elizabeth

Dual Nature

Editing: Inked Imagination Author Services

Cover artist: Ruxandra Tudorica | Methyss Art

www.methyss-art.com

Formatting: Creative Wonder Publishing

ISBN: 979-8-88958-046-1 (print)

You are enough just as you are.

Don't ever change.

AUTHORS NOTE

Dear Readers,

Dual Nature is a book that contains quite a bit of darkness, that could be triggering to some people.

If you feel like this could be a problem for you, please protect yourself.

No work of fiction is worth your mental health.

Elizabeth Knight

The full list of content warnings is available on my website.

Link found here: https://www.elizabethknightbooks.com/omega-assassin

CONTENTS

ONE

FINLEY

As I moved through the crowded streets of downtown Seattle toward my destination, I shifted my black umbrella back to peer up at the sky. A chilly evening was descending as clouds passed overhead, shadowing the last rays of the sun's warm light. Now was the time that everyone was leaving work, and I used the flow of people to my advantage to remain unnoticed by street cameras. As always, I wore a wig and colored contacts to further detract from my usual appearance.

It had taken the past three days of scouting and preparation for me to decide on the best way to get into the apartment building. With various high-profile people living there, the security was tight—but I was better. I pulled my phone out of my pocket and looked at the image of the man I was going to kill. He wasn't much to look at—average, if you will—but he was the brains behind an up-and-coming tech company. I didn't know the specifics as to why someone wanted him dead, but they were willing to pay a lot of money to make it happen quickly. Truthfully, the only thing I cared about was completing the job I'd been given and seeing it through.

Putting my phone away and pulling on my sleek leather gloves, I headed straight over to the sliding glass door of the complex and walked right up to the lobby attendant. "Excuse me, I'm here to see Mr. Matthews. Do you mind calling up to let him know I'm here?"

I knew from her employee file that she was younger than me, her name was Abby, and she was new here. She'd only been on the job for two weeks, having just moved to the city. After watching her through the video tap I'd put in place a few days ago, I knew how badly she wanted to impress everyone here.

"Of course, may I have your name?" Abby asked as she dialed the phone.

"Amy Sanders. If he asks, I'm here with the papers from his lawyer, Mr. Tallister," I said, giving her a bright smile.

We both stood there as the phone rang and rang before going to voicemail.

"I'm sorry. It seems that Mr. Matthews isn't in at the moment," Abby apologized as she hung up.

I bit my lip and started to wring my hands, glancing around the room to make sure we were alone. "Look, I was supposed to be here an hour ago, but I got lost. I just moved here, and I've never lived in a city this big before. This is the first time my boss put me in charge of something this important. Do you think that you could let me up to his floor so I can slide the papers under his door? I wouldn't ask if it wasn't super important..." I begged, putting my hands together like I was praying and making sure I had my eyes wide. *Nothing like earnest helplessness to make someone give you what you want.*

As I pleaded, I could see Abby softening to me. With a sigh, she nodded her head and hit the button that opened the glass door to get to the elevators.

"Oh my god, girl, you are a lifesaver!" I gushed as I hustled over to the open door. "I won't be but ten minutes tops—well, unless I get lost again." I chuckled and gave a little wave.

Pressing the button for the elevator, I stepped in and selected the fourth floor. Once the doors opened again, I dropped my umbrella on the floor, preventing the doors from shutting all the way. This was the time-sensitive part. I hit the button for the remote shut-off I'd hooked up to the electrical system, cutting off all the power in the building. Calmly, I walked down the hall 'til I got to Mr. Matthews' apartment and slipped a manilla envelope under his door. It was important to maintain cover as long as you could. Should any questions be asked later, that envelope would help prove I'd actually come up there with a purpose.

With ten minutes left before the backup generator was triggered, I briskly marched to the end of the hall and took the stairs three more flights up to my true target's floor. His room being only two doors away from the stairs made it just so convenient for me to deal with matters.

With the power out, I didn't have to worry about the cameras or the fingerprint scanner, so I began to pick the back-up key lock to the front door, slipping in easily. I stealthily crept into the living room, closer to the source of the soft muttering that whispered through the quiet space. My target was sitting in his recliner, facing away from me, his dinner balanced on his lap. This was going to be easier than I thought. I stepped up behind him, a thin black case in one hand and a syringe in the other. With effortless practice, the syringe was in his neck, the plunger depressed and solution injected before he could even twitch. My gloved hands gently held him in the chair as he convulsed while the poison did its job, and once his pulse stuttered to a stop, I took a picture. Our client wanted proof of the job's completion as soon as it was done, which wasn't uncommon these days.

When you had vampires, werewolves, and other supernatural creatures to deal with, you could never be too careful. I knew this hit was human, but it only took one time of not being cautious to end up dead or turned. Once HQ sent back their confirmation of receipt, I left just as I had come, taking the stairs down to the fourth floor. Using my umbrella, I pried the doors open enough to slip in, then let them shut, locking me in the elevator.

The wig started to itch, and I desperately wanted to rip it off my head, but I knew it would blow my cover. If everything went according to plan, which it was so far, those cameras would be back on soon enough. Moments later, the power flickered back on, and I was able to descend back to the ground floor. Once the doors opened, I burst out, breath heaving as I wobbled out into the lobby.

"Please don't tell me you got stuck in the elevator!" Abby gasped, rushing up to me.

I let a fake sob out as my body shook. "Could this day get any worse?! Please don't tell anyone about this; how embarrassing to get trapped in the elevator because of a power outage."

"They're doing construction on the building next to us, and they must have done something to cause the power to go out. Oh, hun, I'm so sorry. Can I do anything? Call you a cab, maybe?" Abby asked, taking hold of my hand, her face full of concern.

Shaking my head, I gave her hand a squeeze. "No, I'm good. I think I need to get a drink and then get a cab home. Wine is the only thing that could make this day better."

"Girl, I feel you." Abby smiled, walking me to the door, and waved goodbye as I left.

Letting out a heavy sigh, I mentally shook off the last bit of my fake persona until I was back to my normal neutral personality. I had long since gotten over the rush of the kill, and now, that part was just the job. I enjoyed the strategy, the planning, and sometimes, when the person deserved it, I still got that thrill, but I had been a professional for a long time.

One bus ride later, I ditched the wig, shaking out my natural mahogany-colored hair. A few blocks later, I tossed the gloves in separate trash cans before I hailed a cab to bring me back to my hotel room. I had two hours before my flight back home to Wyoming—plenty of time to get that glass of wine for a job well done.

⸺◆⸺

I stretched and sighed, glad to be out of confined spaces. The flight was easy, but being crammed in with no personal space was my least favorite way to travel. The Organization never allowed us to fly first class unless it was an international flight, claiming it was to help keep us as discreet as possible, but with the money we took in on our hits, we could easily have a private jet charter us wherever we needed to go. Sure, it might be easier to trace the same private plane showing up in the cities where the dead people did, but at least we would be comfortable. On the other hand, it could just be another way to show how they ruled our lives and kept us in line without making a blatant show of force. The Organization liked to keep the leashes tight enough that we didn't forget someone held them.

Grabbing my carry-on from the driver, I strolled up to the entryway of Nature's Healing Wellness Retreat and Spa. What better way to cover up the sins that were committed by the people that lived here than to nurture the well-being of others? The property was littered with settlements of small homes filled with people seeking inner peace. Amongst them, nestled away right under their very noses, were fully trained assassins waiting for their next target. Such is the magic of yoga, cucumber water, and massages.

I headed right to the back of the main building where Margaret's office was. Our fearless leader would be awaiting my arrival, expecting to hear a full debriefing even though it was midnight. Without knocking, I opened the heavy wooden door and entered the warm, cozy office. It was a stark contradiction to the woman herself, but we all had to do our part to keep appearances up.

"Ah, Finley, you've returned," she said, not even looking up from her work. "Take a seat."

Margaret loved to make us wait; she always said it was an exercise in patience, and who could argue with a woman who had been in the industry for fifty years? I watched as she typed away at something on her computer, the picture of poise. Her short white hair was swept up and away from her face in an elegant style, and the steel-colored eyes behind her rimless glasses still held the fierceness needed for the job.

Having been with the Organization since I was five, Margaret was the closest thing I had to a mother figure. Being a hard taskmaster, she had in no way been motherly to any of us, but she'd made us the best—and isn't that what every mother wants for their kids?

Finished with her work, Margaret turned her attention to me, removing her glasses. "Things went smoothly on your end? The client was pleased with the speed you were able to accomplish things."

"Yes, ma'am, everything went without a hitch," I answered succinctly. "He hardly put up a struggle."

"What about the front desk girl? Do you feel certains she won't make the connection?"

Cocking my head to the side, I mentally reviewed the whole situation to be sure. "She will be far too shocked over the matter of a man dying in the building to put two and two together. It was on an entirely different floor from the one I requested access to."

Perching her chin on the back of her hand, she looked at me with an assessing gaze. Having come to some decision, she put her glasses back on and reached for a file, opening it and glancing at it before handing it to me. "Alright then, with that matter settled, this is your next assignment. I know you just got back, but this—this cannot wait."

Inside the folder was a picture of a stunning woman covered in silk and jewels. As I skimmed through the information, I discovered Delilah was a rich socialite in New York City. Her parents were old money, connected to the airline industry, and they funded whatever their youngest daughter's heart desired.

"What's not in that file is that this order has been handed to us by the United Senate. They want the job done in the next two weeks, or sooner if possible," Margaret shared, causing me to gape at her. "What, did you think the Organization had escaped their notice? How foolish. They allow us to function as long as we occasionally do favors for them. This will be one such favor."

The United Senate had been created when supernaturals came out into the open. Each of the major supernatural races were a part of it, along with humans, to make sure all parties were represented. Typically, they handled things related to supers, leaving the human matters to our government.

"So she's not human?"

"No, Delilah is very much human, but she's been keeping supernaturals as pets. They found out she's forcing these supers to turn people for her friends to hunt for amusement. That breaks the number one rule of the United Senate and simply cannot be allowed. The problem lies with the fact that she is too high profile for the legal route. Her parents would just bribe and pay off anyone who tried to arrest her or send her to trial," Margaret explained. "I tell you this because you need to be aware that there are supers around her, and we don't know what kind or how many. There is also no way to tell which could be loyal to her through choice or coercion."

"That makes things difficult," I murmured. My focus had switched to the map in the file. It provided details of the ranch property she had been spending the majority of her time at. The main house was large, with two barns and some other outbuildings set behind it. My gut instinct said, and my gut was hardly wrong, that those buildings would be where the supers were held.

It was the perfect scenario for what she was doing. No one around for miles and plenty of room to keep her *pets* without anyone taking notice.

"The best way for you to get the job done is during one of her parties. Contrary to what the news and other media outlets have been sharing, she isn't stupid. Each guest list is vetted, and only people she knows and trusts can bring a guest. If that guest turns out to be a problem, they become the hunted."

"This chick is fucked up in the head," I said, shaking my head. "How am I going to get close enough to one of her friends by the deadline?" Turning a friend against someone so powerful took time and the perfect strategy. If this woman was as manipulative as it sounded, her hold on the people she kept close would be hard to break in a month, let alone fourteen days.

Margaret gave me an evil smile. "This is where it pays to be friendly with the Senate. They have someone on the inside who is willing to get you into the party. In exchange, they won't torture him while they have him imprisoned for the rest of his life."

"That will help," I said, snapping the folder shut as I stood.

"Finley, you'll need to be smarter than Delilah. This is a difficult job with many unknown variables and hidden players. That's why I picked you personally—not everyone can adjust to changes in the moment like you can. Use all that we have taught you in the past twenty-five years. I have a feeling you're going to need it," Margaret said, her steel gaze piercing. "Good. Now, go get some sleep. Your flight leaves in eight hours."

As I left the office and headed for my room, I couldn't get over the fact that this job worried Margaret. Never had she cautioned me to this extent, and it made me think there was more to this situation that she wasn't telling me. That was the job, though. Margaret was the bow, and we were the arrow—without question, we went where she sent us.

Never once had Margaret steered me wrong, but something about this job made me wonder if there really was a first time for everything...

TWO

FINLEY

The best way to describe January in New York was gray. The sky was cloudy and overcast. The snow had turned to a murky color, no longer fresh and clean, and the trees were barren skeletons of themselves. With all the buildings, lights, and people rushing about, you didn't notice this as much in the city, but out here in the country, it was less than idyllic.

Since I landed two days ago, I'd been holed up in my hotel room, researching everything I could about Delilah and her friends. They had all grown up in the same circle, and Delilah had always been the ringleader—well, gatekeeper, more like. If she decided you were out, then nothing could save you except fixing whatever you did to piss her off.

Maxwell Casper, the gentleman who I was "friends" with, had been a stalwart companion of Delilah's for years. He was a flamboyantly gay man who dabbled in his own line of men's accessories. For the past three months, he had been in Paris, working with a few designers, and Delilah was throwing a party out at the ranch this weekend to celebrate his return. He was bringing me along as his plus one, a fast new friend he'd made on the trip. It was something he apparently had a habit of doing.

Sitting in the corner of the bright pink Hummer limo, I observed the four other people we had picked up along the way. Delilah was already at the ranch, while the rest of us had to drive three hours to join her, giving me plenty of time to study their interactions. My natural disposition was to be more on the quiet side, but my training had taught me to blend in with any crowd. I could be the quiet one when it suited the job, but I knew how to open up when that was the best course of action. Right now, with everyone fighting for the spotlight, it wasn't hard for me to fade into the background.

"Alexia, how is it that Maxwell talked you into coming all the way from France for this party?" Jemma asked, cutting off all other conversation as they looked at me.

Ah, it seemed the interrogation had begun.

"Oh, I'm actually just starting out in the fashion industry, and Maxwell *totally* saved my ass. I was picking out fabric for my next line of lingerie, and the store owner was trying to swindle me on the price. Of course, I don't speak a word of French, so I wasn't even sure what he was trying to tell me! Max was there, doing his own shopping, and swooped in to save the day." I giggled, giving Maxwell a playful smack on the arm.

Maxwell flashed me a bright smile, shaking his head before he turned to the others. "The poor thing looked so lost, I just couldn't in good conscience let that man trick her like that. We have to look out for our own in this fierce business. Especially since Alexia isn't as blessed as those of us with filthy rich parents. This girl has been slaving out of a *rented* workspace in the warehouse district."

The others gasped at this information, eyes wide in horror.

"You poor thing, having to live like that. I hope Maxy paid for your flight out here since I'm sure he didn't give you an option," Lilly said, her plump injected lips giving me an exaggerated pout that I thought was supposed to be reassuring. Instead, it just made me want to roll my eyes at how bad her acting was, knowing she was insulting me.

I turned and glared at Maxwell. "Look what you've done! Now they think I'm some pauper on the streets! Tell them the truth."

Maxwell rolled his eyes and leaned in, causing the others to do the same to make sure they didn't miss a word. "Alexia was on vacation in Paris.

She's from L.A.—her family is invested in the liquor business. She isn't living off Daddy's money right now, but she could if she wanted to."

Now that they'd found out I wasn't as interesting as they thought I might be, they all laughed and moved on to other topics. Halfway through the trip, the drugs and liquor started to flow as they became bored. Cocaine and champagne seemed to be the favorites, but a few blunts were passed around as well. With practiced ease, I went through the motions, sipping my drink and distracting them from the fact that I wasn't partaking.

Now that everyone in the car was buzzed and high, I used the time to ask about the ranch. "So, guys, Maxwell keeps telling me that there's something special about what happens at these parties. I'm dying to know. You have to tell me!"

Brad, one of the two men in the car, gave me a wicked grin as he wiggled in to sit next to me, placing his hand on my thigh. "Oh, it's like nothing you've ever experienced before. Your darkest desires can be fulfilled—you know the ones I'm talking about. The secrets you keep to yourself, that make you worry about what people would think if they found out."

"Will you tell me yours?" I purred, leaning into him so he could easily whisper in my ear.

"I love fucking the brains out of a vamp chick and letting her drink from my neck," Brad said, a shiver running through his body at the thought. "It's even better when I get to beat the shit out of a shifter first; it gets the blood pumping."

Covering my mouth in mock horror, I pulled back from him. "That's illegal! Vampires are never allowed to drink from the vein." Did this idiot even realize how lucky he was that the vampire *chick* didn't just kill him? Seemed Delilah's hold on her supers was strong indeed if she could keep that from happening.

Brad smirked. "Trust me, babe, that is the least of it. Some of these rich fuckers get off to some sick and twisted shit, like hunting them down.

Jemma over there had a lion shifter's head mounted on her wall, tells everyone it's from one of her dad's Africa trips."

Turning, I looked over at Jemma, who was chugging her champagne straight from the bottle. "She seems so sweet."

"Oh, she's almost as cruel as Delilah is. People only see the perfect daughter that heads up all these fundraisers, but she's really a stone-cold killer. Wicked shot with a rifle, too," Brad shared.

I took them all in with new eyes, my mind trying to predict what other secret deviances were lurking beneath each surface. It seemed I wasn't the only one here who was good at hiding who they really were from the world around them. This just made my job all that much harder—no one could be trusted.

Brad let his hand shift under the hem of my tight black bodycon dress, caressing my skin. "What do you say, babe—wanna explore the dark side of human nature together?"

I gave him a sultry smile, grabbing his wrist and stopping his hand from taking its journey higher. "Don't take this the wrong way, but I would hate to limit my options when I haven't gotten a chance to see what they are yet." I lifted his hand and sucked his pointer finger down, holding his gaze as I did it. Pulling away, I let his finger pop out of my mouth with a smirk. "Ask me again later."

"Damn, that's sexy," he moaned, leaning back and biting his lip. "God, I hope you decide to say yes because I can tell we would have a good time."

As much as I wanted to crush all his hopes, I knew keeping my options open was going to be the smart thing. Trailing a finger down his chest, I winked. "You never know what might happen."

"You guys, we're HERE!" Lilly squealed.

Out of the corner of my eye, I watched two guards coming to talk to the driver when we stopped at the gate. We were waved on after a few moments, heading down the long picturesque drive without any other stops. Despite how cold it was, Lilly rolled down the window, screaming her excitement as she hung halfway out of it.

The main house was huge, built out of wood and stone with tons of windows looking out over the four hundred acres of land. It was two stories with a patio that ran around the outside of the whole second story. Massive wooden pillars marked the entrance to the house. Off to the side, I could see out-buildings that would normally be used for the animals and supplies on a real working farm. The only maintained grassy area was the first acre surrounding the house; the rest was heavily wooded. I knew from the maps that a creek ran through the property, ending in a lake.

"Let's get this party started, bitches!" Maxwell yelled as he tossed open the door and jumped out.

Not willing to fight my way out of the car, I waited for everyone else to get out before I did. Seeming overly eager wasn't going to do me any favors. Once I was free, I discovered two guards ready to greet me with stern looks on their faces. I raised a brow at their intimidation tactic, flashing them a carefree smile that matched the others' drugged-up expressions.

"Ma'am, we need you to come with us," the one on the right said before turning and heading off to a small barn just off the house.

The guard behind me put his hand on my back, giving me no option but to go with them. I calmly went along with it; I'd prepared for this, so there was nothing to worry about. Once inside, one took my overnight bag and searched it while the other waved a metal detector over me, both of them finding nothing of interest. I'd arranged for Maxwell to handle my weapons since he wouldn't have to go through this search. My knives, gun, poisons, and black bodysuit would remain tucked away under his bed until I needed them.

"We need your ID and for you to place your hand on this sensor."

I complied, watching as my handprint popped up with my image the moment my hand was on the scanner. Maxwell had already informed us of the security steps for first-timers, so we had made sure to have my fake identity ready.

"Since this is the first time you are a guest here at the Thomas Ranch, we need you to sign an NDA. We have a lot of high-profile guests, and we ask that you refrain from taking any photos or videos during your stay. If we find that you have not followed these rules, we will press charges and confiscate your phone," a guard informed me as he handed over the tablet for me to sign. "Thank you, ma'am. We will escort you back to the main house now."

As they did just that, I looked over the property, making note of things I couldn't see from the aerial photos I'd been working off of while planning. There were twenty guards on the grounds at a time, according to Max, but I had a feeling there might be more since they had to watch the supers as well as the guests. Once we reached the front door, they set down my luggage and gave me a brisk nod before heading off. I stepped into the foyer and was immediately spotted by Maxwell and the others.

"Oh, there she is! Alexia, come over here and meet my bestest bitch in the whole wide world, Delilah!" he called, waving me over.

Aside from a new hair color, Delilah looked just like the photo I had been given. It was now an ombré, almost black at the roots before fading down to a rose gold that set off her bronze skin. Her hazel eyes stood out with the help of her long, thick lash extensions. Everything about her had been primped to perfection, even if most of it was fake.

"Ah, Maxwell's newest victim. What did he bribe you with to come all the way here for his party?" Delilah asked, giving me a welcoming smile as she laughed.

I laughed along with her before I answered. "Oh, he only *raved* about how the parties here were not something to be missed. That they're a once-in-a-lifetime kind of thing." Shrugging, I gave her a smirk. "I'm always up for a life-changing experience."

Upon hearing my words, Delilah's eyes lit up with excitement. "Girl, you have no idea how life-changing this weekend will be! I can't wait to see what you're going to be drawn to. Come on, let me give you a tour of the house and show you where you're gonna be sleeping."

Delilah grabbed my hand and pulled me after her. I glanced over my shoulder at Maxwell, but he just shooed me away. At the last second, I caught the worry in his expression before he could cover it up. Truly, he didn't need to be worried. I couldn't kill her right this moment. The United Senate needed actual proof of what she was doing so there could be no civil outrage once she was dead.

That said, Maxwell better not fuck this up for me, or I wouldn't be the only one in trouble and fearing for my life.

THREE

FINLEY

The whole house reminded me of something you would see in a rustic magazine. Vaulted ceilings, warm-toned wood floors and trim, and a giant stone fireplace with a bear-skin rug. I couldn't help but wonder if the rug was one of her kills or from a real bear. Shaking my head to get that thought out of my mind, I kept my eyes open for anything that might not have been on the blueprints that I'd memorized.

Delilah took me to the second floor and stopped in front of a row of men and women all dressed in what looked like private school uniforms. The jackets were red, and the pants and skirts were red and black plaid. I had no idea what to make of this when she turned to me and swept her arm out.

"Pick one. They'll be your pet for the weekend," Delilah announced.

Even with all my training, I had a hard time hiding my shock. Luckily, it was the expected response. The average newcomer wouldn't be accustomed to Delilah's idea of *fun*. "What do you mean? Who are they?"

"They're all different types of supers that I keep to do my bidding," she answered triumphantly. "Go on, check them out. If you want to know anything, just ask, and they'll tell you."

I walked up to the row of twenty people, feeling nauseous, unable to imagine what these poor supers had endured at the hands of *guests*.

It was moments like this that I was glad I did what I did. There were people in this world that shouldn't be allowed to live, and Delilah was one of them. No one had the right to force people into this kind of life, to take everything from them and expect them to serve others. The idea of adding a few more names to that list was becoming an attractive idea as well.

My instructors at the Organization had always told me I had a natural talent for reading people, so when I stopped in front of an attractive young man, I knew he was the one I had to pick. He screamed 'submissive' to me; he couldn't even look me in the eye, keeping his head bowed. His long mop of curly hair had fallen over, shadowing his face, and he picked at the cuticle on his thumbnail.

"What's your name?" I asked gently.

"Cory, ma'am," he whispered.

"Do you mind if I ask what you are?"

"I'm a werewolf."

Out of everything he could have said, I was not expecting that. In my time doing this job, I'd had many run-ins with werewolves, as they were a favorite choice for bodyguards, but this man standing in front of me couldn't defend himself against a bee. An odd urge to protect Cory took over me, causing me to turn back to Delilah.

"He will be perfect. I like my men to take orders well," I declared with a smirk.

Delilah walked up to Cory and removed a bracelet from him, putting it on my wrist. "He's yours. This is connected to a matching bracelet that he's wearing. With it, you'll be able to summon him to wherever you are on the property at any time. Now, Cory, be a good pet and show Alexia to the Rose Room."

Cory bowed at the waist and gestured to my overnight bag. "May I take that for you, Mistress?"

"Which direction is my room?" I demanded.

Once he pointed, I tossed my bag to him and started heading down the hall, noting that each of the rooms had the name of a different flower on its door. Cory caught up to me in an instant, staying right behind me at my elbow. When I reached the Rose Room, I waited while he opened the door then stepped in, trying not to grimace at the floral explosion before me.

"Is there anything I can do for you at the moment, Mistress?" Cory asked.

Gingerly, I sat on the bed and looked him over. "What is your rank?"

Cory looked me in the eye for the first time, letting me see their amber hue along with the feeling he was reading more about me than I wanted him to. "I'm sorry. What was your question?"

"What is your rank in the pack order?" I asked again, tilting my head to the side, my brows knitting together.

He gaped. "You've met other werewolves before?"

"Is that so uncommon? There are many shifters out in society. Pack order is something they teach in school these days," I said, trying to figure out what I had done wrong. He shouldn't have been reacting this way.

Cory seemed to shake himself out of his shock, but he still looked at me differently. "The simple fact that you asked is odd in this environment. Most of the guests here couldn't care less about knowing anything about us. They just see us as toys to play with, not real people."

This time, I didn't hide my disgust. I might kill people for a living, which of course demanded a certain kind of moral gray area, but I'd never seen the appeal of torturing people for fun. The kind of person who found enjoyment in the suffering of others was the worst kind of living creature.

Time and time again, I'd been told that I wasn't detached enough for this job, but I was good enough in situations like this that they needed me in spite of that flaw. So far, I'd never let it affect my work, but I was starting to get a weird feeling in my gut. This job might just push me over the edge.

"Look, I don't belong here any more than you do. I got roped into coming by Maxwell, and I can't afford to upset people of his status. My family is lower on the totem pole, so having an association with any of these people will help my family's business." I sighed and looked up at him with wide, innocent eyes. "I could use an inside man to help me navigate through this weekend. I'll do whatever I can to help you out, too."

"Omega. I'm an omega," Cory whispered as he dropped his eyes back to his hands. Horror slammed into me at his words, distracting me so much that I almost missed when he kept talking. "I wish I could assist you with that, but I'm practically prey in this house. If you had picked anyone else, they would have been more helpful."

Omegas were rare in the shifter world—so rare they only happened in wolves. When I first learned about them, I didn't see what was so important about omegas. They were the bottom of the pack, a natural submissive that couldn't take care of themselves; they needed the alpha and betas to look after them. If they were left on their own, they would starve because they wouldn't be able to fight for their food. Omegas were meant to be the soul of a pack, caring for everyone in a way that only someone who didn't need to prove they were better than anyone else could. Alphas led the pack while betas protected, but an omega could come alongside someone who was suffering and nurture them, expecting nothing in return. Packs that had an omega excelled in every way, so omegas were treasured for the stability they provided.

But once people discovered what omegas were capable of, they also became the fastest way to destroy a pack. Remove the stability, and the rest would come crashing down.

Focusing my attention back on Cory, I wondered if Delilah had any idea what she had trapped away in her house.

"Cory, how did you end up here?" I asked, unable to move on until I knew.

"Ten years ago, I was taken from my pack and sold to the highest bidder. I bounced around from place to place, owner to owner, until Delilah bought me on the black market. I've been here for six months." He shrugged. "It isn't the worst place I've been."

I chewed on my lower lip as I processed that information. "Does Delilah know what you really are?"

"No, she just saw a pretty face and a replacement for the last wolf she lost."

Sighing, I relaxed a little. I could only imagine what would happen if people in this house figured out they had such a submissive in their clutches. I needed to keep him safe and alive so I could get him back to his pack... if they were even still together after losing their omega.

"Alright, give me the basics of how things work here." I held up a hand when I saw he was going to dismiss his knowledge and usefulness. "Look, I'm not asking you to do anything other than share information. I want to protect you, but I can't do that if I don't know the rules of this place. Something tells me everything is a test and nothing is what it seems—just like bringing me to pick one of you. She wanted to see how I would react to the fact that she had you all here, to see if I would freak out. Now, take a seat and talk."

Cory moved over to the fainting couch and took a seat, clutching a pillow to his chest. "Number one rule is never correct her. She's queen bee, and what she says is law. Even if it's illegal, don't mention it. Just ignore that it's happening. If she gives you something or tells you to do something, take it, drink it, eat it—just say yes. A few weeks ago, there was a girl who was a vegan. She refused to eat the steak dinner, so Delilah drugged her and fed her to the dogs."

"Wait, *real* dogs?"

"Yes. She said, 'Nature doesn't give a fuck if you're protecting them or not, so why should we?'."

Knowing these types of entitled people existed in the world and having to spend the weekend with one were two very different experiences. Being an assassin, I'd studied all kinds of personalities and behaviors, but dealing with psychopaths always seemed challenging because it was harder to tell what was real and what was fake.

"Alright. I'm not a picky eater, so that shouldn't be a problem. The illegal part I kinda figured since she's keeping supers as pets. What else?" I pressed.

"The others here are just as dangerous, if not more, because they're all watching each other to point out when you do something wrong. It's like they think it'll keep it from happening to them someday. Maxwell and Jemma are the only two that Delilah will think twice about punishing. They're special to her for some reason. Oh—then there are the hunts," Cory whispered, hunching his body as if to make himself smaller.

"Brad mentioned something about that," I offered, hoping it would help that he didn't need to explain what that meant.

He peeked up at me through his hair, fear making his eyes glow. "She'll make you go on one. It's the one thing that will bind you to her and her secret forever. Even if you betrayed her and went to the Senate, they would punish you along with everyone else."

I had guessed this would be the case—nothing better to protect you than mutual destruction. It wasn't the thought of killing a super that bothered me. It wasn't even that they were innocent people. No, what caused me to hesitate was the Senate. Yes, they had sent me on this job, but I wasn't living under the impression that I would get a 'get out of jail free' card if I were caught. The more I looked at the situation, the more it seemed like I would have to take out all the guests to make sure no one shared what happened here. I could withstand torture, but none of these prissy trust-fund babies would.

"Thank you, Cory. I would like some time alone now," I said, dismissing him with a wave of my hand.

Without a word, he stood and exited the room, letting the door softly click behind him. Now I needed a new plan since I was adding four more people to the mission, and I would need to act fast. No way in hell was I going to let any of them get away with this; they were all to blame. I knew without a doubt that there would be a hunt tomorrow. With a new person around, Delilah would make sure we all stayed loyal to their secret.

FOUR

FINLEY

I stayed in my room, planning, until Cory came to let me know that dinner was ready. He led me back downstairs to the dining room and pulled out my chair for me. Looking around the room, I noticed it was dim, with only the fireplace and candles on the table providing light. At the end of the table was a round platform covered with red silk.

The rest of the crew was filtering in as well, each followed by their 'pet.' Brad actually had a man and a woman who proudly flashed their fangs when they smiled. Seemed Brad would once again be able to fulfill his dark dream. Delilah walked in last, with a large, buff man, who I pegged as personal security. His bald head glowed in the dim light of the dining room, and his eyes tracked us all even as he pulled out her chair.

He was going to be a problem. Definitely a super, but what kind, I couldn't guess. By the time the night was over, though, I would know—it was my top priority.

"I hope you all settled in and had a good respite because the party has now begun. And you won't want to miss a thing!" Delilah giggled as she clapped her hands before taking her seat. "Alexia, I hope you don't mind if we borrow your pet for the night. He provides the best entertainment, but it will cause him to be unavailable later. I'll make sure a suitable stand-in will be of service for you."

An answer from me wasn't expected, so I remained silent. Staff in white shirts and black pants entered, passing out bowls of soup and filling our glasses with wine. It seemed fine dining was the theme of the night. Once we were all served and the staff had left, Cory walked back into the room with Brad's pets, only this time they were naked.

Continuing to eat, I watched as they walked over to the silk-covered platform and climbed onto it so we could easily see them from our seats. The male vampire shoved Cory to his knees, securing his arms behind him with metal cuffs, as the female vampire crawled toward the omega. An evil glint shone in her eyes as she shoved Cory's legs open wide, displaying him to us. My hands balled into fists under the table as I watched, feeling Delilah's gaze on me as if she were waiting for me to object. Taking her time, the vampire licked and nipped down Cory's chest, clawing her nails into his thighs.

As this took place, everyone else at the table carried on with meaningless chatter, glancing at the performance every so often. I now understood Delilah's game. She had looked up every sick and twisted fantasy that people had ever confessed to, and she was putting them into action. What I couldn't understand was what she got out of it. Did she gain that much power by holding all these people hostage with their sins?

A cry of pain caused me to look back at the *entertainment*, and I saw blood dripping from a series of bites the female vampire had made on Cory's chest. He had cried out from the one she made at the femoral artery in his groin. She lapped at the blood, letting it dribble down her face to coat her breasts. The male vampire had his hand fisted in Cory's hair, baring his neck for him to strike and drink deeply. Cory's eyes rolled back in his head as he whimpered at the forced pleasure that a vampire's venom released. The female had taken his cock deep into her throat, and I wanted to turn away when he struggled to break free from her, but the male held him fast.

"It's hard to look away from something so taboo, isn't it, Alexia?" Delilah called out, pulling my attention back to her. "Sometimes I'm jealous of how they can be so unapologetically primal. They don't see giving into their baser needs as a flaw. Instead, they revel in it."

I paused before I spoke, trying to gauge what would get the reaction I wanted out of her. "It's intoxicating, the thought of giving in to the darkness we all have inside us. Now I see why people are so drawn to your parties and rave about them afterward."

Delilah smiled devilishly, leaning forward on the table, her gaze going past me to what was going on behind me. Following her lead, I was brought back to the performance to see Cory getting pounded from behind by the male. The poor omega was balls deep in the female who was grinding herself on him. In a flurry of panting and moaning, they finished and collapsed in a heap of blood-covered limbs.

Other staff came out, helping the three of them out of the room and removing the platform. Our dishes were taken away and replaced with the main course while a new wine was poured. As I started on my meal, the sound of snarling and the clank of chains came from the hall. Moments later, a wolf and a tiger were brought into the room, their chains secured to the far end of the wall. There was enough length for them to get at each other, but they weren't close enough to harm us.

Delilah signaled her bodyguard, who carried over a plate with a slab of raw meat on it. He tossed it in the middle, just out of reach of both animals, and it immediately had the desired effect. The wolf lunged for the meat, but the tiger batted him away, sending him skidding along the floor. The wolf turned his attention to the tiger now, rage glowing in his amber eyes.

"Shifters are nothing but animals. Starve them, beat them, and look—you can't find a speck of humanity in them any longer," Delilah said, popping a piece of fish into her mouth.

Frowning, I cocked my head to the side, knowing this was going to be a risky question. "I don't understand. Do you like supers or despise them?"

"Oh, Alexia, that is *much* too black and white a question. I thought you understood." Delilah scowled at me. "We are what we are, but we have a choice to let it control us or not. I know the darkness within me, and to make sure I control it, I have these parties. We let our animalistic side out, rejoice in our darkness, then we take back control and rule over our urges. There's a whole underground society out there if you really look for them. I'm not the one who came up with this idea. I simply perfected it."

"You're right. That was very small-minded of me," I admitted, falling back into character to distance myself from this situation. "Thank you for enlightening me to something I didn't see before."

Content with my acknowledgment, she turned her attention back to the battle that was waging at the end of the table, but I had no desire to watch two lost souls destroy each other at the promise of a meager meal. The tiger ended up winning, and Delilah's guard kicked his prize closer to him so he could eat it. With the end of the fight came the end of the meal, and we were all brought to a sitting room filled with couches, pillow nests, and overstuffed chairs.

The pets entered the room in nothing but lingerie, carrying trays filled with all kinds of drugs, liquor, sex toys, and condoms. A man walked over to me as I chose an armchair to sit in, handing me a glass with some kind of amber liquid in it. I took the drink, and he fell to his knees in front of me. He was a pretty boy with a muscular physique, but not overly so.

His dark brown hair was slicked back, and his bright green eyes looked up at me with hunger in them. Slowly, he ran his hand up my legs with the barest hint of nail making contact. He reached my knees, then let his slender fingers slip under my dress. "Mistress told me to please you so well you'll forget you don't have the pretty wolf tonight," he purred. "You'll let me do my best for you won't you, Mistress?"

"Oh, lucky Alexia! Delilah is letting her play with Antonio," Lilly announced from her perch in a large black man's arms.

"Seems like you have a fine hunk of man to entertain you tonight, Lilly," I offered as I felt Antonio shifting up my dress.

Lilly looked up at the man in question and planted a kiss on his cheek. "Berry is a sweetheart, but he doesn't talk all that much since he lost his tongue. Shame—he was really gifted with that thing."

The only thing to distract from my slowly building rage was the fact that Antonio had reached my underwear and proceeded to rip them off me. I gasped at the surprise of it as he scooped up my ass and pulled me forward so I was on the edge of the cushion. It didn't take a genius to figure out where this was going, and good thing too, because I was not about to let this man stick his dick in me.

I was far from a prude, but I liked to choose who my partner was and set expectations before letting things get intimate. If this man wanted to let his mouth do the work and help me keep my cover, then so be it, but I would kill him if he pushed me further. It would speed things up, and I would have to make a new plan on the fly, but worse things could happen. As Antonio got to work, I took a sip of my drink, discovering it was brandy, but there was something else laced in it. I tossed my head back and set the drink down on the table as I pretended to be in the throes of bliss thanks to his tongue.

Eyes slitted, I watched the rest of the room. People snorted coke off their pets, shot up, and tossed back shots like there was no tomorrow. Delilah was in the pillow nest with her bodyguard, but to my surprise he'd stripped down and shifted into a fucking silverback gorilla. He charged at Delilah, ripped off her dress, pulled her up by her ankle, and tossed her down on the pillows face first. Shifting once again, he landed behind her, yanked her to him, and fucked the ever-loving shit out of her while roaring his pleasure.

I was so surprised that my own orgasm hit me out of nowhere, causing a moan to burst out of my mouth and my back to arch. Antonio pressed on, wringing every last bit of pleasure he could from me. Once I came back to my senses and laid limp in the chair, Antonio moved to grab a condom out of the bowl on the table.

"No," I snapped, pulled out of my haze. Antonio looked surprised, but he stopped what he was doing.

"Go play with Lilly and her man. I want to watch," I stated. If I showed interest in another sort of kink, it would help explain why I wasn't taking my own use of his body. Plus, it would be further help in keeping Lilly distracted, giving me one less person to deal with if things went south.

Antonio nodded with a grin.

It worked, and I was able to make it to the point where everyone had passed out from all the fucking and drugs. As I moved around the room throughout the night, I discovered there were no cameras, obvious or hidden, in this room. I was sure the risk of anyone seeing what went on in here would destroy any of their credibility in the human world, and this left me with an ideal opportunity to do my job in one fell swoop.

With plenty of drugs and syringes around, I had the perfect way to deal with this disgusting mess. I could easily make it look like everyone had overdosed. The potential issue I had to work around was making sure that none of the supers woke up and tried to stop me. Drugs and alcohol didn't work or last in their systems the way they did in humans, but I had a plan to ensure their cooperation. I would offer any super the chance to escape so that they wouldn't be blamed for the dead bodies.

Delilah was in the most challenging position to work around, so as much as I wanted to start with our hostess, I had to get rid of the potential witnesses first. If there was any kind of struggle on Delilah's part, it could rouse others and make my job that much harder.

I began with Jemma, who was sprawled out on her back with another woman sleeping on her stomach. Swiftly, I injected her with the drugs and stepped back as her body started to convulse before she threw up, choking her own vomit. The female super sleeping on her didn't stir, so I moved on to the next person. The guys were easy to deal with, having larger veins to hit, which then left me with two more.

Lilly was wedged in between both Berry and Antonio, curled up in a little ball, so I had to handle this delicately. The other problem was that she was one of the only people who hadn't gone overboard with the drugs, which increased the risk that she could possibly wake up. As if he could sense me watching them, Berry shifted onto his back, giving me access to her legs. Luckily, many junkies shot up between their toes if they didn't want it to be noticeable, so that would be easily explained away if Delilah's family connections didn't manage to hide away evidence of the deaths. Slowly, I grasped her big toe and pushed it to the side so I could get to the webbing in between. A few moments passed after I injected her, and I thought I was in the clear, but she shot up, gasping, her eyes wide with terror. Just as she was about to scream, Berry rolled back over, smothering her with his body until she started to convulse. It seemed he was done playing pet.

Looking up, Berry's eyes were on me, and he gave me a nod as if he understood what I was doing. I returned his nod and got up, turning toward Delilah and her gorilla man, only to find them awake and watching me.

FIVE

FINLEY

"**W**HAT HAVE YOU DONE?!"

Well, fuck. This is going to make things harder.

Delilah crawled out from under her pet, still screaming at me as she took in the rest of the room. Only the supers were starting to rouse, all her so-called friends lying there dead, surrounded by puddles of piss and vomit.

"What the fuck are you doing?! Kill her!" Delilah shouted at her gorilla man. Instantly, he shifted and started to charge at me.

Without any kind of weapon, I wasn't going to do any damage against a silverback. Turning on my heel, I ran out of the room, slamming the door closed behind me, and raced down the halls toward the back of the house. I knew where the guns and other supplies for their hunting events were stored. I just had to get there if I was going to have a chance of getting out of this alive.

An alarm went off, blaring through the whole house and around the property. In moments, guards would come running, so my only option was to get some space between me and them.

The cold winter air bit at my skin and bare feet as I tore across the gravel driveway, but I reached the large barn doors only to find that they were locked with an electronic keypad. I slammed my fist against the door, pissed that I didn't have what I needed, but this was why the

Organization had given me the job—to deal with and succeed despite all the unforeseen variables. Taking a moment, I slowed my breathing and ran through what I knew about the property.

An idea struck me, so I took a few steps back and looked at the barn as a whole. Seeing what I needed, I ran to the side and climbed up onto the pallet of bagged salt they used on the driveway. I jumped, catching the edge of the roof, and pulled myself up until I was crouched low on the shingles. Just as I hoped, I caught sight of a skylight that I could use to get access into the building. It was made of hard, foggy plastic, but I easily kicked it out and sent it crashing to the ground. Not the most subtle of entrances, but I didn't have time for stealth at the moment. Grabbing the lip of the opening, I lowered myself until I was dangling into the space, taking in what was below me.

It was a concrete aisleway with cell doors instead of your typical stall doors for horses. I dropped down, rolling into the fall so I didn't break anything as I landed, then popped up and started moving to the gun safe. Breaking into safes was not a particular talent of mine, but I knew enough that I'd be able to get into the old spin rods and lever-style safe. Crouching down next to it, I put my ear near the dial, closed my eyes, and took deep breaths to slow my heartrate down until it wasn't thudding in my ears.

It took me ten tries to get it, but when the final click sounded and the handle turned, I couldn't help but be impressed with myself. I grabbed two shotguns and a box of shells labeled "pure silver" and loaded both guns before I grabbed the rifle and loaded that one up with silver bullets as well. I found a Carhartt jacket that had been left behind and shrugged it on, filling the pockets with ammo. Climbing up to the hayloft, I headed to the door and unlatched it from the inside, sliding it open just enough to see out.

I could see the guards scouring the property alongside wolves. If I was going to have any chance at getting to Delilah, I needed to take out some of these guards and supers before I even thought about going back into the house. Pure silver bullets could kill any shifter if it was a fatal shot, and they would also work on vampires if hit directly in the heart.

With the barrel of the rifle propped up on the lip of the hayloft door, I took two deep breaths before I wrapped my hand around the stock and placed my finger on the trigger. Adjusting to looking through the scope, I took in what was going on around the house. Many of the guards had scattered into the forest to search for me, but I caught sight of a werewolf who had picked up on my scent. *Easy enough to deal with from here.* I let out an easy breath as I squeezed the trigger, hitting it right between the eyes. The wolf dropped hard, and before the one right behind it could tell what had happened, it was dead too.

If any supernatural creature was going to protect these people after all they'd done to them, they didn't deserve to be brought back into the real world. With the amount of abuse and mental torture I could only guess they'd endured, they were a lost cause anyway. This was the kindest option to give them their freedom.

Sweeping back to the right, I saw a guard walking toward another barn, and once he slid open the door, I could hear all the noise from the animals inside. Trusting my gut, I took him out with a head shot before he could get any further. Two more ran over to check on him, lining up nicely for me to finish them off as well.

Now halfway through my clip, I pulled back, knowing I would need to change locations. I quickly reloaded, keeping one bullet in the chamber, ready to shoot in an instant. Heading to the back of the barn, I noticed something huddled in one of the cells, but I didn't want to chance getting caught to see what it was. I got to the back door and opened it, but the pitiful whine made me pause. Leaving the door closed but not latched, I went back to the cell. When the head of a wolf lifted, I was met with an amber gaze filled with fear and sadness.

I *knew* those eyes. "Cory?"

The wolf let out a whine and crawled over, keeping himself low to the ground, his tail tucked between his legs. Everything about him screamed 'submissive prey,' to the point where he rolled on his back, giving me his belly, when I walked closer to the door of his cage.

"Cory, I'm gonna get you out of this cell. When I do, I need you to run and hide in the woods because I'm going to wipe this place off the map. Keep low and hide well so the guards don't find you. Can you do that for me?" I whispered as I looked around for something to break the lock on the door.

I noticed a rusted long-handled axe in the corner by other castoff tools. Setting aside my guns, I grabbed it and swung it as hard against the lock as I could. Sparks flew, but it didn't do much else, so I swung again and again until it finally fell away. "Alright, let's go, Cory," I urged, trying to shoo him out of the cell. If anyone was near the barn, they would have heard the noise.

Cory didn't move, though. He just whined and scratched at his neck. In the dim light from the moon, I hadn't noticed he had on a collar that was chained to the wall. Letting out a growl of irritation, I rushed over to him and reached for his neck. If he were a normal wolf, this would be a risky move. However, since Cory was such a submissive, it should have been safe. Without warning, Cory bit me on the forearm, his teeth sinking deep into my skin. *So much for being submissive.*

"Fucking hell," I gritted out through clenched teeth. "Why the fuck did you DO that?! I'm trying to get you out of here! I'm sorry if I scared you, but you didn't have to go and fucking bite me!"

This is bad. This is very, very bad. I was just bitten by a werewolf, and there are only four days before the next full moon. Margaret is going to kill me if I make it through this alive.

"Cory, I need you to let my arm go so I can get us both out of this hellhole alive," I murmured, trying to keep my voice calm and gentle. "That's it, good boy. Now, I'm going to take this collar off, then you will be free to run and hide like I said before. See, there we are, no big deal. Now, RUN!"

Cory bolted out of the cell, crashing through the back door of the barn and continuing into the woods. Thankfully, with the thick jacket on, his bite wasn't as bad as it could have been, only breaking the skin but not tearing into the muscle. Although the damage was enough that it was going to change my life forever. With werewolves, one break of the skin was all that it took. The Organization did have supernatural assassins, but they were greatly limited in what jobs they could take. I put that thought on the back burner to deal with if I made it out of this alive needing to stay focused.

Going back to my weapons, I slipped out of the barn and into the woods, heading to the left of the house. I had no idea how many supers or guards were searching for me, so I kept one of the shotguns at the ready. Moving along the backside of the barn the guard had opened, I peeked through a grungy window. Shifters of all kinds were locked away in small cages, their animal forms looking crazed. These must be the ones they hunted because they would be far too dangerous to let loose otherwise.

A guard rushed into the barn and hit the large red button on the side of the wall, opening all the cage doors, setting everyone free. Within seconds, the guard was attacked by the feral shifters, unable to get into the secure room in time. As much as I wanted to sneak back to the house and finish this mission by taking out Delilah, I wasn't going to be able to with the fifty or so rabid shifters this close to a full moon. For now, the plan was to stay alive and finish the job another time.

Looking deeper into the woods, I spied an old oak tree that had a thick trunk and sturdy branches, so I bolted toward it. I ran as far up the trunk as I could before I grabbed a sturdy branch, pulling myself into the tree. With no leaves to hide me, I needed to get higher into the denser branches to obscure my presence.

Tucked away, I watched a helicopter take flight. I just knew Delilah was on it, but I wasn't worried. I was patient, and she wouldn't get away again.

━━━━◆━━━━

Even though the guards were still on the lookout for me, they had retreated to the security of the guard house with the release of the crazed shifters. Some fought against each other, filling the air with the sounds of snarling and howls. Perched in the oak tree, rifle in hand, I picked off any shifters that came near until there was a wide circle of dead animals around me. When I didn't see movement for a good half hour, I started my way downward, keeping my senses alert to anything that might be stalking me in the darkness.

Dropping to the ground, I paused and crouched. Watching, waiting, listening. The air had gone eerily quiet, as if a new predator had entered the playing field. Keeping low to the ground, I headed back to the house. I needed to make sure all evidence of my presence was removed before what happened here was discovered. Ditching the guns, needing to move unencumbered, I darted across the open area to the back door of the house.

I snagged a handgun from one of the dead guards as I passed, checking to see what ammo they had in the clip and swearing when I saw it was loaded with normal bullets. They would slow down a super, but they wouldn't kill them. It was better than nothing, though. I just had to get to Maxwell's room, where my personal weapons were hidden. Taking the stairs two at a time, I moved as efficiently and quietly as possible until I found the Sunflower Room. I burst into the room and dropped to my knees next to the bed, pulling out the hard-shell briefcase that held everything I needed. Entering the code and pressing my thumb to the fingerprint reader, the case popped open. Snugly packed inside were two black-coated silver daggers and my favorite Smith & Wesson 9mm handgun with a silencer attachment.

Shrugging off my clothes, I pulled out my black spandex bodysuit from the upper portion of the case, then grabbed the extra clips of silver ammo, forearm sheaths for my daggers, and my shoulder holster.

I paused a moment to look at my arm and the bloody mess it was. *Probably not a great idea to pull the bodysuit on over that.* Heading to the bathroom, I rinsed it off then scrubbed it with soap, trying to lessen the scent of my blood. It was a losing battle since it was still weeping, and my arm throbbed with a deep, dull ache. But that didn't mean I could rest. Unless we were knocked unconscious or had a fear of bleeding out, we weren't allowed to stop. The Organization had trained us better than that. Pushing through the pain was as much a mental exercise as a physical one.

Grabbing the toilet paper, I wrapped up my arm the best I could, knowing it wasn't going to do much at this point. With the arm temporarily tended, I tugged on the black spandex and zipped it up to my chin. Ripping off the wig I'd been wearing, I pulled my hair up into a bun and secured it with some hair pins I found in the medicine cabinet. It was stocked full of anything you could have possibly forgotten.

Suited up and armed, I was ready to wipe my existence off the map of this place. I walked over to the bedroom's fireplace and turned on the gas after blowing out the pilot light. Systematically, I did this in all the bedrooms until I made it back to the room with all the dead bodies in it. As far as I could tell, the house was empty of anyone alive. Then, as I passed through the kitchen, I turned on all the burners, making damn sure nothing remaining on this property would survive.

Knowing I didn't have long before this bomb of a house went off, I booked it out the door and into the forest. With a plan in place to get off the property and to the vehicle hidden miles away, I started to jog my way through the dense trees. The clear sky and the almost full moon gave me enough light that I wasn't too worried about falling and hurting myself. Moments later, the ground shook as the sky lit up with the explosion of the house, the echo of explosive force almost knocking me off my feet.

With the added light of the fire, I was able to pick up my speed until a dark shadow burst out of the undergrowth, crashing into me and slamming me to the ground. A panther stood on my chest, its glaringly white teeth bared at me. Claws dug into the skin of my shoulders, causing me to hiss as I took the butt of my dagger and slammed it into its skull. Once it was dazed, I was able to shove it off me, and when I rolled out from under it, I crouched low, both daggers at the ready.

Shaking its head clear, the panther turned and growled at me before it tried to pounce again. This time, I was ready, slamming into the big cat and tossing it to the side with all my body weight. Once we landed,

I shoved my dagger up and under its jaw, praying it was long enough to reach the brain. The thrashing panther tried to dislodge my hold, but I put more weight behind the dagger and twisted, ignoring the claws marring my flesh. Finally, the panther went limp, its body sagging to the ground.

Dislodging my dagger, I fell back on my ass, panting as I took in the scene. I had just bested a *panther* with nothing but a dagger. There was no way I should have survived that, but now that I had shifter DNA already flowing through my body, it seemed I was a little tougher to kill. Was this supposed to happen so fast? That wasn't taught in any of our training. Once my heart rate started to lower, I heard soft cries in the direction the panther had come from.

Slowly, I got to my feet and staggered toward the sound. It really was a terrible idea, but I didn't like to think someone was suffering. A killer I might be, but I was fast and efficient. I like clean, simple kills. The world was filled with enough suffering of its own.

Naked and curled up in a ball, Cory laid on the ground in his human body. As I got closer, I could see he was trying to hold his guts in as he sobbed. The damage the panther had done was too great for him to shift back to try to heal it. Dropping to my knees by his head, I reached out and combed my fingers through his blood-soaked hair, trying to offer what little comfort I could.

"Cory," I whispered, "I can help you. Would you like me to do that for you?"

He looked up at me, tears streaming down his cheeks, before he latched on to my other hand, his skin slick with his own blood. "What's your real name? I want to know the name of the person who will end this life of pain."

"Finley. My name is Finley," I answered.

I didn't know if it was because I liked Cory as a person, or if it was something to do with the fact that he'd bitten me, but I needed him to know why I was here. That I was going to fix what had happened here, that I had failed my job... and him, in a way.

"Cory, I'm an assassin." His eyes widened at this. "The Senate put out a kill order on Delilah, and I was the one who was supposed to do it. I failed, but know this—Delilah *will* die by my hand. That is a promise, and I don't make those lightly."

Cory clutched my hand tighter as he looked at me with a glimmer of hope. "An omega who's an assassin. There might be a chance for you to survive this life." He gasped and started coughing up blood. "Find Colt Harris—my brother. He will keep you safe. Finley, I'm sorry..."

I couldn't handle listening to him suffer anymore, so as he talked, I deftly slid my knife between his ribs and into his heart. "Shh, it's all over now. Be free to run unafraid into the next life."

The light dimmed in his eyes, and I knew he was gone. Wiping my dagger off on my leg, I slid it back into the sheath, then closed Cory's eyes for the last time.

I waited a moment before I took a deep breath and got to my feet. There were still miles to run before all this was over, and I needed to get somewhere safe to lay low.

SIX

FINLEY

In the soft light of dawn, I pulled into the empty barn in the middle of nowhere. The plan was to ditch the vehicle here and make my way to the safehouse on a dirtbike that was waiting for me. As I got out of the rustbucket of a car that I was amazed still worked, my poor battered body started to protest being forced to move again. Now that the adrenaline had left my system, the damage done by the panther was taking its toll. Part of me wasn't sure I could manage riding the dirt bike, but the safehouse had everything I needed to keep things from getting worse.

Not really having a choice, I pulled the bike out of the barn and kicked it into action, heading off through the open field where I seemed to hit every rut and bump in existence. Finally, deep in the forest, I found the safehouse. Well, it was more like a bunker than a house. It looked like something a hobbit would live in, what with it being mostly underground. Stashing the bike and covering it with camouflage, I logged into the access panel, and the door clunked open. Pulling the steel door wide, I headed down the steps and into the bunker.

It was a simple space with two sets of bunk beds, a table with four chairs, and a small kitchenette for cooking simple meals. The bathroom was a brick room with a toilet and a showerhead coming out of the wall. Stripping out of my bodysuit, I washed myself, making sure to scrub all the cuts. They should have been gashes, but along with increased reflexes and strength, it seemed that super healing was already kicking in. At least I could be grateful for that one. Clean, clothed, and safe, I couldn't put off crashing any longer.

The moment my head hit the pillow, I passed out.

⸺◆⸺

After sleeping for who knew how long, I finally managed to get out of bed. My body hurt all over, and not just from the battle with the panther. Even my joints ached. Stumbling over to the airtight pantry, I grabbed an MRE, not caring what was in it. I just needed to stop my stomach from wanting to eat itself. Ripping the main package open with my teeth, I didn't bother to heat it up before I tore into the meal, supposedly some kind of beef stew. I even ate the so-called biscuit that was nothing more than a tough, thin puck. It wasn't enough, so I grabbed another and ate everything in that one too.

Feeling completely out of control, I refused to let myself eat another. Instead, I combined both protein shake mixes from the MREs and drank that, along with heating up some water for the coffee. My hands shook as I tried not to panic about what was happening to me. It was then that I noticed all the damage I'd received yesterday was gone. I'd noticed increased healing before I went to sleep, but my brain had been far too overtaxed to think much about it. Now, after sleeping, the bite on my forearm was nothing but some pink scars where the teeth had penetrated my skin. Pulling the collar of my t-shirt away, I saw the same thing had happened to all the wounds I'd received from the panther.

"This is happening way too fast," I muttered, standing and heading over to the safe where the laptop and satellite phone were kept. The need to understand what was going on with my body drove me to find the person who could help me figure all this out. The Organization might know a fair amount about the supernatural world, but they didn't know how to help a newly bitten wolf like an alpha would.

Back at the table, I typed in Colt Harris's name, searching for him in any register of the werewolf packs in the US. From what Cory had said and the lack of any distinguishable accent, I didn't think he'd been brought in from overseas. I got five hits on the name, finding them listed alongside the names of their associated packs. I dove deeper, looking into the history of each to see if they had any siblings or had contacted the Senate about a missing omega in their pack, and that brought it down to two.

Expanding my search, I pulled up all social media and anything else tied to these two men. As soon as I pulled up the profile picture for Colt Harris, one of the alphas of the Knoxville, Tennessee pack, I knew I'd found the right one. Cory and Colt could have been twins because there was no denying how closely they resembled each other. Colt was older, with a thick, full beard, but they had the same honey-blond, curly hair with amber eyes. His gaze was so commanding, even from just a picture, that I almost couldn't look at it; the need to submit was so strong.

Closing the picture, I was able to take a deep breath once the pressure was gone. *Okay, let's try again* without *the picture.* Pulling up his information, I found a few phone numbers listed, but I wasn't sure which was current. I picked up the satellite phone, pausing before I dialed.

Am I really going to call this guy? If I did this, by law, he would have to take me in and be responsible for me because his brother had turned me. Everything would change instantly. Once he was my alpha, I wouldn't be able to work for the Organization without his permission, and being that I was an omega, he wouldn't give it. Especially since his brother had been taken from him all those years ago. But what did I know about being a werewolf? My life was going to change, one way or another, but right now I had to make a choice that would directly impact just how much it changed. And how much help I'd have with managing those changes. This wasn't a decision to be made lightly.

Maybe I should just call Margaret and let her know what's going on. She would already know I was alive since I'd accessed the bunker. Then again, I would have to tell her I fucked up and got bitten by a werewolf... and was an *omega*, at that. Hell, Margaret might tell me that I had to contact this guy since we would be in hot water with the Senate for not following their shifter laws. And that was on top of fucking this job up.

"UGH!" I yelled, slamming my fist on the table, which proceeded to leave a crack in the wood.

Taking a deep, calming breath, I typed in the first phone number and hit the call button. *"I'm sorry, the caller you are trying to reach—"* Hanging up, I went to the second, then the third, the fourth.

"Who the fuck is this, and how did you get this number?" a deep voice growled. I almost dropped the phone, his tone alone making me want to run and hide. Before I could stop myself, I whined, curling up into a ball on the chair. *What the hell is wrong with me that I'm acting like a scared child? I've killed some of the worst of humanity, yet I'm cowering because of a voice on a phone?!*

There was a sharp intake of breath on the other end before he spoke again. "Easy, now. I'm sorry. I didn't mean to yell," he murmured, his voice soft and comforting. "This is a protected number that not many people are supposed to have. Can you tell me how you got this number, little one?"

He thinks I'm a kid.

"Cory. I'm looking for his brother, Colt Harris," I answered, my voice hoarse from nerves. "He told me to find him, that he would help me. Cory didn't mean to bite me; he was scared, and I moved too fast. Everything is changing so fast I don't understand what is happening to me. I haven't even shifted yet."

The more I spoke, the more irritated I was with myself. I sounded like a scared child, not the seasoned assassin that I'd been for the last twenty-five years.

"You know my brother?! Where is he? Tell me right this second!" Colt barked.

This time, I did drop the phone, backing away from it to crawl under the bottom bunk. Shivering, I felt tears of anger and frustration running down my cheeks at my inability to fight this reaction.

"He's dead," I whispered, afraid of the reaction my words were going to bring. "I couldn't save him."

The sounds that came out of the phone next seemed like someone was destroying everything in sight, crashing and banging, along with lots of swearing.

"Colt, what the fuck is going on?" another voice asked. "Who are you talking to? Give me that before you break it."

There were sounds like someone was trying to take the phone from Colt, then it was silent for a bit.

"Hello? You still there?" the new voice asked.

This voice was warm and smooth, with a little bit of a Southern lilt to it. Crawling out from under the bunk, I reached for the phone again.

"I'm here."

"Would you tell me your name, sweetheart?" the man asked.

I licked my lips, wanting to give him a false name just in case I hadn't called the right person—even though the reaction to my news told me I had—but the pull to do as he requested was too strong.

"Finley," I blurted, my voice cracking with the urgency to answer.

"Holy fuck." The voice came back, shocked. "Finley, did you feel that you had to answer my question? Fuck, sorry! I'm guessing that didn't help."

"Yes, I can't seem to fight against your request. Are you an alpha as well?" I inquired, thinking that could be the cause of this irrational behavior.

"Are you telling me that you feel my dominance that clearly through the phone?"

"Yes. Now, please, I'm begging you, stop asking me questions. I don't even know who you are," I gasped, putting all my resistance into my request.

"I'm sorry, Finley. I've never interacted with an omega before. My name is Lane Cunningham, and I'm the second alpha to the Knoxville Pack. Now, I really don't want to do this, but I need to know where you are. We need to come get you," Lane coaxed, keeping his voice soft.

"I'm in New York, about three hours north of New York City. I'm in a safe location, and I can stay here for a while if I need to. I am not in any immediate danger and can defend myself if the need arises," I rattled off just like if I were talking to Margaret. "I was on a job when I met Colt's brother. He bit me, and before he died, he told me to find his brother."

Lane cleared his throat, giving himself a moment before he answered. "Alright, we'll go over all of that in more detail once we get to you. Colt and I will be on the next flight out. How can we get ahold of you when we arrive so we can find a meeting point?"

I gave him one of the emails I used with informants. "When I get your email, I'll call back on this phone to arrange our meet-up location."

"You're oddly prepared for this kind of situation, not to mention extremely calm," Lane mused without actually asking what he really wanted to. "How are you feeling?"

"My whole body aches, I'm starving, and my reactions to things are not normal to who I am and how I've been trained," I responded, kicking myself for adding that last part on.

"You were hurt?!" Lane demanded.

"I'm fine now. When I woke up, I was healed." I sighed, feeling a wave of tiredness hit me.

"Take a nap, then eat more food. Your body is working overtime to heal you. Once you shift for the first time, it will be easier and not so taxing."

I gave a hum of agreement and headed over to the bunk, curling up once again with the phone laying by the pillow.

"We'll be there soon. Be safe until then—that's an order."

"Yes, alpha," I murmured before I drifted off to sleep.

SEVEN

LANE

Hanging up was the hardest thing to do when all I wanted was to crawl through the phone and wrap her up in my arms. That was crazy, right? *Definitely crazy.* I hadn't even met this woman, and I already felt a great loss by not having her at my side.

Crashing continued behind me in our office that Colt was determined to destroy in his grief. Colt had never given up hope that his brother was still alive, that we would find him one day—even without the United Senate's help. I could only imagine what he must be feeling, finding out he was dead just after we'd received intel that he was spotted in New York.

We would get through this just like we had everything else—as brothers.

Ten years ago, when Cory was taken and Colt's original pack was destroyed, I found him on the side of the road, a bloody, broken mess. As a paramedic, I couldn't just stand by as he died, so I went to help him. In his confusion and pain, he cut me with his claws when he tried to defend himself. That day, I saved his life, and he changed mine.

He helped me through my transition, and we became best friends. Together, we moved here to Tennessee, where we founded our own pack. Before we settled here, the two of us had roamed as lone wolves, searching for his brother. I refused to let him do it alone, so when he finally decided to set up a homebase, I was right there at his side to help him. I didn't know the first thing about being a pack leader, but many things were instinctual, and everything else I learned along the way. Our pack wasn't massive, but it was full of stable, healthy wolves, which was unusual in the supernatural world these days.

Taking a deep breath, I walked back into the office. Colt was slumped on the floor, his back against the wall and his hands covering his face as his body shook.

"I didn't find him in time, Lane," Colt rasped. "He's dead, and I wasn't there."

Maneuvering my way across the room, I cleared a spot next to him and sat. I rested my head against the wall and stared at the ceiling, silently supporting my friend. There was nothing I could say to make this better, and I wasn't one to waste words. Not that he needed them from me. He always said that actions spoke louder than words.

"Did you find out who that was on the phone?" Colt asked. "I don't really remember much after she said Cory was dead."

"Her name is Finley, and she's an omega, says she was made by your brother. We'll be leaving shortly to go get her," I explained, watching the information sink into Colt's grief-stricken brain.

Colt dropped his hands and looked at me with wide eyes. "*What?*"

"It seems your brother bit her, and before he died, he told her to find you."

"No, that's not possible. Omegas can only be born; they can't change a person. They aren't strong enough to do that. If they could, everyone would be having omegas create others," Colt explained.

I looked at him and tilted my head. "What happens to the person they bite, then?"

Colt shrugged. "I can't think of a time it's happened. Most don't even think to defend themselves; they freeze. I never saw my brother fight back or attack anyone."

"Whatever the case, there is no doubt in my mind that this woman is an omega, and we need to get to her before anyone else figures it out. Something about her seems a little off, but I can't put my finger on it." Standing up, I reached out a hand and pulled Colt off the floor. "Come on, we have a flight to catch."

"Should we bring the twins or Elias with us?" Colt asked as he brushed the drywall dust off himself.

After thinking for a moment, I shook my head. "Too many of us leaving might bring attention. I think it's best if we keep this as lowkey as possible. Our pack is growing, but we don't have enough people to guard our lands, let alone the women and children. Who knows what kind of crowd having a surprise omega will cause."

"We have to invite Zander if we want to use his plane," Cory countered as he pulled his phone from his pocket.

"Remind me again why we're friends with him. The man insists on being a lone alpha on the outskirts of our pack, getting all the benefits without putting in any of the work," I grumbled. My wolf was getting agitated at the mere thought of him. The man acted like he was a prince and everyone around him was there to cater to his whims. Sorry, but he wasn't going to get that from me.

Colt just gave me a look, letting me know my pettiness was showing, as he held the phone up to his ear. "Zander, it's Colt. We need the jet—it's an emergency. Yeah, as soon as we can fly out. Oh, New York, upstate I think." He looked to me for confirmation, and I nodded. "Great, we'll see you in an hour."

Shoving his phone back into his pocket, Colt glanced at me over his shoulder and headed out. "*That's* why we're friends with him. Didn't even ask a single question as to why, just where and when. We should feel lucky he's taking the next few months off after his last tour."

"Fine, but you have to promise to knock me out if he starts talking about how amazing he is the whole time. I don't give a fuck if he's a platinum-record recording artist; he's a prick."

Colt just smirked at me as we headed out of the office to go pack. The house we lived in was supposed to be for the alphas and their families, but since neither of us were mated, we had decided to share it with our three betas, our seconds in command. There were still plenty of extra rooms for whenever the time came to support a mate or pups once we became more established.

I was surprised when the United Senate had given their approval for our pack since neither of us had led a pack before. Although Colt's father was the alpha of his childhood pack, Colt personally had no experience. They checked in from time to time, but it wasn't like they ever did anything to help. The Senate was more of the cautionary tale that you told kids to make sure they behaved. Coming from more than twenty years of being a human, I'd had a lot to learn about how much the Senate worked on this side of things. Most importantly, I'd quickly learned to keep a low profile and not to gain their notice, good or bad, because it never worked out in your favor.

Entering the two-story house with its wraparound porch, I found Mason on the couch eating a bowl of cereal. Mason and his identical twin Noah were large brick walls of pure muscle. When they weren't working for us, they moonlighted as bouncers at the clubs in Knoxville on the weekends. The only way I had learned to tell the difference between the two was scent, because in the looks department, they were carbon copies. They kept their hair buzzed close to the scalp, same with their facial hair, and had matching light green eyes that stood out against their dark onyx skin.

"What are you two doing at home in the middle of the day?" Mason asked, his deep voice filling the room.

"Colt and I are flying out to New York with Zander," I answered, heading down the hall.

The sound of heavy footsteps following me up the stairs let me know Mason was right on my heels and wanted me to know it. Like all shifters, we could walk silently, but as a common courtesy, we often made sure our presence was known. It was unwise to trespass into an alpha's personal domain without permission, no matter how close you were with them.

"Do you need any help?" Mason inquired, leaning against my door jamb. "The twin and I don't have any jobs tonight."

Turning, I looked at him, and he stood up straight. "What I need you to do is be here and watch over the pack. I'll let Elias know we'll be gone. Tell Noah to clean out the spare room up here and make sure it's ready and stocked with basics for a woman to stay there."

Mason frowned at me. "Alright…"

I could tell how badly he wanted to question me, but doing so would be a direct challenge. Walking up to him, I placed a hand on his large shoulder. "Trust in your alphas; we will explain everything once it's safe to do so. Right now, we have to keep things quiet, or someone's life could be in danger."

Nodding, he turned to head back downstairs.

"Mason, if you ask Colt and I find out about it, there will be consequences." As born wolves, the twins were the only werewolves who had the option of fighting for a higher ranking in the pack. Those bitten were relegated to their status for life, for better or worse, no matter who or what they were in their previous lives. I didn't often fear that the twins would make a move on Colt and me, but there were times they would test the waters and push the limits of their station. Now was not the time for it, however, so I needed to know that what I'd asked would be done.

Glancing over his shoulder, I could see in his eyes that he believed me and wouldn't press the issue. I listened a moment longer until I heard him return to the couch and start munching away on his cereal once again.

I swore when I checked my watch, realizing I only had fifteen minutes to grab whatever I thought might be needed to usher an omega into our pack. I pulled a soft blanket from the end of my bed since it smelled like me, then walked to the hall closet where we kept spare sweatpants and t-shirts that were new and unscented. I wracked my brain, trying to remember what Colt had told me about his brother and what an omega needed from a more dominant wolf. Giving up, I knocked on Colt's door before I swung it open and leaned against the doorframe.

"I'm at a loss here. I have a blanket and sweats…" I paused when I saw him grabbing every soft pillow and blanket out of his room. "Umm, do I need to grab more blankets?"

Colt growled, the sound full of frustration, and tossed the pile onto the floor. "Every omega is different, but in a way, they're all the same. They want comfort and security, but *how* they get that is personal preference. My brother always liked to nest in piles of pillows that had our family's scents on them. But in this case, she doesn't know us or what would work for her."

"So, should I grab things from the betas as well? Since she'll be living here, it could help to get her more acquainted with their scents," I offered, unused to seeing Colt so frazzled.

"Yes, let's do that, then she can pick whatever comforts her the most. Even though she hasn't shifted yet, her instincts will be riding her hard to seek out what she needs," Colt said, wrapping up everything he'd gathered with a large blanket and tossing a hoodie on top.

Leaving him to his project, I headed downstairs. "Mason, I need something from you and Noah."

"Care to narrow that down a bit?" Mason asked, standing from the couch.

"A shirt or sweatpants, even a blanket or pillow would work for what we need," I clarified as I headed into the kitchen.

Opening the pantry, I grabbed jerky, a package of cookies, and a few other snacks that were higher in protein. She said she'd healed, and depending on how much damage she'd taken, she would need food to replenish herself. Grabbing my phone, I called Elias.

"Alpha," he answered.

"Colt and I are flying to New York. Stick close to the pack lands. If something should happen, Mason and Noah are here as well," I explained, knowing Elias would follow orders without question. "Oh, and I'll need to grab something out of your room."

"You are alpha. Take what you need," Elias stated before hanging up.

Others would have seen that as disrespectful, but he knew I always led with what was important. Also, in his mind, he had given me permission to do what I thought was best for the pack. Eight years ago, during our search for Cory, we had come across Elias and adopted him, for lack of a better word. He was a lone wolf looking for a pack, and we decided to take him in, which in turn made him the most loyal beta I had ever witnessed. I knew that he would give us anything we needed, big or small. Heading to his room, I looked around the stark space and decided on one of his pillows.

Okay, that should do it.

Back out in the living room, I found Colt with his blanket full of pillows, along with the clothes that Mason had handed to him. "Time's up. We gotta go."

Snagging the bag of snacks, I followed him out the door and to the large black truck. We tossed everything into the bed, and then we headed off to grab Zander on our way to the airport.

EIGHT

FINLEY

Yawning, I stretched out, cursing when my hand punched into something hard. I opened my eyes to see that I was still in the bunker in the middle of the woods in New York state. It took me a moment to go over everything, confused as to why my brain was so fuzzy about the details, but once my memories fell into place, I shot up and out of the bunk, heart racing.

How long has it been since I fell asleep? Margaret! I still need to call her and explain what happened. Grabbing the phone, I called the secure line. I immediately realized I couldn't stand still; there was way too much anxiety-driven adrenaline coursing through me right now. I climbed out of pace, starting to pace as the phone rang.

"Nature's Healing Wellness Retreat and Spa, this is Tiffany. How may I help you?" a chipper voice answered.

"I would like to inquire about the ebony package; I was told Margaret was the one to speak with," I answered, giving the necessary code phrase.

"One moment. Can I have your name?"

"Foxtrot-seven-nine-five." The line went dead for a moment before it started to ring once more.

"Finley, what the fuck happened? Did you really blow up the house and let Delilah get away?" Margaret asked in a voice as cold as steel.

I took a deep breath through my nose, needing to keep a level head considering how furious Margaret was. Margaret *never* swore, so she only did that when she was about ready to send you to a week of isolation in the small basement cell to think about what you did wrong. "Matters were worse than we thought, ma'am. As you stated when you gave me the job, I had to improvise for the best outcome."

"You're telling me the *best* outcome was this?" Margaret demanded.

"The info that Maxwell gave us was only the tip of the iceberg. I walked into a situation that would have made matters worse between you and the Senate. If I'd allowed things as Delilah intended, I would have been responsible for the death of innocent supernaturals too. I had to destroy the property because they had my prints and other information about me that couldn't get out," I explained.

A sound that I would have qualified as a growl came out of Margaret, surprising me. "Something tells me the Senate didn't give me all the correct information so that they could take you out and keep this situation under wraps."

"That would be unwise of them, seeing as Delilah is part of an underground organization that believes they have every right to embrace their *animalistic* side. It seems that Delilah is just foolish and far too open about it. She had a bodyguard with her at all times—a silverback gorilla," I said, going into further detail.

"I will be sure to share all that with the Senate when I speak to them. As for you, we can send evac to you in a few hours. I would much rather have you where I can keep an eye on you than stranded out in the woods when the Senate learns about all this."

"There's one more thing that you should know," I ventured, knowing this was the moment everything would change for better or worse.

"Well, spit it out," Margaret ordered. "It's not like you to need me to draw it out of you."

"I've been bitten—by a werewolf... an omega."

The silence on the other end was deafening, telling me all I needed to know. My time with the Organization was over.

"That can't be possible. There is no way that you could have been changed from the bite of an omega," Margaret blurted. "What makes you believe it was an omega that bit you?"

"Because I talked to him and he told me. I was his Mistress for the weekend, and he had to answer any request." I didn't understand why this was so odd. Wasn't it common knowledge that if you got bit, you changed? To me, that was just common sense. Or at least according to what I knew of shifters. What made Cory so special that Margaret, of all people, was reacting this way?

"Still, it shouldn't have changed you. Are you certain that you're a shifter now?" Margaret pressed.

"Yes, ma'am. I was mauled by a panther shifter, but I healed overnight, not a scratch on me once I woke up. Then there's the reaction that I had to the alpha I spoke to on the phone..."

"Stop, go back. Did you say you spoke to an *alpha*? Why would you do that, Finley? We could have protected you!" Margaret yelled, causing me to flinch at her disapproving tone. As the one person I'd looked up to all my life, hearing her so upset with my choice gutted me. What other choice had I really had?

Pulling the phone away, I took a moment to settle my nerves before I answered. "The omega who bit me ended up getting killed. Before he died, he told me to find his brother, said he would protect me. It's the law. The shifter's pack must take responsibility for the person their packmate bit. How could I get the Organization in more trouble with the Senate than I already have?"

"You foolish, foolish girl. I might have been able to protect you from the world of the supernatural and let you have a normal life, but you've thrown that all away." Margaret sighed, suddenly sounding so tired. "Since you have made your choice, know that once you leave the safehouse, you are no longer a member of the Organization. We will not be responsible for you. For all intents and purposes, you will be dead to us. Never contact this place again, and if you do, know that you risk death."

My heart clenched at her words. I knew this might be the outcome, but what choice did I have? If the Senate caught me, it wouldn't just be me that was affected. The Organization had given me a home, a purpose. I owed them this attempt at protecting them.

"Understood, ma'am. And since it will be the last time we speak, please know I am grateful for all you have taught me," I whispered, unable to keep my voice strong in this moment.

There was a pause before I heard Margaret take a breath. "Finley, you truly were one of our finest, a rarity in this line of work. You might be dead to the Organization, but you are not dead to me. You know how to get ahold of me if you need to, but I will stress that the need must be great indeed to ask for that favor."

"Thank you, Margaret, I will keep that in mind... Goodbye," I said, closing my eyes as the line went dead.

There was no turning back now. Everything I'd ever known and once was... was now over. After I took a few moments to collect myself, I called the alpha again.

"Finley, is that you?" Colt asked, sounding much less upset than he had the last time we'd talked.

"Yes, alpha," I answered immediately, feeling the need to keep him from getting upset with me again.

I could hear other voices in the background of the call as I waited for him to tell me where he wanted me to meet them.

"Do you have a vehicle?" Colt asked. "Some way to meet us somewhere? Or do we need to come get you from where you're hiding out?"

"No, alpha, I have a dirtbike that I can use. I'm about three hours away from New York City. If it's easier, I can come to you—"

"Absolutely not, Finley. You will not enter that city without us there with you, do you hear me? You might not be a full omega yet since you haven't had your first shift, but that doesn't mean that you won't be taken like Cory was," Colt snapped, causing me to let out a whine and hunch low.

I could hear someone else yelling at him not to be an ass, then the phone was taken from him once again. "Finley, it's Lane. Are you alright? Did you get some rest like I told you to?"

"I did, alpha," I said, answering his direct question even though I felt the need to tell him that I was most assuredly not 'alright.'

Lane grunted his approval. "Good. Now, we're going to drive out to meet you. Are you familiar enough with the area to know of somewhere quiet for us all to meet?"

Taking a moment to think about where I was and the maps I had looked at, I figured the small town an hour away might be the best place to meet. "There's a small town called Merryville. It's off the main highway and easy to find. There's a diner I can meet you at if you think that's best."

"That sounds perfect. Give me a moment to see how long it will take us to get there..."

"An hour and fifteen minutes if you go the speed limit and the traffic isn't too bad in the city. Since it's a Sunday and there's no work traffic, it might even be less than that," I answered, feeling the uncontrollable need to ease his worries about the situation.

Silence greeted me on the other end before I heard a snort from someone trying to cover a laugh. "Who is this chick?"

"Fuck off, Zander," Lane barked, making me yelp. Lane groaned, and I heard him walking away from whoever was still laughing. "I'm sorry, Finley. I didn't mean to use my bark around you. We'll meet you where you suggested in what sounds like two hours or less. Zander and Colt both have a lead foot, so I don't think we'll be going the speed limit."

"Alright, I'll meet you there. I only have MREs here, so I think I'll leave soon. That way, I can eat and be ready to leave once you all arrive… unless you all need to eat as well. I am more than happy to wait for you to arrive if you want to eat," I offered, feeling uneasy about assuming I could do that without their approval.

"No, Finley. If you're hungry, you need to eat. A new wolf burns a lot of energy. It's important that you don't get too hungry because it can make you irritable and more likely to bite or scratch someone, and we can't have that," Lane instructed.

I didn't want to disagree with the alpha, but I wondered if a normal wolf's experience would apply to me since Margaret said I shouldn't have even been changed by Cory's bite. Before I could say anything, a new voice came over the phone.

"My, my, are we coming to get an omega?" the voice purred.

A shiver went down my back—not one of fear, but a feeling that I hadn't felt in such a long time. We trained ourselves to be in control of our desires so that they couldn't be used to sway us. On more than one occasion, I'd had to use my body to lure someone in close enough to kill them, and to allow yourself to get lost in the charade was dangerous. So when heat flared in my chest at the sound of his voice, it caught me off guard.

"I don't know how to answer that, alpha. Are you coming with alphas Colt and Lane?" I asked, trying to keep my voice even.

A soft chuckle drifted along my ear. "Yes, I'll be arriving with them to get you."

"Then yes," I said, going back to his original question, refusing to give in to the need to bare my neck to this man with a voice of velvet.

"These boys always seem to have a surprise up their sleeves. I'll see you soon, my little dove," he murmured before the line went dead.

Dropping the phone to my side, I slumped into one of the chairs, then leaned forward to rest my head on the table. What the hell had I gotten myself into? Now I wasn't dealing with just one alpha, but three! How big was this pack of theirs to need so many men keeping it in line?

I had sealed my fate already. There was no turning back time to avoid facing the choices I'd made.

NINE

ZANDER

I shoved the phone into Lane's chest as he opened his mouth to say something, glaring at him. I pinned my gaze on Colt next, who was leaning against the blacked-out SUV I'd had ready and waiting for us. He had earned my trust and respect many times over during the past six years, but stealing an omega was asking for a whole new level of trust. When he told me it was an emergency, I thought one of his wolves had gotten into trouble with the big city wolves, but this situation was going to be way more challenging to manage.

"You didn't think to tell me that we would be smuggling an omega out of the state?!" I snarled. With how rare omegas were these days, each one was guarded to the point where the Senate wouldn't hesitate to kill those who dared to touch an omega that didn't belong to them.

Colt's head shot up, and he met my gaze, just barely flinching at my aggression. "It's not smuggling when your own brother is the one who changed her, Zander. I have every right to be here *and* to take her back to our pack."

Tossing back my head, I started to laugh, a loud belly laugh that almost made me shed a tear. "You think that, do you? Well, I have news for you, pup—if she gets noticed by anyone else, then you can kiss your omega goodbye. She has no pack scent nor a mate mark to keep her safe. How the hell did you even know about this?"

"She called me earlier, right before I called you. Cory bit her, and she hasn't had her first shift yet. They might not even know who or what she is," Colt challenged, stalking over to me.

Before it could come to blows—as it often did between alphas who weren't pack—Lane cut him off.

"Easy, Colt, we need to get moving. She said she was going early to get food, so if we don't want her sitting alone at a diner in some strange town for too long, then we need to get a move on."

Colt just growled at me, shoving Lane off, and stomped to the SUV, yanking open the door so hard the hinges groaned. I didn't even try to argue with him as he slid into the driver's seat, knowing that Lane was right about this situation. Even a pretentious prick like myself would put the needs of an omega before my own. *But the little omega doesn't need Lane to be in the front seat.* Smirking at the frown on the stuffy alpha's face, I cut him off and claimed the front passenger seat. I made myself comfortable, sliding my Gucci shades on and pushing the chair all the way back. It was far too easy to ruffle Lane's feathers, so it made for easy entertainment.

Pairing my phone with the radio so I could control the music, I flipped to my newest album, knowing it would piss Lane off to no end. "I'm guessing you guys haven't heard this yet since that pack of yours likes to live under a rock."

"Staying out of werewolf politics doesn't mean we live under a rock, Zander," Lane grumbled as he sighed heavily from the backseat.

I peered at him over the top of my shades. "You keep telling yourself that. Just know that ends once you tell the Senate that you have an omega in your pack. Especially when they find out she's a *changed* omega. They are goddamn fucking rare."

The SUV came to a screeching halt. "What the fuck did you just say?"

"Fucking hell, man! You trying to get us killed before we even leave the airport?" I snapped. "If you're going to be like this, then it might be better if I drive the rest of the way."

"Explain what you meant about a changed omega. Why would the Senate care?" Colt said, his hands gripping the steering wheel so tightly it was making his knuckles white.

I looked at him closely, trying to understand what had made him so upset. "Um, okay... Well, some omegas can come about by being bitten, but two conditions have to be met. One, the bite has to come from an omega. Two, the bitten individual must be a person who would have been a natural omega had they been born as a wolf. I would say there aren't many of them. I mean, how many omegas do you know that would attack someone instead of running away?"

Colt shook his head slowly. Was that sincere disbelief on his face? "Why don't we know about this? How many omegas could be out there in the world, so scared to ask for help that they end up dead or captured?"

It was then that I figured out he was envisioning his brother in this woman's place, what could have happened to him if he hadn't been born into the pack he was. From the few things I knew about Cory, I was aware that Colt had taken on the role of guarding him and keeping him safe within their old pack. When an omega was raised in a healthy pack, they were given a protector to keep an eye on them until they were mated and under the protection of an alpha. Cory had never gotten the chance to find a mate, or even to live much of a normal life.

Through some of my connections, I'd caught wind that he was being kept by Delilah yesterday, and if that was true, I shuddered to think what his life had been like in her care. I'd planned to tell Colt once I checked a few things out, not wanting to get his hopes up. I had heard whispers of some of the shit Delilah was into, and given her reputation, my own hopes hadn't been very high. This led me to wonder how Finley had wound up being on the receiving end of an attack by an omega. It never would have been Cory's first reaction to lash out—he had to have been left with no other option but to attack.

"What do we know about this woman?" I turned slightly so Lane knew I was directing the question back at him.

I could hear Lane stiffen as if he didn't want to share anything with me, but that was pointless because I was an older alpha than him. If I wanted him to back off, I could make him. Before this woman stepped foot on the pack lands where I resided, I was going to make sure she wasn't a threat. I might not want to be bound to a pack, but I would always protect those who gave me protection in return.

"I don't know much other than her name, that she was bitten by Colt's brother, and that she was hurt. Thanks to her new abilities kicking in this close to the full moon, she's healed," Lane answered begrudgingly.

I rubbed my hand over my jaw as I mulled that information over. "She said she was staying in a safe place that only had MREs to eat, the phone she called us from was blocked, and she was surprisingly knowledgeable about our journey. Something about this doesn't add up to me. No omega would be able to survive being attacked; they don't have the drive to fight back like other werewolves."

"Well, she hasn't shifted yet, so her nature wouldn't be changed as much... Right?" Colt interjected.

"Possibly, but I plan on having all those answers before she's on my plane back to Tennessee," I growled, feeling my wolf's hackles rise along with my suspicions.

***

It wasn't hard to find the town. It was just as she'd described; Maybelle's Diner was right off the short two-block strip they called their 'downtown.' Colt took a parking spot right in front near the door so that she wouldn't be out in the open for long when we left.

With it being so close to the full moon, I was more worried about her shifting early. If that happened, it could bring on her heat and, subsequently, our rut, and I did *not* want that to happen with an omega I'd just met. The chances of marking her would be too high, and I wasn't going to bind myself—and all the danger that came with who I was—to some stranger.

The moment Lane opened the door to the diner, I was smacked in the face with her scent. There was a bite of cardamom and clove, but it was sweetened with a hint of vanilla that made you want to bury your nose in its warmth. My wolf sat up, eyes alert, seeking out the owner of this addictive scent, and seconds later, I found my gaze landing on a slight woman sitting in the back corner, staring at us with wide eyes. The bright cobalt blue of her eyes was just as alluring as her scent, and before I knew what was happening, I was standing before her. Her long brunette hair had hints of red running through it in the sunlight, and her frame was so small, almost as if, were I to hold her too tightly, I would break her.

Mate. That scent rocked me to my core.

My wolf let out a growl, not liking how skinny she was. She needed to be healthy if she was to be a good mate and give us strong pups.

Mate? Pups? What the fuck was I thinking? I didn't even know this woman, and I was already planning to keep her. I'd heard the call to your true mate was one you couldn't fight, but I'd always assumed it was still a choice. After all, we weren't purely animals. But this right here felt like an obsession, like this woman was a drug, and I needed my fix *now*.

It was then I noticed that Lane and Colt were on either side of me, both as rigid as I was, attempting to keep themselves from pouncing on her. Out of the corner of my eye, I saw Lane take a deep breath, pulling in her scent and closing his eyes as his chest started to rumble. Hearing this, my wolf thrashed inside me, furious that this other alpha would dare lay claim on something that was ours. Colt echoed the sound, causing me to whip my head in his direction and snarl, rising to my full height.

A whimper of distress pulled my full attention to the omega trembling in the booth in front of me. The need to fix whatever had made our omega whine had me tossing the table out of the way so I could kneel in front of her, oblivious to what was going on elsewhere in the diner.

"What's wrong? Are you hurt?" I demanded, her flinch letting me know my voice was too harsh.

Shaking her head, she curled into a ball, peeking out at me from behind her arms. I turned around and surveyed the diner, making sure there wasn't some unseen danger, though nothing but shocked faces stared back at us. I looked back at her, and, unable to take it any longer, I reached out and scooped her into my arms, holding her tightly to my chest and letting out my alpha purr. Instantly, she snuggled into me, clutching my leather jacket as two echoing snarls sounded from Colt and Lane.

"What do you think you're doing, Zander?" Colt demanded.

He and Lane blocked me when I tried to carry my omega to safety.

Narrowing my eyes at them, my purr changed into a warning growl. "What does it look like I'm doing? I'm getting my mate the fuck out of here."

"*Your* mate?!" Lane snapped. "She's ours!"

The sound of a shotgun cocking drew all our attention to the portly man who was rounding the counter. "I think it's best if you leave. We don't welcome your kind here."

My vision went red at the sight of this gun-wielding man threatening my mate. Gently, I handed her off to Colt, trusting him far more than I did this trigger-happy bigot. Waiting a moment, I saw her burrow against him just as she had with me, setting my wolf at ease before I turned all my attention to the diner's owner. Stalking over to him, rage pumping through my veins, I snatched the gun out of his hand and broke it over my leg in one swift movement.

"What kind is that, exactly?" I asked through a clenched jaw. "Because from where I'm standing, you're the one threatening a defenseless woman."

The color drained from the balding, fat man's face as he stared down at his gun. When supers had come out, humans realized that they were no longer on the top of the food chain, and they'd taken to resenting us. Supers, just like any human, could be good or bad, but because we weren't like them, we were considered 'evil' or 'abominations.' The fact that I was as huge a star as I was despite how open I was about being a werewolf was almost unheard of, but I'd spent my entire career trying to educate people.

"Zander, we should just go. We need to get her back home—quickly," Lane said, resting a hand on my shoulder.

Glancing over at my little dove wrapped up in Colt's arms, her gaze taking everything in with uncertainty, I knew he was right. Nothing I did here would change this man's mind anyway. Shoving the asshole out of my way, we headed out of the diner to the SUV. I opened the back door so that Colt could get in easier with her in his arms, and I slid into the driver's seat. Once everyone was in, I slammed on the gas, and we shot out onto the road, getting out of this shitty little town.

TEN

FINLEY

There weren't words to describe the feeling I had while sitting in the car with three alpha males, but the only description that came remotely close was a soul-deep sense of safety. I'd never once experienced this, but it was more than a feeling—it was as if I'd always been missing a piece of my life that I never knew was gone—until now. The instant I locked eyes on them, I knew I was in so much trouble. One, because I wasn't going to want to leave them, and two, they would want to coddle me and put me in a protective bubble. I could kill a man with only the prick of a needle, but now I'd be nothing more than a wilting flower in their eyes.

"I'm sorry things went down like that on our first meeting, Finley," Colt murmured as he rubbed a hand up and down my back.

It was so soothing; along with his evergreen scent wrapping around me, I was put into a daze that wasn't entirely comfortable. My omega side was pleased beyond measure at this attention, but the independent assassin that I'd been for the past twenty-five years was irritated.

I might crave their protection, but I didn't need it. Before that diner owner had even thought about pulling his shotgun on these men, I'd known it was there. That was why I'd chosen to sit in the corner, so I could keep an eye on whoever walked in and out. I was a trained soldier, and I remembered my lessons even while scrambling to keep myself together inside.

Would these alphas still want to hold me, comfort me, once they figured out what I was? Having an assassin in their pack could change a lot of things for them and provide a level of protection they'd never had before—at least if they let me be *me*. Should I keep silent and just let them assume what they would about me, or did I take a risk and tell them the truth?

Lane turned in his seat, looking back at me with a soft smile on his face. He had warm brown eyes that held flecks of gold, adding an interesting depth to them. His hair was covered with a baseball cap, but I could see light brown strands peeking out around it. With the slight accent he had and the style of clothing he wore, I guessed he was originally from somewhere in the South. Not quite a true Texas cowboy, but he had that Southern charm about him.

"Were you able to eat before we arrived?" Lane asked.

The need to please him was far stronger in person, but I fought against the instinct and chose to answer with a simple nod. Some of the urge dissipated, the nonverbal response taking the edge off. I was too afraid to open my mouth, not trusting what would come out. How much I was willing to tell them? Knowing that I was going to be part of their pack for the rest of my life didn't mean they needed to learn everything about me right away. I had a gut feeling that right now might not be the time to drop certain bombshells. My assassin's instincts were still stronger than my werewolf, and they had kept me alive this long, so I didn't see the point in ignoring them.

"If you're still hungry, let me know. We can easily stop somewhere to pick something up along the way," Lane assured.

Zander, the largest of the three, let out a low growl. "We are not feeding her fast-food shit; she deserves good home-cooked meals. Nothing but the best will pass her lips if I have anything to say about it."

I knew who Zander was—he was far too famous a super for the Organization not to know about him—and it wasn't just because he was a very talented singer. He'd managed to do well in hiding his family connection, choosing to do things on his own without their influence, but the Organization's reach went far. It was hard to keep secrets from them.

Everything about him was imposing, and to have him sharing the small space with me was overwhelming my omega nature. When he tossed that table out of his way and squatted in front of me, I'd been unable to move, trapped by his silver eyes and the heady scent of whiskey and leather. He was bulky, with muscles threatening to burst from his shirt each time he moved. I could tell he liked the finer things, from the fabric of his clothes to the watch he wore on his wrist. He kept his hair buzzed short, and since it was so blond, it almost looked like he kept it shaved to the scalp.

I could feel him watching me in the rearview mirror, but I refused to meet his gaze to prove that I wasn't going to be a pushover. Then a purring hum filled the car, and I instantly locked on to his eyes, instinctively knowing that he was the one producing the tantalizing sound. His silver eyes glittered with triumph, pleased he'd gotten me to look at him.

"Little dove, tell me—how did you end up out here at one of Delilah's parties?" Zander asked, even though I knew he wasn't really giving me the choice not to answer.

Licking my lips, I took a moment to decide what my next move was going to be, but it seemed they didn't want to give me an option.

"I don't know who this Dalilah person is but if an alpha asks you a question, Finley, you answer it," Colt pointed out as his hold on me tightened, turning me to face him. "We understand this is new to you, but let this be your first lesson—alphas are *always* to be answered."

Emotions warred inside of me. I wanted to refuse them to show them I couldn't be manipulated, but my omega side was begging for me to give in.

"I was there to kill her," I blurted, unable to fight against the command in Colt's voice.

The car went silent at my answer, and I quickly darted my eyes between them, taking in their expressions. Lane was shocked to the point his mouth was hanging open, and Zander seemed intrigued, but Colt was the hardest to read. I saw a flash of surprise followed by a wave of anger. I innately knew he wasn't angry with me, but it was still hard to handle while being so close to him, causing me to shake a little.

"Did the Senate send you?" he asked through clenched teeth.

Tilting my head, I thought about that question. "Yes and no. I'm an assassin for someone else—*was* an assassin—but the Senate hired my company to do the job they couldn't."

"Did you finish the job?" Zander inquired.

"No," I answered, letting my eyes fall to my hands. "I wasn't given proper information, and the situation I found myself in devolved too quickly."

This seemed to upset all three of them, and I started to panic at the thought that they would be upset with me for my failure. Closing my eyes, I took a few deep breaths and tried to calm my new rioting emotions.

"Allow me to make this clear," I stated, needing to prove my worth. "In my twenty-five years in this profession, I've never failed to finish a job. I do not plan on letting this one be any different. She is the key. Through her, I'll be able to find out the identities of the others in her radical-minded group and present that to the Senate. I will find her, and I will end her—just as I have been asked to do."

"Not gonna happen, sweetheart. There's no way we'll ever allow you to hunt down someone who's known for abusing and killing supers. Not to mention that she had Cory, and it's Colt's place to seek revenge for his death," Lane informed me, putting an end to that discussion. "Now, I want you to rest. The full moon is only three days away, and too much stress before your first shift could cause problems. We can't have you changing early in the plane or someplace we can't manage your reactions."

I fought against the urge to release a frustrated huff, knowing they wouldn't like it. Seemed I was going to have to do this job on my own after all. I refused to give up so easily.

As if sensing my mood, Colt tucked me in tighter against him and wrapped a blanket around me that carried the same scent as Lane—fresh warm laundry. Then he started to comb his fingers through my hair, and his chest rumbled with a deep, bone-rattling purr that made me melt. Within moments, I knew I wasn't going to be able to fight against the urge to slip into slumber, so I stopped trying.

I felt myself being lifted and shifted into another set of arms, waking me up. Cracking open my eyes, I found Lane's gaze meeting mine with a look of such rapture and devotion it shocked me. These men knew nothing about me. How could they look at me that way? Was this a wolf thing? Could an omega's scent really have that much of a pull that it made alphas such as these fall to their knees? Would it work on betas and other wolves of the pack as well?

My mind wandered to how that could be useful that way if I continued on as an assassin. It would be so easy to render someone into compliance with nothing more than my presence. I would be in hardly any danger... as long as they were werewolves, anyway.

Lane's eyes narrowed as he watched me. "Why do I get the feeling that I won't like what you're thinking?"

Quickly, I wiped my face of all expression, surprised that I had been giving so much away. "Seems we have a lot to learn about each other," I whispered, tucking my head under his chin so he couldn't look at me.

Lane gave a noncommittal grunt as he walked aboard the private plane. Squirming, I tried to get out of the blanket in hopes I would be set down on my own two feet, and Lane begrudgingly let me go, tossing the blanket on top of a pile of pillows, more blankets, and some clothing. Zander was up by the cockpit, talking to the pilot, and Colt was coming up the steps with what looked like bags of food. Slowly, I walked down the length of the jet, peeking behind doors to find a bathroom on one side and a very well-packed liquor cabinet on the other.

"Do you drink?" Zander asked from where he'd tried to sneak up behind me.

I turned and looked up at him with a shrug. "With my job, it's frowned upon to eat, drink, or smoke anything that would impair my ability to perform well. Occasionally, I've needed to drink to play a part, but it's not something that I indulge in."

Zander cocked his head as he studied me with so many questions floating around behind his gaze. "Tell me, how does the nature of an omega mix with being an assassin?"

"Not well so far," I answered, my shoulders drooping with my sigh. "I can't tell if the fight between my dual natures will be easier or worse once I have my first shift. The omega instinct is so strong already... I can't imagine what it'll be like after the transformation is complete."

Zander reached out and gripped the back of my neck, using his thumb to brush against my cheek comfortingly. "You won't have to do this on your own; we'll be there every step of the way. It'll help settle your wolf nature once we're back on pack lands, knowing you're safe and home. The rest will come with time."

"We're ready for takeoff," the pilot called back.

Using the hand he had on my neck, he pulled me to him and scooped me up before he plopped me in a seat, securing my seatbelt before taking the chair next to me.

"I *am* able to do these things on my own, you know," I ventured, a smile tugging at my lips.

"Did she just make a joke?" Colt asked, looking up from his phone. He smiled at me, his eyes dancing with humor, making me feel all warm inside. I was pleased that I'd done that, given him a small amount of happiness.

"I would count that as a joke," Lane agreed, giving me a bright smile.

With a halfhearted growl, Zander turned away from me. "Makes me feel better to know I did it." It would appear that this was a new development for Zander, seeing how uncomfortable he was about it.

Reaching over, I gently placed my hand on his arm, causing him to snap his attention to the contact, then to me. "Thank you."

With another grunt, he took my hand in his and laced our fingers together before looking back out the window.

Once we were up in the air and able to move around, the guys unbuckled and moved to various spots around the plane with laptops or a book. It appeared that they might be trying to give me a little space, but they didn't look all that happy about it. I was grateful for it though, not at all used to being overwhelmed with so many different emotions. Getting up from my seat, I wandered over to the pile of things that was set in the corner near the most open part of the plane. I grabbed the first pillow, giving it a slight squeeze, and was hit with the scent of evergreen and fresh mountain air that instantly told me it was Colt's, and I also found a blanket that smelled like him. Kneeling next to the pile, I sorted everything out by scent, interested to see what else I might find, especially when I caught whiffs of unknown males in the mix.

Before I knew what was happening, I had my face in a pillow that had a sharp tang of sea salt followed by undertones of citrus. I could feel the pull from my omega senses, telling me this wolf *needed* me. He was in so much emotional pain. Instinctually, I knew that I would be able to soothe him and ease this pain of his if I could spend some time with him. Keeping the pillow in my lap, I grabbed a sweatshirt and pulled it on over my t-shirt, loving the fact that I was surrounded by the warm scent of chocolate and hazelnuts. I took a deeper sniff and caught the hint of coffee somewhere in the mix, leading me to pounce on the remaining items and burrow through them to find out if there was more of that somewhere in here. Sure enough, I found a shirt to curl up with, letting the coffee and cinnamon envelop me as I lay in a pile of comforting scents.

I didn't know how I knew this, but there was no question—these were my pack, *my* wolves.

ELEVEN

MASON

I t'd been hours since our alphas left with the odd order to clear out the spare room for a woman they were picking up in New York, of all places. As far as we knew, there hadn't been any talks with the packs there to allow a potential mate to visit with us. In fact, I didn't know that I'd ever seen our alphas actively interested in finding a mate at all... but I couldn't think of another reason this would need to happen so quietly—and quickly. It had taken everything in me not to challenge Lane, but I knew that if I did, I would lose, just like I had every time I tried. Even if I was on the cusp of being too dominant for a typical beta, I wasn't quite up to snuff as an alpha. But there was an instinct inside me; I just felt like I was meant for more than what I was doing now, but I couldn't quite figure it out, so I kept trying.

"Twin, did you bring those towels I asked for?" Noah asked, popping his head out of the bathroom.

"Yeah, I got 'em right here," I mumbled, handing them over. "How can you calmly do all this without knowing why?"

Noah scowled at me before he grabbed the towels out of my hands. "Twin, you know the answer to that. Just because *you* refuse to see that being an alpha isn't all it's cracked up to be doesn't mean I have to. Besides two other people, Elias, you, and me are in charge of this pack. We have all the power we need to do what is best for the pack, but the perk is that we aren't held responsible in the eyes of the Senate."

"I know all that," I growled, sitting down on the twin bed we'd pulled out of storage. "You know that I respect Colt and Lane, but I just know that I need something more, and becoming an alpha would do that. Or at least I think so. What else is there?"

"So you want to prove you're an alpha and work alongside them?" Noah asked, leaning against the bathroom door.

Just when I was going to answer, we both heard tires on the gravel driveway. In seconds, we were downstairs and out the front door, meeting them as they made it to the front of the house. The hair on the back of my neck stood on end, and my wolf paced under my skin, telling me there was something in the car that was putting him on edge.

Colt pulled up right in front of the house instead of parking in the garage off to the side, and when Lane opened the passenger door, I caught a scent that set my blood on fire. Next thing I knew, I'd ripped off the back hatch with a snarl, then frozen when I saw what had set me off. Curled up in a ball on a pile of pillows and blankets, clutching my shirt to her chest, was the most beautiful woman I'd ever seen.

Her slight body screamed how delicate she was, and she carried a spicy, warm scent that I wanted to bury my nose in, making sure it was imprinted on my brain. I'd reached out to brush a strand of hair off of her face when a body suddenly tackled me, slamming me to the ground before tossing me far enough from the SUV that I skidded into a tree. Rolling, I shot up and shifted, my clothes shredding and bursting into the air as I charged at Zander, my teeth bared.

Just as I was about to launch myself at the man, the woman burst out of the back of the car, spreading her arms wide to protect him. My body locked up in an effort to stop my action, causing me to trip over my own feet until I skidded to a halt only inches from her.

"Stop this," she ordered, and despite the slight quiver in her soft voice, she held her ground.

Zander wrapped his arms around her waist, lifting her up and away from me. "What the fuck were you thinking, Mason? You could have scared her by acting like a damn beast."

A deep growl rumbled in my chest, warning him I didn't appreciate him speaking to me like that. Even if he lived on pack lands, he wasn't my alpha. He had no right to scold me like a pup.

"Zander, please put me down," she asked, placing a hand on his chest. The contact caused him to look down at her with one of the softest expressions I'd ever seen.

Who is this woman?

Once she was back on her own two feet, she slowly walked over to me. I could see the wariness in her vibrant blue eyes, and my wolf didn't like that at all. She should never be scared of us—it was our job to protect her. Instinctively, I knew that I'd just discovered my purpose. Here I was, just bitching and moaning about my life, not meaning anything, then minutes later, *she* appeared before me. Looking at her, I knew that nothing could have filled the void like she just did with a glance.

When she reached me, I lowered my head and relaxed my ears, reaching toward her, needing to be closer to her. Her hand came out, and she ran her fingers through the fur on my neck, causing me to lean into her touch. No self-respecting werewolf would allow themselves to be pet, but damn, I didn't think they knew what it felt like. My wolf wanted to roll on his back and show her his belly for extra scratches. *That's it. This woman, whoever she is, isn't allowed to leave—ever.* I took a few steps forward and sat my ass right on her feet to keep her right where she was, taking advantage of the position by leaning against her. She let out a soft chuckle that had me perking up and giving her a wolfish grin, slowly wagging my tail.

"Holy shit, she just turned my brother into a lap dog! Who are you? More than that, *what* are you?" Noah asked, cocking his head to the side, watching us from where he stood with the alphas.

I could see it in his face that he was drawn to her as well, but as always, he had much better control over his actions. I was the explosive twin who acted first and thought about it after... maybe.

"I'm Finley, the newest member of your pack, and I'm an omega," she shared, turning her attention to my brother.

I heard my twin gasp, but I was distracted by the fact that she'd stopped petting me. I butted my head against her stomach, letting out a short, sad whine. Giving me a half smile, she started combing her fingers through my fur again. Who knew being petted was such an amazing feeling?

"Needy bastard," Colt grumbled, glaring at me, to which I let out a yip of agreement.

When I felt her freeze, I snapped to alert, taking in our surroundings and trying to see what had made her nervous. There was no way in hell I was going to let anything harm this woman while I was around. Then I heard the sound of someone walking through the woods off to the left side of the house. Lifting my nose, I scented the wind, letting out a snort. I knew who it was. There wasn't any threat to Finley, so I was content to stay where I was. It seemed that she had other ideas, though, once she saw the person exit the woods and start toward us. To my surprise, Finley shoved me off her feet and took off like a streak toward the newcomer.

"Finley, wait!" Lane called after her, but I didn't think she heard him. When she finally reached Elias, she threw her arms wide and launched herself at him, but what shocked us all was the fact that he caught her and allowed her to wrap herself around him.

Elias had become like a brother to me, but that cold bastard *hated* to be touched. Generally, werewolves were big fans of physical touch, but not Elias—he rarely let anyone get that close. I knew he had a dark past that he hadn't really told anyone about, so it was understandable even though I didn't know the details. Needless to say, seeing him with Finley wrapped around him like an anaconda was something I never expected to see. She was burying her nose into the crook of his neck as he looked at us with wide, startled eyes, but he made no movements to dislodge her hold.

"Um... Do we help him, or just let her do what she's gonna do?" Lane asked, nudging Colt with his elbow.

Colt actually looked relieved, and even Zander didn't seem at all bothered by what was going on.

"No, we let our new omega do her job," Colt answered cryptically.

We all looked at him, confused... Well, all but Zander, who appeared quite pleased with the scene unfolding before us.

"Many omegas have empathic tendencies. It helps them in their role as caretaker of the mental well-being of a pack. They instinctively know who needs them, and depending on how needed they are, they'll respond accordingly," Zander added when Colt ignored us.

"So you're saying that based on that reaction, Elias *really* needed a hug?" Noah asked with a smirk.

Lane punched him in the arm with a frown. "Knock it off. None of us really knows what he's been through, but we all know how much he's changed since becoming part of our pack. This will help bring him out even more."

"True. He talks now, and he doesn't stay in his wolf skin as much," Noah agreed, crossing his arms. "But we have our work cut out for us once the rest of the pack finds out about her, not to mention when other packs find out we have an omega."

Zander looked back at us, his brow creased in worry. "We have something far worse to worry about—she was found at the same place where Colt's brother was being held. If the Dark Ring finds out that the assassin sent to kill Delilah was turned into an omega, we are well and truly fucked."

Shifting back, I got right up into Zander's face, buck naked. "What do you mean *assassin*?! And the Dark Ring is just a made-up scary story to teach pups to be careful of strangers."

"I would take a step back, *beta*, or I will put you in your place," Zander threatened, the rumble of a growl echoing in his words.

Glancing over at my alphas, I saw they would let Zander make good on his words, so I followed his order. Zander was far older than my alphas, and even though he lived the life of a rock star, I knew he was one scary motherfucker under the act.

"That woman is a trained assassin who got bit by an omega during a mission. The Senate sent her to kill one of the known members of the Dark Ring. Believe me when I say that they are *very* real, and once Delilah tells them what happened, they will start to hunt my little dove down," Zander explained, his expression growing darker and darker. "The other problem we have is that she plans to finish the job like the good little trained soldier that she is, regardless of what we say."

"She also hasn't had her first shift yet, so there's no telling what changes might happen once she's fully an omega," Colt interjected.

"Alphas," Elias called out, startling us all.

We had been so distracted by the conversation that we didn't notice when they walked up, Finley still in his arms.

"I was just about to call you when I heard the car," Elias explained, a flash of worry in his eyes as he looked down at our newest pack member. "There's a news report saying that you three kidnapped a woman from a diner, which I'm guessing was Finley. Since they have video footage and Zander is a well-known celebrity, they know where to start looking. Once they figure out she's an omega, more than one person is going to come after her..."

Zander started swearing, Lane ripped off his baseball cap and ran his hands through his hair, while Colt's face looked as dark as a storm cloud. I met my twin's gaze, and we both nodded at each other in agreement. It didn't matter that we'd just met her; no one was taking our omega.

TWELVE

FINLEY

It was so odd for me to see so many people worked up about my safety. Everything I'd been taught was about survival and, most especially, avoiding getting caught. I should have known the diner had cameras and that they might be used against us. I'd been in a fog all day, making it hard to think clearly. My only guess, and it wasn't any comfort, was that the closeness of the full moon was messing with my whole body. I thought I'd likely have my first shift any day now.

Being around all these alphas and betas wasn't helping matters. All I wanted to do was snuggle up with them and sleep. The sense of peace I'd gained from being surrounded by their scents on the plane was addicting, and even now I craved to nuzzle up to Noah and that sweet chocolate scent he gave off. It seemed to match his personality, versus the spicy coffee and cinnamon scent of Mason. Despite being twins, I could easily tell they were as opposite in personality as they were identical in appearance. Even the energy they gave off was vastly different. Noah was more calm and controlled. There was something else that was hiding just under the surface, but I couldn't put my finger on it. Mason was like a firecracker; he was fast to ignite—whether it was good or bad—making his personality shine brightly. My intuition told he was the one people gravitated to for his confidence, but it was also what probably got him in trouble.

Elias had set me down on the porch before returning to the others who were still talking, and Noah opened the door to the pack house, ushering me in. I paused, taking in the open concept of the house, needing to understand the layout before I went any further. There was no way I'd be able to settle in before I knew where all the exits were. The living room was large and inviting, connected to a dining area that had a massive wooden table, easily fitting twelve to fifteen people. Everything was very masculine, with deep rich tones and a lot of wood and leather, but it still felt welcoming and comfortable.

"Our pack house is a little different from a normal home. Typically, the betas don't live in the pack house, so I guess that makes us lucky we get to be close by. If you need us, our rooms are down the hall past the dining room," Noah explained as he led me deeper into the house toward a staircase to the left of the living room. "Upstairs is where Colt and Lane's rooms are and where yours will be."

"Zander doesn't have a room here?" I asked. At the top of the stairs, I was surrounded by my alphas' scents, causing me to pause and take a deep breath. I had to force myself not to run off and roll around in their beds. When I opened my eyes, Noah was standing in front of me, his own eyes wide and pupils blown.

Oh god, can he tell how deeply affected I am by their smell? This is going to take some getting used to.

Noah cleared his throat and shook his head as if to clear it. "Right, ah, Zander has his own house elsewhere on the pack lands. This is your room here."

A little put out, I looked at my new space. Of course it would be the room inbetween both alphas because being this close to them wouldn't be torture enough. Stepping into my new room, I found it was set up very simply, containing a twin bed with a nightstand next to it, and an attached bathroom. I opened the only other door and discovered a closet with a set of built-in drawers for all the things that I didn't have any longer. Walking back out into the room, I sat on the end of my bed and looked around, feeling the true impact of what had happened to me. It wasn't about not having my things from my apartment at the Organization; that could all be replaced. What I couldn't change was never being allowed to return to that part of my life ever again. As far as they were concerned, I was dead, so all my possessions would be destroyed and forgotten. Finley, assassin for the

Organization, was no longer, and I didn't know how to process that. A hand brushed my cheek, startling me. I had all but forgotten that Noah was in here with me.

"Sorry, I didn't mean to startle you. I just couldn't take seeing you so sad," Noah murmured.

I brushed a hand over my cheek, checking to make sure I hadn't cried or anything equally as pathetic. I was alive and had a place in this new life. There were lots of other people out in the world who weren't as fortunate. "It's nothing, just these new emotions to get used to. They never talk about how much your wolf nature affects your personality."

"Yeah, I'm not the best person to help you with that. Mason and I are born wolves, not changed, so we've always had our wolves with us," Noah explained. "Lane was changed by Colt; he would be able to give you some pointers on learning to deal with a second person in your brain."

I took a deep breath, closing my eyes, and centered myself to calm my emotions. Thankfully, it still worked as it always had. I needed some things to stay the same.

"Are you hungry, or do you want some time to yourself? I'm sure the alphas have been a little overwhelming... It's kind of their nature," Noah said with a grin.

My stomach growled at the offer of food, making the choice obvious. "I'm fine to make something myself if you show me what I can use."

Noah's brows shot up in surprise. "Why would there be rules on what you can eat?"

"I'm an omega, the last in line... Isn't that how it works?" I hedged, his look of horror telling me that I was mistaken.

"Finley, we might be created from wolves, but we're human as well. Yes, there is hierarchy in the packs, but one thing that will never happen in a healthy pack is allowing *any* member to go hungry. Our bodies burn so many more calories than a normal human that we have to eat frequently and in larger amounts. To withhold food would be cruel."

Now that he'd explained it, I could see how my question showed my ignorance of their world. The main things the Organization had taught us about supers was how to kill them, not how they lived. It would seem that I needed to go back to basics and learn all I could about my new environment. Knowing the rules would keep me alive, especially now that I would be under the critical eye of the Senate.

"Just so we're clear on things, you are welcome to anything you can find in this house. No one will stop you or get upset. If they do, ignore them because it will most likely be my brother, and he's an idiot. Now, it's been a long day, so why don't you let me fix you something? I'll show you where things are for next time," Noah offered, rising from the bed and offering me a hand.

Without hesitation, I reached for his hand, enjoying the warmth of his touch. It only made me crave more contact with him.

Jerking my hand back, I blinked at it a moment before looking up at him. "Is that a wolf thing too? I mean, it makes sense from what I know about werewolves, I guess. I've just never been one for physical contact, but it's like I *need* it now."

"Oh yeah, that's totally your wolf. As pack animals, we need to feel each other for comfort as well as scent marking. If a rogue wolf were to enter the pack, we would all know right away by their strange scent. It also works if you get lost, letting another pack know where you came from."

Grasping his hand, I let him pull me up and lead me back into the hall. Other than our three doors, I saw more rooms down the hall and what looked like a library or study. "Are there books here about being a werewolf?"

Noah contemplated that for a moment as we headed down the stairs. "I don't know that we have any, but Zander might. I know he loves to collect old and rare books, so you'll have to ask him."

"Ask me what?" Zander asked from where he was cooking something on the stove.

It smelled heavenly; lots of garlic, butter, and other rich flavors assaulted my nose in the best way. I let go of Noah's hand and drifted over, letting my nose take over my brain until I was leaning against Zander, eyes half closed. "What are you making?"

"It's a parmesan garlic sauce to put over some noodles and chicken. I figured you were going to be hungry after all the traveling," Zander answered, nuzzling my head with his cheek.

Hearing what he said snapped me out of my daze. "You're making that for *me*?" I can't even remember the last time someone cared enough if I was hungry and made me something.

"I sure as hell wouldn't be cooking it for any of these assholes, little dove," he chuckled. "This isn't my home. I live on the edge of the pack lands, in my own house. You'll have to come see it and pick out a room. Since it's only me that lives there, you've got plenty to choose from. If you don't like any of them, I'll take down some walls and have one custom built."

My mind added this information to what Noah had told me, trying to put it in order with everything else I knew about him so far. If he didn't live in this house, then he wasn't a pack alpha—he was a lone alpha. Back at the diner, he had claimed that I was his mate, but so had Lane... Could a werewolf have that many mates? Was it an omega thing? God, I hated not knowing what the hell was going on in my own life.

"Little dove, what's wrong?" Zander snapped, making me flinch away from him at the tone of his voice.

I made to move away, but his hand shot out and gently grasped my throat, making it known I wasn't going anywhere.

"No. I asked you a question, Finley. We covered this already. If an alpha asks, you answer," Zander scolded, making it impossible to resist him any longer.

"Nothing is wrong," I stated. It was the true answer to the question he'd asked, and I didn't plan on giving him more than I had to. I had always followed orders from my superiors, but they always made sense and were for a reason. What Zander wanted from me was purely personal, and I was *not* playing that game.

"Are you lying to me right now?" Zander growled, all but causing my legs to give out in a mixture between terror and pleasure.

I wanted to please him and make him stop growling at me, but I also wanted to kick him right in the dick for being an ass. "No, you asked what was wrong, and there's nothing wrong."

"Looks like she's got you there," Mason interjected. "Leave her alone. You're being a dick for no reason."

I heard the stove turn off, the pot shift, then Zander picked me up, carrying me out of the kitchen and back up the stairs. He kicked my door open and sat on the bed with me over his lap and my ass up in the air.

"What the hell are you doing?" I snapped, squirming to get out of his hold.

That was when the first slap echoed in the room, followed by the sting of where he'd hit my right ass cheek. "You should know better, Finley. You're a trained soldier, and I'm your commanding officer. When I ask you a question." *Smack.* "You." *Smack.* "Will." *Smack, smack.* "Answer."

With each impact of his hand, I shattered further from who I was. My omega nature wept at upsetting our alpha, whereas my assassin side boiled with rage at how I was being treated. No matter the war inside me, I was unable to do anything to fight his strong hold. I gritted my teeth, refusing to let the whimper that was stuck in my throat come out. I would not let him best me in this.

"The longer you fight me, the longer this will go on. Submit, and this will be over," Zander ordered, continuing his assault on my ass.

As my skin began to burn more intensely, he picked up the speed and force, letting me know he'd been taking it easy on me. It was at that point my omega nature won out, a whine slipping past my lips as I started to shiver. Something inside of me suddenly started fighting for control, clawing its way to the front, and instead of a whimper, I screamed and started to convulse.

"Fuck!" Zander swore as he shifted us down to the floor. "Colt, Lane, get up here now! She's starting to shift, and it looks like it's gonna be one hell of a battle!"

I lost all track of time, senses, and self; stuck in an endless loop of pain, I fought back against what was trying to take over my body. *I won't lose to you, damn it. I'm not an omega. I'm a motherfucking assassin who can take care of herself!* Unfortunately, my wolf didn't give a shit about what I thought. It was here and moving in whether I liked it or not.

THIRTEEN

COLT

Entering that room to find Finley on the floor, drenched in sweat, screaming, and convulsing, terrified me. This was nothing like any transitions I'd seen in my life; she looked more like she was demon possessed than shifting into a wolf. I'd been with Lane when he went through his first shift, but I'd had enough time to help him accept the fact that he was going to be a werewolf. My ferocious little mate hadn't had even forty-eight hours to come to terms with being bitten, let alone losing her job, home, and life as she knew it. Add on the knowledge that this was happening way too fast *and* she was going to be an omega, the complete opposite of what I knew of her so far, and it was no wonder she was fighting this.

Shifting closer, I pulled her head onto my lap, brushing her hair out of her face. I started to talk to her in a soft, low voice I'd used when my brother was a baby. "It's going to be okay, little one. Let the shift happen; your wolf is a part of you. I know this isn't fair and you never wanted this, but we'll help you through it. Come on, Finley, don't do this. There are worse things than needing to lean on others."

I had no idea if she could hear what I was saying or if it was just our presence, but she finally stopped screaming. Her body was still twitching, but not as violently as it once was. Glancing up at Zander, I found him sitting there, watching her, his body frozen as if he were afraid to do anything.

"What happened? Something must have triggered her shift. The full moon isn't until tomorrow night."

Zander met my gaze, and something that almost looked like guilt flashed in them. "She wasn't submitting when I asked her a question, so I was disciplining her. I should have known it was too soon to push her that hard. She hasn't had her first shift, and even if she's acting like an omega, she isn't one yet."

This made far more sense. When bitten wolves, particularly people who were turned into submissive ones that conflicted with their human personalities, fought against their new nature, their instincts tended to fight back. The new werewolf genetics were stronger than the human, forcing them to submit to their new role in life.

What we were witnessing right now was a battle between dueling natures. Would they be able to find balance? I'd never known a person who was bitten by a wolf whose nature was incompatible with their own. Lane didn't see himself as an alpha, but he'd taken to it like he'd been born that way. Sure, he was more gentle about things than I was, but that was his personality, and one could still be a strong leader while having a softer touch. He hadn't lost himself just because his wolf was more dominant. In fact, I thought his designation had simply shown another side of who he truly was. Would that be the same for Finley? Could there be a part of her, however small, that actually craved submission? That wanted to be cared for, pampered, and provided for?

"Zander, you said that for a bitten omega to be able to happen, the person needed to be innately compatible, right?" I asked, running my fingers through her hair as she quieted even more.

He shifted to take her hand in his, rubbing his thumb on the back of it. "I've never met one, but from what I've studied, yes. It's the only way that the mutation can happen from a bite."

Lane got up from the floor beside me and walked over to the bathroom. I heard the sink running before he returned with a damp washcloth and set it on her forehead. Always a medic first, no matter what the situation. I couldn't argue how useful that training was.

"She's going to be alright, isn't she?" Lane whispered, eyes locked on her face. "Should we strip her out of her clothes so she can't get twisted up in them? I think that would just freak her out more."

I felt like an ass for not thinking of it myself. Between the three of us, we stripped her and placed a sheet over her stunning naked body. Even though I tried to be as respectful as I could, there was no way to stop the raging boner I now had thanks to the knowledge that her bronze glow was natural. Unless she sunned out in the nude...

She let out a sharp gasp, eyes snapping open to reveal her now-glowing breathtaking blue eyes. Her wolf was close, meaning her shift was too. "Guys, I think we should give her some space. I don't think she's going to be happy when her wolf emerges."

Rolling onto her stomach, she got up on her hands and knees before her skin began to ripple, then burst, replacing the beautiful woman with an equally gorgeous pure black wolf with shining cobalt eyes. Finley whined and dropped to the floor, panting, her sides heaving and tongue lolling out of her mouth as her body tried to compensate for the stress it was under. Happening without the pull of the full moon, everything about this transition was rougher and faster. I wasn't sure what the right move was at this moment; typically, I would also shift to address things as a wolf would, but being an omega, I feared it might be too much for her.

"Finley," I murmured, shuffling a little closer to draw her gaze to me.

The look in those haunting blue eyes made me pause—that was *not* the look of an omega. No, that was the look of an assassin. My wolf charged forward, and a growl trickled out of my lips as I narrowed my eyes on her. As if a switch had been flipped, the look was gone. She was on her back, belly up, head back, offering up her neck. There wasn't a more submissive pose she could take to convey her apology. I cut off the growl and moved closer until I was right beside her head, studying the way her ears flattened, as if she was waiting for me to hit her, when I reached a hand out."Finley, you have nothing to fear from me. I'm your alpha and protector. No harm will come to you," I promised. We were werewolves, and we loved our mates fiercely.

My hand settled on her head between her ears. Her fur was like silk to the touch, and it made me want to bury my face in it. As she shifted back to lay on her stomach, tail wagging, she watched Lane and Zander's slow approach with a guarded stare.

"Easy, little dove. The first shift is always the worst, but it will get easier. You put up one hell of a fight, that's for sure," Zander shared as he ran a hand down her back. "Any idea who won?"

Her ears pricked up as she tracked him with her eyes, but that didn't give anything away.

"Guess I can't get mad at you for not answering my question when you can't speak... very clever," he teased. Finley made a chuffing sound that almost made me think she might be laughing.

Lane stood and started to take off all his clothes, tossing them on the bed. "Come on, guys. We have to take her for a run and a hunt so we can feed her wolf."

"Ah, yeah, about that... It's a little different when it comes to an omega. They can't make the kill themselves. If we want this to work how it normally does, we'll have to do it for her then give her part of the kill," I explained. "She might have better luck making the kill if we let her go with some of the less dominant wolves."

"You want to send our mate out on her own?!" Zander snapped, causing Finley to whine and jerk away from us, hiding under the bed. "Look at her! She's a four-legged chew toy. There is no way that I'm letting her go without one of us."

"I'm not saying we can't be around, but we have to stay out of sight and downwind," I argued. "Giving her the chance to get even a taste of a kill will make her that much stronger. I've seen omegas that can fend for themselves if the need is dire, and I *need* to know that Finley can be one of those few. If the Dark Ring is really after her, then we owe it to her and ourselves to give her the best possible chance to survive. She's different, a trained assassin who's been changed into an omega. Who knows what odds she could defy."

The two of them frowned at me, not at all on board with what I was proposing.

"There's no need for her to survive when she has us looking after her," Zander challenged.

That was when I snapped and got right up in his face. "Yeah, well, so did my brother, and now he's DEAD!"

Suddenly, there was a shaking body wedged in between us, someone licking my hand. Finley had come out from under the bed to try to stop a fight between alphas. I took a deep breath and squatted down in front of her, holding her face in my hands as she licked at my cheek.

"Do you know how stupid that was?" I asked, leaning my forehead against hers. "Don't ever do something like that again. A fight between alphas is bound to happen, and it's not your place to stop it."

She let out a sharp, disapproving bark and butted into me.

"Seems as if she disagrees with that," Lane chuckled. "What if we send her out with the betas and see how things go? We'll watch from a distance and make sure nothing disturbs them. Zander, did you get ahold of your contact at the Senate?"

"I left a message. If they don't get it in time, we still might have visitors coming after her, but if we prove she's a werewolf, then the human police have no jurisdiction here," Zander pointed out. "Although if it's the Dark Ring, they won't give a fuck about the rules."

"The sun is starting to set. If we're gonna go, I'd rather everyone be back home and safe before it's pitch black outside." Lane sighed then shifted into his wolf and shook out his black and tan fur.

"I'll go find the others while you two head to the hunting grounds," I called as I headed downstairs. A giant white and silver wolf shoved past me, running out the specially made werewolf-sized doggy door that we had installed. "No need to be such a dick, Zander!"

Mason and Noah were in the kitchen eating what Zander had been making. "Where's Elias?"

"When the screaming started, he went to his room. I'm kind of shocked he didn't leave the house," Mason said, shoving another forkful of pasta into his face. "What? It's wrong to let good food go to waste."

Shaking my head, I walked down the hall to Elias's room and rapped on the door. "Hey, you up for taking Finley on her first hunt?"

"What the fuck, Colt! You're not gonna ask us?!" Mason yelled from the kitchen.

Elias opened his door, and the haunted look in his eyes told me that something wasn't okay. "She's alright? It sounded like she was being torn apart."

"Finley is fine... I think. She just had some trouble wrapping her head around being an omega, so she put up one hell of a fight," I answered, gripping his shoulder gently. "You okay?"

He nodded and stepped out of his room, shutting the door behind him. "Is there a reason you three aren't taking her?"

I motioned for him to follow me back to the kitchen. "There have been a few rare cases of omegas being able to have a proper first hunt if they're with less dominant wolves. Our hope is that Finley might be one of these since she's unlike anything we've dealt with before. You guys up for the task?"

"Fuck yeah, who wouldn't want to take snuggles out for a hunt!" Mason cheered, shoving Noah so hard he all but knocked him off his seat. "Come on, twin, let's go play with our new packmate."

"What if we're too much? Mason and I are strong for betas, and Elias isn't a slouch either," Mason questioned.

"Look, all I can ask is that you guys try. Even if she can keep pace and join in, it would be better than slinking in the trees, watching and waiting to be able to pick the bones clean." I sighed. "The first hunt is important, even more so because it bonds the person and the wolf together. Right now, they're not doing well with that. Her shift was the worst I've ever seen; she fought it the whole way."

Noah's face fell at this news. "Then we'll do all that we can to help support her. No one should be at odds with who they really are."

FOURTEEN

FINLEY

"Give yourself a moment, then come down when you're ready," Zander murmured as he stroked my head. "Everything's going to be alright. I promise, little dove, we will all help you through this."

Seconds later, he shed his clothes and shifted into a massive white wolf with hints of silver running through his coat. He was stunning to look at, and my wolf preened at the knowledge that this male was our mate. Zander licked my muzzle before bounding down the stairs, making Colt curse him out as he left the house.

Now alone, sitting on my haunches in my new room, I looked around, seeing everything as a wolf would. My eyesight was sharper than anything my human brain could have imagined. I stilled when I caught sight of myself in the mirror over the bathroom sink, hitting me with the urge to stand up so I could see all of my new body. My coat was jet black, but my eye color had stayed the same, if not slightly brighter, as my eyes glowed with that primal intensity that all wolves had. In the back of my brain, I could sense my wolf was pleased that I approved of her form, and that had our tail wagging. It was odd to feel like myself yet... more. My wolf didn't take over my brain like I thought she would. Instead, she sat on an equal plane as if we shared space side by side. The closest way I could think to explain the feeling was what the Organization had tried to teach us about working with a partner—two parts of a whole working in tandem to get the job done.

My wolf had the feeling of her own personality, one that would likely have a strong influence on my behavior, but I still felt like I hadn't lost who I was before getting bitten. Finley the assassin was here, but that was no longer *all* that I was—I was now an omega too. I could feel her excitement to go run in the forest as well as a reminder that she was very hungry because *I* hadn't been doing a good job of feeding us. Her thoughts running through my head was the part that was going to take some getting used to, but there was nothing I could do to change that. I slowly padded out of the room and down the stairs, knowing that the others would be there. I'd heard them talking but was too focused inward to listen in on what they were saying.

Once they saw me, the talking dropped off, and the twins gawked at me while Elias gave me a shadow of a smile.

"Damn, snuggles, you look good as a wolf." Mason grinned, coming to squat down in front of me. "Can I touch you?"

The human part of me wasn't sure how I felt about being pet like a dog, but my wolf was all for it. Surging forward, she shoved my head into his chest, rubbing my cheek to mark him with my scent. His large hands started to scratch behind my ears in a way that felt no less than magical, and a sound I'd never heard before started to rumble in my chest. He chuckled as he kept up the attention.

"Would you look at that? I got her to purr," Mason boasted.

"Little one," Colt called, forcing me to lift my head to look at him. "You ready to go on your first hunt?"

I yipped and wagged my tail like the excited puppy that I *wasn't* convinced I was. In this body, I was finding that she had more power to control our actions, so I was hoping the opposite applied while in my human form. I wasn't thrilled with how things were going at the moment, but I didn't know how to stop her from acting like an idiot.

"This hunt will help you and your wolf settle in together. If you want to eat, you have to catch it and take it down yourself," Colt explained.

Okay, easy. How hard can that be? As a trained killer, all I have to do is figure out how to use this new body.

"These three are going with you. If you need one of us alphas, just call out to us and we'll find you. It's going to be fine, little one. I have faith in you and your wolf to figure this out. All you have to do is stop fighting her," Colt stated, giving me a scolding look.

My ears dropped, as did my gaze, when the fear of disappointing him became too strong. Then I felt a snout nuzzle under my jawline, bringing my head up to meet a set of light green eyes on the face of a dark gray wolf. I could tell by his scent that it was Noah, so I booped him on the nose with my own, letting him know I was okay. Another dark gray wolf stepped up, giving me a toothy grin. Mason had a little more white mixed into his coat, making it easier to tell them apart by sight. Finally, I spotted Elias sitting by the doggy door, watching me with a cautious hazel gaze. He was a beautiful deep red mixed with black. I'd never seen such a color on a wolf before, but it gave him something of a regal look. Seeing that he had my attention, he jerked his head and exited the kitchen with me right on his heels.

We left the house at a quick trot, and I couldn't help but get distracted by all the sights, sounds, and smells that assaulted my senses. Birds flitting about in the trees, squirrels dashing through the underbrush, and the scent of so many wolves, it made my head spin. The guys kept me in the center of the pack as we moved deeper into the woods, following some unknown trail to what I assumed was their hunting grounds. In all my experience I couldn't say that I'd spent much time out in the boonies of Tennessee, but it was beautiful—all tall trees, rolling hills, and mountains. The fresh air was crisp with the winter chill, but nowhere near as cold as it had been in New York. My ears swiveled, picking up every snapped twig, as I focused on finding my first kill as a newly shifted werewolf. The guys slowed and spread out a little more, giving me a chance to get a sense of where we were and how I wanted to handle this.

Hunkering down low, I kept to the shadows, using my dark coloring to my advantage. My attention shifted to the wind as I approached. If I stayed downwind, I'd have a better chance of keeping my scent from giving my location away to any prey. Just as I was about to break out of the dense foliage and into a clearing, I spotted a rabbit feasting on some plant off to the left-center. Through the eyes of my assassin training, this was a perfect score, an easy hit. How threatening could a bunny be to a predator?

My wolf, however, had other ideas. It was too out in the open, and if we missed, the others would steal it from us, forcing us to go hungry. I had to fight back the urge to growl, knowing it would scare the rabbit, but I refused to let this chance pass us by. Squaring up into position, muscles tense and ready to attack, I grabbed hold of my wolf and took control, charging forward. The speed that I had in this body was fantastic, and I easily made it across the clearing, but what I didn't count on was a fox making for the same rabbit that I was. The bastard snatched the damn thing right as I was about to pounce, then darted back into the dense underbrush with his prize. Snarling, I took off after the fox, but, being smaller, he easily evaded me by diving into a burrow with a swish of his tail as if to flip me off.

That little asshole! I swore, which came out as me barking like a damn chihuahua.

My three escorts appeared out of thin air as I started to dig at the hole, letting out frustrated yips. Elias brushed up alongside me and pushed me away from the hole, urging me to get back to the matter at hand. I sneezed at him in irritation, and he swatted at my nose before giving me a warning snap of his teeth to show he didn't appreciate my actions. This caused my wolf to turn into a puddle of despair, sinking to the ground and army crawling over to him, whining for his forgiveness.

Get the fuck up! He isn't that mad at you. It was a simple scolding because you were behaving like a child, I groused at my wolf, but she was having none of it. Elias needed to forgive us, right here, right now, or she was going belly up and begging.

Thankfully, Elias took pity on us and licked my face, urging me to get up so we could go hunting again. Somehow I had a feeling this was as new to everyone else as it was to me. If I was going to be prostrate on the floor any time they were upset with me, it was going to make for a very interesting day. My nature was to push my limits until I found where I couldn't cross the line; those were the boundaries that I lived by. Indulging in a full-body shake, I got my head back in the game and dragged my wolf along with me, running further into the forest. As we picked up speed, she seemed to calm down, the two of us flowing into one symbiotic unit. Now I understood what Colt had said about this helping us meld together. I just had to help her get with the hunting program.

A deer darted out in front of us, and my wolf wanted to slam on the brakes when we saw the antlers on the buck. In my very basic knowledge of the animal, I knew it was still young, only having a few sprouts that didn't seem too dangerous. *We are gonna take down this deer. Do you hear me? Think of how full you'll be when we're done. Won't that be the perfect ending to our first hunt?* Begrudgingly, my wolf agreed. Taking in my surroundings, I noticed the guys following a little further back. If I wanted to get this deer into the right spot, I was going to need their help. Unfortunately, this was where my wolf drew the line. Omegas did *not* tell other wolves, let alone betas, what to do. If we wanted the deer, we had to do it ourselves or abandon the idea altogether. Growling in frustration, I started working on the next plan of action. That was when I saw the fallen tree leaning at a forty-five degree angle, providing the perfect place for me to get the right takedown.

Digging my nail into the wood, I streaked up the tree, and just as I'd planned, the deer ran right by it, right in line for me to drop on its back. Latching my jaw around the base of the deer's neck, I used my weight and momentum to take it down to the ground. Quickly, I had to switch my hold on it and sink in closer to the head, shaking it back and forth as I clawed at it with my front paws. The deer was strong, and it kicked out at me, catching me in the side. I yelped and lost my hold. As the deer struggled to get up, I swiped my paw over its eye, sending it reeling back, off balance, giving me the chance I needed to finish the job. Ripping out its throat sent blood spurting everywhere, and I was thankful that I wasn't white; otherwise, it would have looked like I'd been in a horror movie. Dropping the pound of flesh I had in my mouth, I watched the last few minutes of its life drain away. Elation shot through me from my wolf as we let out a howl to announce our achievement for all the pack to hear.

The betas trotted up to me and started to lick my face clean of blood. Mason and Noah both gave yips of excitement as they tried to get me to play with them, while Elias backed off to sit out of the way. He watched closely with his tongue lolling out of his mouth in a way that felt much too silly for both the man and his wolf. My wolf knew the moment the alphas arrived, and before I could stop her, she backed us away from the kill and laid down, her wagging tail the only display of accomplishment. Zander sniffed the deer, checking it over, before he padded over to me and licked my face in approval. Colt and Lane took hold of the deer and started to drag it to a more open area where they could feast on my kill.

Once the alphas had dug in, the betas ventured closer, testing to see if they were welcome. Colt and Lane didn't seem to mind, but Zander snapped at them to chase them off. He tore a chunk of meat off and plopped it right in front of me then took a step back before sitting to watch me eat. I crawled forward and licked at the gift, still not sure if I was allowed or if he was testing me—we had been in trouble with him before all this happened. Zander nudged it forward and took another set back, giving me no doubt I was expected to eat this, which I did with great pleasure. When I was done with that portion, Colt and Lane both offered me more which I gobbled up the feeling of being cherished by my mates making it taste all the better.

Finished with the deer, everyone having eaten their fill, Colt sat down and lifted his head, loosing a howl that was quickly followed by Lane and Zander. The rest of us got pulled into it as well, binding us all in this moment while inducting me into their pack.

Only there was something else that it triggered as well...

FIFTEEN

FINLEY

Heat flooded my body, and I didn't mean my temperature was rising. No, this was a feeling I'd never experienced before. It was almost like my body was aching, yearning, and demanding to be filled. My wolf pulled back from me, triggering my shift. Somehow, she knew that my needs couldn't be tended to like this. What we were desperate for had to be taken and given in our human body. The feeling of being thrust back into a body with two legs and arms was just as awful as the first switch to being a wolf, only not as drawn out. Crouched in the mud, I gasped for air as a blinding need took over, making me feel like I'd been drugged. My body pulsed, forcing a cry out of me when it felt like I'd just wet myself. Swiping a finger along my leg, I realized it was slick like lube, which only made me panic more. That was *not* normal for humans. What the fuck was happening right now? Looking up, I found all six wolves circling around me, eyes bright with desire. They were taking deep shuddering breaths of my scent which was thick in the air.

"What's happening to me?" I begged, worried even as my wolf tried to reassure me. As much as my human brain was freaking out, my wolf was excited. She was practically pacing in my mind, trying to tell me something that I just wasn't understanding. Lane shifted first, making it look so much easier than what I'd experienced so far. His golden brown eyes were filled with lust as he moved toward me with slow, cautious steps as if I might run away from them.

"Finley, I need you to stay still. Do you hear me?" Lane instructed.

I gave a jerky nod, but when I caught his scent on the light breeze, warm, clean, and comforting, I gasped. My body was begging me to go to him. I felt so empty, incomplete, and wanton, needing something only he could give me.

"Tell me what's going on, Lane," I whispered, afraid to do anything that would make this worse.

"You're going into heat, and in doing so, you're sending us into rut. Do you know what that means?" Lane bit out through clenched teeth, letting me know this was serious.

"No. I mean, kind of? Going into heat is when dogs breed... Is that what's happening to me? If this happens, does that mean I could get pregnant? Do you want kids? I never planned on having kids. Assassins don't have kids! Wait, I'm on birth control. Will that matter?" I rambled, so utterly lost at the reality of being unable to control my own body.

Never in all my twenty-nine years of life had I been more scared than I was right now. Everything about this was out of my control, and that was not okay with me in the slightest.

Colt shifted, and the others followed, leaving me surrounded by six naked men who were very much interested in whatever pheromones I was putting out. I was used to one-night stands, the nature of my job not allowing much more than that, but these men were built on a whole other level that I wasn't sure any woman could handle. My nerves must have finally bled through to my wolf, and for the first time in the last few minutes, she reacted as something other than a lust-drunk schoolgirl. It occurred to her that we might be in some kind of danger from these men, and she wanted to hightail it out of here. It took everything I had to fight her desperation to run, knowing that Lane had told me not to do that very thing. What would a wolf do if its prey took off? Chase it, of course, and at this moment, their prey was me.

"Little dove, we need to get you somewhere safe. You can't be out like this or else every male in the pack will be after you," Zander said, his voice rough like he was fighting off a growl. "I can feel you fighting the urge to run, but that's exactly what we need you to do. My home isn't far from here. Head straight east and don't stop until you see my house. You won't be able to miss it, I promise."

"What happens if you catch me before I get there?" I questioned, feeling like this was a stupid plan.

Zander closed his eyes and took a deep breath as if to calm himself, but it seemed to do the opposite. "You'll either get fucked in the dirt or in a bed, but one way or another, I'll be pounding into that pussy before long."

A shiver of delight went down my spine. I should not be turned on by what he'd just said; any other woman would freak the fuck out if they were in my situation. Must be an omega thing. That was the only explanation that made sense for how fucked up this was.

"Think you can hold off long enough to give me a head start? I don't know these woods, but you do," I asked, praying they said yes.

The betas looked to their alphas who never dropped their gazes from me.

"We'll do the best that we can, little one. You're gonna need all your skills to make this work," Colt warned, not giving me much hope. "We'll close our eyes, and that should give you a minute or so to get moving."

Taking a deep breath, I pulled my wolf to the front, using her need to flee to help the shift along. I waited until I saw them all close their eyes, then I bolted, digging my nails into the soft dirt as I ran like my life depended on it. Seconds later, I heard snarls from behind me, followed by a chorus of howls that alerted the forest to their hunt. Using the fact that I was smaller and lighter than the boys to my advantage, I ducked and darted, making sure I didn't run in a straight line. A flash of white appeared to my left as I dove through some brush to hide me from sight. They could scent me, but without being able to lock eyes on me, I had a chance. I pushed my new wolf form to the breaking point, stretching my legs out as far as they could reach, knowing I needed to move as fast as possible. Bursting out of a bush, Colt tried to cut me off, but I kicked off a tree trunk and sailed over him, landing a safe enough distance away to start running again.

Two gray wolves tried to box me in just as I saw the house. It was a massive modern-style three-story home with tons of glass windows. Its warm light beckoned me to reach it. Mason tried to take advantage of my distraction, but I dug in my heels, causing him to miss me and slam into Noah. The two of them tumbled to the side. I hadn't seen Lane or Elias, but I couldn't focus on that when the goal was in sight; all I needed to do was make it the last few feet. The threat of other wolves coming after me was enough to keep me single mindedly lasered in on the finish line. Knowing there was a chance of six men fucking me tonight was a terrifying mixture of "I must be insane" with a dash of "oh my god, I think I got turned into a whore." Because the idea of being owned by these men brought the need I'd been restraining back into high gear. There wouldn't be a second chance for me to get away. If this had to happen, it was gonna happen in a house—with a bed.

Ten feet from the house, I got sacked by a streaking red blur that sent me skidding across the dirt with teeth on the back of my neck. Where I would think a normal wolf would try to save themselves from dying at the hands of their attacker, my omega forced us to go limp. The act was one of pure and effortless submission. Meanwhile, Lane stalked up to us, teeth bared as he snarled at the beta holding me. His mouth still full of my fur, Elias snarled back, placing himself over me to claim me as his—or that was how my wolf viewed it. Lane, on the other hand, was not having it. He attacked Elias, and the two of them became a whirlwind of teeth and claws, leaving me a chance to make it the rest of the way to the house... or so I thought.

Zander was the next to claim me as his prize, leaping off the porch and rolling me onto my belly. Carefully, he wrapped his teeth around my throat, causing me to once again lay there like a lamb to slaughter. Unable to handle my wolf running the show, I pushed her back and shifted, Zander instantly following suit. He nipped and licked up my neck, his fingers fisting into my hair as he ground his dick along my thigh.

"Zander," I gasped when he latched on to my nipple. "Please, the house is right there. Don't do this in the dirt."

He looked up at me from his place on my breast, snarling, and I released a pleading whine. That seemed to do the trick, snapping him to attention long enough that he hauled me up, wrapping me around him, and carried me up the steps to the sliding glass door. He charged up two flights of stairs to the third floor which was completely open with a massive bed along the far wall. Glass windows along the length of the bedroom flooded the room with the glow of the sunset, but I didn't have a chance to really admire it since I was flung onto the bed. Zander pounced, engulfing me under his large body.

"Little dove, this is not how I wanted our first time to happen. I'll try my best to avoid marking you, but know that as your true mate, I'm not sure I can," Zander explained between kisses. "With this being your first heat, it could possibly be completed faster if you just let us mark you, not to mention being safer in the long run."

"Don't you dare fucking pressure her into that," Lane roared before he tossed Zander's body off of mine. "She doesn't even know what you're asking her to consider!"

Noah and Mason crawled onto the bed and flanked me, letting their hands run down my arms and over my chest, which surprisingly eased some of my fear. The scent of so many alphas and strong betas permeated the air with their wildly different scents. Chocolate and cinnamon were strongest with the twins around me, but hints of whiskey and evergreen wafted around as well. My body began to convulse, and the flood of slick resumed its gushing. Like a fire being stoked into a raging inferno, I was lost to it. The only awareness I had was of how much I *needed* something to fill me, to complete me. Never in my life had I felt so incomplete or lacking in some way, but I didn't know how to fix it. Then I felt it, the blunt head pressing at my entrance, his nearness sending me into an orgasm before he even penetrated me.

I screamed with the release. "Please don't stop. Fill me, please!"

All my prayers were answered when the cock slammed home, pumping in and out of me at a speed that was deliciously inhuman. The fog cleared enough for me to see it was Colt who was balls deep in me, arms wrapped around my waist and teeth buried in my neck to give him better leverage. If I had still been human, this would have broken me in two, but I wasn't anymore. This was everything I ever needed in life—comfort, connection, and the sense of belonging to something bigger than myself. I clung to him, my hands on his back and my legs wrapped around his waist, holding on with everything I had for fear he would stop fucking me. The sound of slapping flesh and grunting filled the room as the other men watched Colt take me like a man possessed.

Lane looked equal parts worried and hungry as he focused on Colt's face at my neck, but I couldn't think of what he possibly could be upset about. Colt's thrusts became deeper and more forceful, something I hadn't thought possible. Then I felt it—Colt slammed home, snarling into my skin, as the base of his dick grew three sizes larger, pushing my pussy to the point I thought it would break, but it didn't. Oh no, quite the opposite happened; it sent me into another earth-shattering orgasm as his hot cum shot out, filling me. His cock swelled to the point he couldn't thrust any longer, even with all the lubrication I was providing. Instead, it changed to a slow rocking motion that had me losing my everloving mind. The connection between us triggered climax after climax until I wasn't sure what my own name was.

At some point, Colt stopped thrusting, and we just laid there wrapped up in each other as he licked the bite mark he'd left on my shoulder. I tried to shift away from him, but I quickly discovered that we were absolutely still connected to each other. I could still feel the heat and need lingering in my body, the sensations warning me it wasn't over.

Fuck me, this was just the eye of the storm.

SIXTEEN

FINLEY

"Anyone coherent enough to tell me why I'm stuck to Colt?" I rasped, my voice raw from screaming my pleasure.

"Well, snuggles, that would be because you are hella knotted up at the moment," Mason shared, peeking his face over Colt's torso.

Relaxing into the bed, I combed my hair out of my face and scowled at him. "Pretend I'm a new wolf who doesn't know what that means."

"When alpha werewolves have sex with their mate, they swell at the base of their dick, locking them in place to make sure that their seed has the best chance of getting their mate pregnant. You, as an omega, are like crack for an alpha because you were built to take their knot—in both holes, I might add. Some females of other ranks struggle or can't accept an alpha's knot, so they just don't go as deep or hard during sex. Us lowly betas aren't equipped with the extra *pleasure button*, but we can still manage to rock your world, don't you worry." Mason grinned as he wagged his eyebrows as if he was sure he'd get the chance to show me.

I peered down at Colt, who was done licking my mark but had yet to relax his hold on me. Lifting a hand, I combed it through his hair. With that motion, his chest began to rumble which, in turn, made other things vibrate. I moaned as it echoed through my body from his cock wedged deep inside me. Colt deepened his purring even more, bringing me into a state of complete and utter contentment. It wasn't the fact that I had been fucked better than ever in my life.

More importantly, I felt wholly taken care of at this moment. I was in the arms of my alpha, my mate, safe, warm, and with my pack who would always look after me. A feeling my wolf craved and I had never experienced before, it was as if in this moment both sides understood each other. *Is this what it could be like with my wolf? Seems I have a lot to learn. Good thing I have so many teachers.*

"Mine," Colt growled as he shifted my head to kiss me for the first time.

It was odd to think that a simple meeting of lips could be more intimate than his dick still being inside me. Knowing that my trysts were just that, I didn't typically involve kissing. What was the point of that when all I wanted was to be fucked? This... this moment was like my soul was reaching out to Colt, just as his had reached out to me. Something settled into place between us, and I knew that I belonged to him in every way possible... which terrified the human side of me. Now I understood why Lane had looked so worried about what might happen between Colt and me.

Colt pulled back and looked down at me with such tender love, swirls of lust mixing in as he playfully nipped at my chin. He shifted so I was on my back, then he gently pulled out now that his knot had relaxed enough to do so. Before my brain could register that I was once again empty, I whined, reaching for him, but he caught my hands in his and kissed the backs of them.

"I know, little one, we've got you. The need is going to come back, but it's Lane and Zander's turn to take care of you," he reassured as both men crawled over. "I'm going to find us some food and drinks because you won't be leaving this bed for a while." His words calmed me as Zander slid in behind me, running his hand up and down my arm.

Lane gripped my chin, turning me to look at him. "Sweetheart, do you understand what happened between you and Colt?"

"Yes, I'm now his," I answered the best I could as that need started to build in me once again. Having Lane's scent so close to me while adding in the heat of Zander's body melded to my side, I was losing all reasoning—fast.

His grip on me tightened, pulling me out of the haze; my wolf was worried we'd upset him somehow. "Do you understand that if we take you, the same thing will happen with us? We can have the betas take care of you. They don't feel the need to claim you as strongly as we do."

My wolf and I both started to panic that our alphas didn't want us. "No, please, don't reject me, Lane!"

"That is *not* what I'm saying at all, Finley. I don't want to take the choice from you as to who you mate with. I know that our wolves have decided we're mates, but we aren't animals," Lane clarified, stroking my cheek.

When he put it that way, I could see this was more of a struggle for him to come to terms with the situation than it was for me. In that brief explanation, he showed he didn't like the fact that his werewolf instincts were winning out over his human control. So I did what any omega would—tried to ease his concerns.

"I'm already mated to Colt. This is my home, where my pack is," I explained, giving him a soft smile as I started to rub my legs together. I was feeling the slick starting to pour out of me again.

"Lane," Zander cut in, "Colt already sealed her fate. Her heat won't end unless she's marked and seeded by both of us."

Lane growled as he glared at Zander. "I know, but this isn't how I wanted to take a mate. What happens when she wakes up from the heat and realizes what we did?"

"What we already planned to do—help her," Zander countered. "You think I like how this is turning out either? This whole day has been one unknown after another, but this isn't something we can fight. She's ours, and not marking her will only hurt her in the long run."

I tried as hard as I could to follow along with the conversation, but I was drifting in and out of my needy haze while they figured their shit out. A hand brushed along my hip, and I whimpered, spreading my legs wide so they could get better access to where I needed them most. Empty, I was so utterly empty. What an odd feeling... I never thought

I would be in such a state where I would beg to have a cock shoved into me. Large, strong hands cupped my face as lips descended upon mine, and I moaned, wrapping my arms around Lane's neck, letting him lift me so I was seated on his lap.

"I need you," I whispered into his ear. "Please take me, Lane. Make me yours."

Lane growled into my neck as he curled around my body before lifting me and sliding me down onto his thick cock. He was longer than Colt, and I wasn't sure if I was going to be able to take all of him, but with the magical power of being an omega, I managed. Lane took long, slow strokes, letting me settle onto him. Shamelessly, I draped myself against his chest, trusting him to take care of me however was needed. Another hand stroked down my back, sending lightning shooting through my skin, and I began to writhe on Lane's cock.

"Do you feel full enough, little dove, or can you take more?" Zander murmured against my ear.

"More," I sighed, reveling in the thought that I could please two alphas at once.

Hands trailed down my hips to my ass, and a finger started to massage my asshole. With the abundance of slick, it glided in easily. Like Mason had warned, I was more than ready to handle Zander without much prep, but my alpha wasn't taking any chances with my care. Lane stilled, holding my body steady, and Zander sank into my ass, causing me to cry out in bliss. I was filled to the brim. It took them a few moments to find a rhythm that worked, but once they got the hang of it, they didn't hold back.

Zander gathered up my hair so he could kiss up the back of my neck while Lane feasted on my breasts, kneading one with his hand and sucking on the other with his mouth. Never had I felt my body so stimulated. It was like I was no longer in my own skin but looking down at what was happening to me. That was when I felt the shift of their intentions, but before I could stiffen or fight them, Zander latched on to the nape of my neck and Lane at the swell of my breast. A scream was torn from my mouth as I was hit with an orgasm like a freight train had barreled into me. Both thrust, locking us together with their knots, then proceeded to torture me with aftershocks as their knots hit all the right places over and over again. The need cooled as I was flooded with their essence, my body hungry to accept their marks on my soul.

The same connection that I felt with Colt snapped into place with Lane and Zander. It centered me and my wolf more than the hunt had, as if this was what we needed to successfully bond us together.

Once they'd marked me, my alphas chased the betas out of the room, refusing to share. I only remembered bits and pieces of the next day as the need drove my every move. My mates filled me, over and over and over again, in any opening that I had. Zander was down my throat as Colt filled my pussy and Lane filled my ass, the three of them drowning me with their seed. As time went on, it got to the point that I couldn't tell my own scent from theirs. During moments of clarity, they would help me get food and water down before the next wave would take me, but I noticed that those breaks were eventually becoming longer and longer. Then, just as suddenly as it came on, that desire vanished, leaving me raw, sated, and in the middle of a nest of men that were wholly mine.

⸺⬦⬥⬦⸺

"Little one," Colt whispered as he ran his fingers through my hair, "it's time to wake up." I wriggled in his hold, burrowing deeper into his chest while sighing in contentment.

Colt chuckled as he scooped me up and hauled me off the bed. Instinctively, I wrapped my arms around his neck, cracking an eye open to see he was taking me to the bathroom. I hummed my pleasure, happy with the idea of being able to clean myself up after all the fluids I'd been coated in during my heat. Colt set me down then started the shower, giving me a chance to check out his ass and marvel at the fact that he was mine to keep. *Wait... am I basically* married *to three men?* That idea struck me two-fold. My human logic was slightly panicked at the commitment I'd just signed up for with these men I'd only known for a day or two. Being in heat, my brain was so muddled I didn't actually know how much time had passed. My wolf, unbothered by what just happened, was napping in the background of my mind, content.

"Where is everyone else?" I ventured, trying to hide how unsettled I was.

"Downstairs, getting lunch ready. We figured you would be pretty hungry after everything," Colt said, turning back to me, a hand extended.

I looked at it, then back at him, hesitating before I took it. He gently guided me into the large glass-walled shower and backed me under the spray of water which was just this side of scalding. It helped to relax some of my aching muscles, and I took a deep breath, steadying myself. Colt grabbed a loofah and body wash, proceeding to scrub me from neck to toe with gentle care. I let my eyes close and allowed myself to indulge in his soft touches. This level of care wasn't something that anyone had shown me before.

"It's okay if this is overwhelming for you, Finley. None of us expected this to happen as fast as it did. Truth be told, I should be apologizing to you. If I hadn't marked you, then the others would have been able to hold back," Colt said as he scrubbed my back. "These days, not many wolves meet a mate, much less one that's an omega. Packs don't intermingle, and as you've gathered, omegas hardly venture from where it's safe. I want you to know that we will respect how you want to move forward with this, but there are some things neither of us will be able to resist, like touching each other. Newly mated couples tend to hide away for a few weeks, like a honeymoon, so that they can be near each other all the time. You lucked out and got three of us, but we can't leave the pack unattended for that long with the threat of someone coming after you. Now that you're mated to us, though, there's nothing they can do about it. Mate marks are the most protected claim a wolf can make."

"I didn't mark you, though?" I questioned, turning to face him. "How will they know that *you're* taken?"

The moment the question came out of my mouth, I snapped my jaw shut with a click; my wolf didn't like the idea of another female sniffing around what was ours. Not that she would fight the other wolf, but she definitely wouldn't be happy. *Don't worry, I have no problem explaining things to anyone who tries to steal from us,* I assured her, but she shook her head at me and went back to her nap as if I just didn't understand.

"Your scent marks me, little one," Colt answered with a grin. "That, and the fact that I have zero problem telling a woman to back the fuck off. Wolves mate for life. Other than pack matters, I have absolutely no interest in spending time with any other woman. Besides, you're part of the pack. It's not going to be a secret that we're mated or who you are to the rest of the pack. An omega is someone who is very involved in everyone's lives."

I mulled all that over as he started to wash my hair, his fingers massaging my scalp in a way that was simply addictive. I became putty in his hands, languishing in the contact until he wrapped me up in a towel before darting back in to clean himself up. I took that time to rummage through the drawers, trying to find a brush of some kind to deal with my hair. Thankfully, it was naturally pin straight, but I still needed to work the tangles out.

I glanced up into the mirror, feeling someone watching me, and wound up staring into Zander's silver eyes, noting their possessive heat and the grin on his full lips. Without breaking our stare-off, Zander approached me from behind and settled his hands on my hips.I bared my neck to him, instinctively requesting a kiss, and a purr rumbled in his chest.

"My little dove seems well looked after," he murmured, running his cheek along mine to scent mark me. "I figured you might need a hand finding a few things, like clothes to wear, before coming down. What does my mate need, hmm?"

"Clothes would be good, and a brush if you have one," I answered.

Pressing a soft kiss to my lips, he tugged a drawer open and pulled out a brush and blow dryer. "I'll be back with some clothes."

Is this what life with mates is going to be like?

SEVENTEEN

FINLEY

Hair dry, I left the bathroom and found women's clothing sitting on the bench at the foot of the bed. I couldn't stop myself from sniffing them to make sure I wasn't going to put on another woman's clothes, but they smelled brand new. My wolf relaxed and chuffed in approval, knowing that they were new and hadn't touched another woman's skin before. I, on the other hand, was frowning as I checked the sizes. They would definitely fit well; even the bra was the right size. Slipping on the dark-washed jeans and the warm, soft knitted sweater in a blue color that almost matched my eyes, I felt back to normal. Not bothering with the socks that were left for me, I padded down the stairs on silent feet, pausing before heading down the second set to the main floor.

"How did she seem when she woke up?" Lane asked, voice full of concern.

The sound of a cup hitting the counter quickly followed. "She's fine, alright. I know you wanted to be all noble about the situation, but it's done. Finley is our mate, and I for one am thanking whatever gods might be listening to end up with a woman like her," Zander snarled.

A growl that I somehow knew was coming from Lane echoed up the stairs. "Don't presume to know what I'm thinking, Zander."

"Your assassin skills might typically serve you well, but don't forget you now have scent to contend with," Elias said from directly behind me.

I spun on my heel, lashing out at him with a kick, but he deftly moved out of the way. He apprised me with those haunted hazel eyes for a moment before his lips seemed to fight a smile. "Never thought I'd see the day where an omega would attack another wolf, let alone a beta."

"I guess my training is too strong for my new nature to remove it entirely," I offered, not understanding it myself. I didn't mind his inspection, but my wolf was now awake and utterly concerned that Elias was going to be upset with her.

"That type of conditioning must have started very young, makes me wonder what other surprises you hold. Come let us set your mates at ease now that they know you're close," Elias suggested, letting his hand gently run across my lower back as he brushed past me.

Catching on to what he said, I paused to listen, noticing that the talking had stopped. When I looked down the stairs, there they were, looking up at me questioningly.

"You planning on coming the rest of the way down, or lurking?" Zander inquired, letting me know I hadn't been quite as successful at hiding myself as I thought.

I followed Elias into a kitchen that was just as impressive as the rest of the house. Everything was modern, sleek, and top of the line, making it very clear that the owner of this house had plenty of money to spend. The island was covered in plates, bowls full of fresh fruit, and platters of piping hot food, making my mouth water. Lane came up and rested a hand between my shoulders, guiding me over to the plates before handing me one, indicating that I should help myself. My wolf who'd just started to relax and curl in the back of my mind shot up, extremely unsettled at being asked to go before anyone else had gotten their food.

"I can't go first," I murmured, not wanting to broadcast it because the whole thing made no sense to my human brain. My wolf was adamant about it though. I could *not* take from others of higher rank.

Thankfully, Lane caught on right away and took the plate from me. "Anything you don't like or can't eat?"

I shook my head and dropped my eyes to my hands, pissed that I couldn't shake these omega instincts even while in my human body. A hand grasped mine, squeezing it gently, and the stark color difference and the whiff of warm chocolate told me it was Noah.

"Come on. Let's get you a spot at the table, hmm?" Noah suggested as he led me through the kitchen to the large round table and pulled out a chair. "Are you a coffee drinker?"

"Yes, I certainly am," I answered, smiling up at him.

He brought a mug, the coffee carafe, milk, and sugar over to the table for me to help myself. Surprisingly, he didn't linger while I doctored up my morning brew. Without him right next to me, my wolf relaxed enough to do this simple task ourselves. Knowing it had been given to us seemed to make all the difference. Knowing that they weren't interested in it, that they were actually providing it to me, gave me the freedom to take what was left for myself without fear of upsetting them. Forgoing the cream, I scooped way more than an appropriate amount of sugar into my cup. This was my one and only vice; I *loved* sugary sweet things but rarely let myself indulge. With my training and job, I normally needed to be at peak health and performance, but something told me I didn't need to worry about that quite so much now.

"Bit of a sweet tooth there, sweetheart," Lane teased as he set a plate down and kissed the top of my head. "Good to know."

The plate was overflowing with food, so much that I wasn't sure anyone could eat this amount, but all the others had even more on their plates when they sat down. The alphas dug in first, then the betas, while I watched, slack-jawed, all of them going to town on their meals.

"Still can't eat?" Mason asked, pausing with half a waffle hanging off his fork.

Much to my own surprise, laughter slipped out when I went to answer him, causing everyone else to pause. "Do you guys have any idea how ridiculous you all look? No one should be able to eat a full waffle in two bites, and I'm pretty sure that is a *serving* spoon, Zander."

Zander looked down at the utensil in question and shrugged. "I hate cold eggs."

For some reason that struck me as hilarious, and I broke out into a full belly laugh. The guys just looked at each other, unsure of what to do.

"Oh god, I can't remember the last time I laughed that hard," I wheezed, wiping at my eyes. "If I didn't know you were wolves, I would have guessed I was around bears storing up for the winter."

Colt cracked a smile and shook his head. "Can't say that we spend much time with people outside our pack or anyone who isn't used to the amount shifters eat. If you think this is a lot, then I can't picture what you'd think about *actual* bear shifters. They cook a whole pig to eat themselves—never get tricked into an eating contest with them. You'll lose."

"Ha, if you think that's impressive, you've never seen a whale shifter eat before," Zander countered.

"No one has seen a whale shifter eat! They're the most reclusive bunch I've ever heard of," Lane shot back, stuffing potatoes into his mouth.

Zander growled at him but stopped after what sounded like someone kicking him under the table. Colt gave Zander a warning look before both of them turned to me as if I was supposed to know what was going on.

"His growl didn't bother you?" Colt asked, perplexed.

"Why would it? I wasn't the one in trouble..." I ventured even though the reason sounded odd to my own ears.

Colt canted his head as he thought that over. "Interesting, and you lashed out at Elias earlier, which no one else would do seeing as the pack all think he's scary. It seems you are turning into a different kind of omega than I've ever seen before. Must be the assassin in you," Colt chuckled.

"Elias wouldn't hurt me. He's my Sentinel," I answered, knowing in my gut that the term rang true even though I didn't really know what it meant. I wasn't even sure where the word had come from; it wasn't something I'd heard before.

Elias' head snapped to attention, his eyes wide. "What did you call me?"

"Ah... Sentinel?" I answered.

"What about Mason and Noah?" Elias pressed.

I turned to look at them sitting there side by side, eyes locked on me with great interest. "They're Companions. Wait, no. Noah is a Companion, but Mason is a Hunter... yet somehow also a Companion." Turning back to my mates, I frowned in confusion. "What does any of that mean?"

"Finley," Zander said, starting to make me tense by using my name, "what's your family heritage?"

"I have no clue. From what the Organization told me, I was pulled from an orphanage at the age of five. They put me into training right away, and it's all I've ever known... Why?"

"Do you know which orphanage or if it's still around?" Colt continued, ignoring my question.

My hands fisted in my lap as irritation bubbled up, making my wolf whimper at my distress. I took a deep breath, closed my eyes, and focused on bringing myself to a calm center before opening them to answer. "There had been no need for me to learn that information since I had no desire to find out anything about my past. Could one of you please tell me what's going on?"

"You might not have ever been human," Elias spoke up.

"These terms you used for them are Elvish in origin—Light Elf, to be more specific. Sadly, elves haven't been around for quite some time... or so we thought," Zander added on. "Being creatures of the forest, shifters typically had a good relationship with them. They were honorable and proud people who kept to themselves, but they always came to our aid if we needed it. There were also the Dark Elves, though they were not so kind or honorable."

"They were creatures of darkness who slipped into people's dreams, living off fear and nightmares. A hundred years before supernaturals came out, there was a war among our kinds when the Dark Elves tried to take over and cast the world into chaos and darkness. The Light Elves took it upon themselves to destroy them because the Dark Elves were created from Light Elves who'd been tainted by dark magic. The battle was of epic proportions, and in the end, the Light Elves won at the cost of their own lives. It was presumed that they were all dead, but it might be that there was a survivor or two."

"You make this sound like such common knowledge, so why haven't I heard of this before?" I demanded. My nails lengthened into claws, digging into the table as irritation turned into anger.

Colt reached over the table and took my hand in his, steadying me. "You've seen what the world has done with the information that it currently knows. Do you blame us for not sharing everything about our past? The elves gave a great sacrifice to the world, but the only ones who know about it are the supernaturals. The world knows of elves in theory only. They were private people, gifted healers who loved their community and the nature around them."

"Okay, so I used terms that they would, but that doesn't mean I'm an elf," I countered, trying to grasp at anything that meant my whole identity wasn't a lie.

"There aren't many in the supernatural world who take more than one mate—shifters *never* do. It's not how we're built. We mate to one woman for life, and one woman only. For three alphas to sit here without trying to kill us or each other is a miracle. In any normal circumstance, they would've torn each other to pieces, which leaves the reasoning that it has to be because of you," Mason explained.

I looked at all of them, feeling even more lost than I had after getting bitten by Cory. My training had only prepared me to handle problems

I could fix—*this* I couldn't fix. "None of this makes sense. I have no magic, pointy ears, or anything at all that's unusual about me."

"Elves have a lifespan of eight hundred years or more. They don't mature into their full form until they turn thirty... Are you sure you know your age?" Colt questioned.

Wracking my brain, I thought back through my life. The Organization didn't really spend time on acknowledging individual birthdays, so they had everyone age up on New Year's. It could very well be that I wasn't thirty like I believed I was.

"There's a strong possibility that I might not be thirty yet although I know it will happen this year. I just have no way of determining when my actual birthday might be," I answered. "Plus, I feel like we might have bigger issues to worry about. Has there ever been an elf that's gotten turned into a werewolf before?"

The guys all looked to Zander who was absently scratching at his jaw as he thought. "I'll have to do some research, but I wouldn't say that it was a common occurrence. Elves didn't believe in mating outside of their own kind."

I was trained to handle things that got thrown at me, to absorb them and find the best move to make while going forward. Doing this was default, but it also kept me level-headed when I felt like everything around me was shifting sand. First, I became a werewolf, then I found out how rare it was to become an omega. So far, I'd been navigating this, but I knew nothing about elves, so what the hell was I supposed to do with that? Everyone assumed there weren't any left alive. Me being alive was a clear indicator that was incorrect, but what did I do with that information? I needed to know more. The more I knew, the better I would feel.

"Alright, do you guys know more about these terms or what mating is like between elves?" I urged, trying to get any kind of answer to my situation.

"Female elves are treasured since not many are born, and they also have more magical talent. Through the years, many other supernaturals have tried to kidnap and enslave female elves to gain access to their powers, and that danger was responsible for the creation of their elven mate units—called a *Nos.* They're a support system to share the burden of protecting females and offspring."

"Alpha Mates are the ones best suited to be a strong leader for the female in all ways; they also tend to be better breeders. Sentinels are just like they sound, guardians. They're there to back the Alpha Mates up with protection if they aren't around. A Hunter is the best tracker and provider for the female, and he supports the Sentinel. Companions are mates who mesh with the female on an emotional level. They tend to fill the role of confidant, and they help manage domestic matters," Zander listed, then paused as if he were hesitant to continue. "The stronger the female, the larger the *Nos.* Only the female knows who belongs in the unit. Seeing as you haven't come into your magic yet, there could be more of us..."

EIGHTEEN

NOAH

The look on Finley's face told me that she couldn't handle any more shocks for the day; she was holding it together by sheer willpower. I looked at all the others, trying to gauge how they were feeling, but I couldn't shake the pull to wrap Finley up in a blanket and help her through this. Seemed that her claim of me being a Companion was right on the money.

"I think that's enough for now," I broached. "There's a lot that we don't know and need to do some research on, so why don't we focus on what we want to do today?"

Finley flashed me a look of thanks as she started to eat.

"Well, Lane and I have to get back to check in with the pack, also need to check on a few business matters," Colt shared, draining the last of his coffee and bringing his plate to the sink.

I knew he was talking about dealing with people coming after Finley. We'd decided not to bring it up just yet since Zander seemed to think he could get the matter dropped. After having this whole conversation, I was glad that we didn't add that on top of it.

Early this morning, we'd had one of our pack show up, letting us know that federal marshals had come looking for Finley. Obviously, since she wasn't there and neither were any of us, they said they'd come back later, but truthfully, they didn't have any standing here on pack lands.

If they brought a Senate rep with them, then that would be a whole different story.

"Want to explore the pack village or see what mischief we can get into here, snuggles?" Mason asked, wagging his eyebrows at her.

"Why snuggles?" Finley questioned with an arched brow.

Mason grinned, thrilled that she'd asked about his ridiculous nickname. "You looked so cute all snuggled up in bed that I just knew it was the perfect nickname. Besides, you're an omega, total snuggle material."

Finley looked unconvinced but didn't argue with him about it. Good thing too because my twin would make it his mission to change her mind about it.

"Still want to be an alpha, twin?" I asked through our mental connection.

Surprise flickered over my twin's face as he tried not to react to me using that mode of communication. *"Nah, this sounds way more interesting, and she's way cuter to hang out with than the alphas."*

"We need to think of something fun to take her mind off of what's been going on. You sure a pack tour is the right move?"

"Tree fort?"

"Tree fort is perfect."

Both of us were grinning at each other like fools as Zander talked about something with Lane and Colt. Elias gave us a calculating look, but he chose not to bust us on talking through our twin connection.

"Mason, Noah, you're with Finley today," Colt instructed as he walked up behind Finley, setting his hands on her shoulders. "I need Elias with us, and Zander got word back from his contact, so he's going to meet with them."

"Don't worry, Colt. We'll keep her safe," I answered as Mason shared his agreement.

"We're gonna have a pack dinner tomorrow night so that everyone can meet Finley. I was going to wait longer, but we think it's better that we have introductions sooner rather than later," Lane added as he walked up to stand by Colt. "The sooner our pack can help integrate our new omega, the less trouble we should have with outside scores. Also, the Senate will advocate for us being that omegas are highly protected."

Colt leaned down and kissed Finley on the temple, whispering something in her ear before heading to the door. Lane did the same, but he pulled her into a half hug as if he didn't want to let her go just yet. Eventually, both our pack alphas and Elias headed outside, shifted, and raced into the forest to our pack village.

"Little dove, this is your home now as much as it is mine. As your mate, what's mine is yours. Between all of us, you will always be provided for. I took the liberty of ordering some clothes for you. Once they're delivered, they'll be placed in the master bedroom closet. If you give me a four-digit code, I'll add it to the security system so you can come and go as you please," Zander said, pulling her out of her chair. "There's nothing off limits in this house, so you should feel free to go wherever you like. Snoop in any drawer you want. I have nothing to hide from you."

"I don't even know what to say to all that," Finley murmured, looking around the house with new eyes.

Zander gave her a tender look as if he understood how overwhelming this all was. "Let me show you something before I have to leave." Finley nodded and followed after him.

Being the nosy beta that he was, Mason was hot on their heels, which meant I was going too. Someone had to keep my twin out of trouble with Zander and Mason both having hot tempers. On the second floor, the right side was a large open living room with the latest and greatest flatscreen TV, video game systems, and sound system to boot. To the left was a hallway that led to the guest bedrooms that we betas had been relegated to once the alphas had gotten lost in the rut. At the end of the hall was a door, but seeing as there were five guest rooms and only three of us, we didn't bother to snoop—that, and it had a code lock on the door. Zander typed in the code and pushed open the door.

I held back a gasp as we entered what looked like an indoor greenhouse with floor-to-ceiling windows and plants that filled the room. The floor was covered in a really fucking soft carpet that your feet sank into, making you just want to roll around on it and stare up at the sky since even the ceiling was made of glass. In the center of the room was a gauzy canopy with a fucking gigantic bean bag chair in the middle of it, all in soft blues to make it look like a cloud.

"What is this room?" Finley asked, amazement written all over her face.

Zander led her over to the bean bag, and without any hesitation, she crawled right up on it, snuggling into the plush fabric. "I'd always hoped to find a mate one day, but with my career and lifestyle, I'm gone for months at a time. Knowing this, I wanted my mate to have a space of her own to do with what she wanted while feeling like a princess. In my limited dating experience, I found many females feel like omegas are treated differently and catered to more than is normal, so I fashioned it after what an omega nest would be like."

The blissed-out look on Finley's face told me that he had absolutely made the perfect nest. Even if she didn't know it yet, we would definitely find Finley here often. Yeah, she might be an elf, but she was fully omega too. This would be the perfect place to decompress after dealing with all the emotions that tended to fly around in the pack. "Zander, are you saying this is *my* space?" Finley asked, sitting up to look her mate in the eyes, conflicting emotions running over her face. Could it be that she hadn't ever been given her own space before we came along?

He cupped her face between his large hands and rested his forehead on hers. "Yes, my little dove, this room is yours to do whatever you want with. If you want to toss everything out and start over, we can. Want to change the paint, say the word. Need to add something, point it out, and I'll have it here the next day."

The romantic in me was envious that he could provide such a big gesture for her while Mason and I had more humble offerings. The two of us got paid from the tithe that pack members gave, and we worked as bouncers for extra cash, but Zander came from money. Even without his music, you could just tell. All I knew was that even if I couldn't buy her the world, I wanted to give it to her one way or another. If that was through supporting her and being a shoulder to lean on, I would do a damn good job of it. Now I needed to find out everything I could about being a Companion so I could be exactly what she needed.

Nineteen

FINLEY

As I was still trying to wrap my head around the fact that Zander was giving me this room to call my own, he gently caught my chin in his hand. I glanced up at him, getting captured by his cool silver gaze that looked at me like I was his whole world. He leaned down, pressing his lips to mine, and the instant they touched, I melted, my wolf overwhelmed.

"I'll be back tonight, hopefully with more information about you and the elves in general. Be good. Don't make trouble for Mason and Noah, or else I'll have to do something about it," Zander warned, but I wasn't worried. The hunger in his eyes told me I wasn't in any real danger.

"Wait! Before you go, I had asked Noah about books on omegas. He thought you might be the best source to have them," I inquired.

Zander smiled at me, caressing my cheek with his thumb. "The library is downstairs. Feel free to read whatever you find in there, but I know for sure there are a few that match what you're looking for."

With a quick kiss, he left the room, giving the twins a meaningful look. The moment the door closed behind Zander, Mason darted across the room and leapt onto the bean bag chair with me. He wrapped his arms around me and pulled me close, giving enough space for Noah to join us in a snuggle pile. All the anxious feelings that I'd been having since breakfast drifted away as I was cocooned with these two large betas. Noah started to play with my hair, something I found oddly comforting.

"Still not sure that snuggles is a good nickname for you?" Mason teased, poking at my side, making a giggle slip out.

I froze at the sound of it and looked between the two of them. "That never happened..."

Noah grinned and gave me a wink. "What do you mean? Twin, what could possibly have not happened just now?"

"I don't know, twin, but it might have been the most adorable thing I've ever not heard before. Think I should see if I can get her to not do it again?" Mason asked, his finger skimming down my side, threatening to poke me again.

Shifting to lay on my back, I pulled my knees up to my chest then shot them out, vaulting me forward and out of their arms. I tucked and rolled forward, somersaulting away before I stood and looked back at them over my shoulder. "Sorry, boys, but that's not gonna happen."

Both Noah and Mason gave me a look that told me I'd just triggered something primal in them. They turned to each other next, and the conspiratorial smile they exchanged had me racing out of the room with them hot on my heels. At the bottom of the stairs, I had a split second to guess what direction I was going to take before I spotted the library. I darted into the room, just barely managing to slip behind the couch before they entered.

"Oh, snuggles, you're gonna need to try harder than that to hide from us," Mason taunted. "You forget that we have super hearing and smell. Your heart is racing awfully fast."

"Twin, that's creepy! Don't say things like that to her," Noah scolded.

I squeaked as Mason's face popped up above me. "Gotcha!"

Laughing, I came out from behind the couch. "Just you wait. Once I figure all this out, I'll make it so it's impossible to find me."

"Ah, but you forget you named me a Hunter, the best there is at tracking their prey," Mason pointed out, grinning from ear to ear.

"That's the challenge, right, to be better than the best? I was once one of the best, and I plan on getting back to that some day, sooner than later," I announced. "You know what helps make you the best?"

Mason frowned at me. "Practice?"

"Knowledge. Before any job was started, I spent a few days learning, researching, and stalking my hit. All of this is beyond overwhelming, so I'm going back to what I know, and I'm going to learn what I don't know," I shared as I took in the library. "Sorry to say it's not looking to be a very exciting day."

"Love, as your Companion, I am happy to help support you in any way that I can. If that means we spend the day curled up reading, helping you figure out this new life, then we are all in. Right, twin?" Noah called out to Mason who was sprawled out on the couch.

"Yup, what he said. All in, snuggles, whatever you need," Mason agreed.

My heart warmed at their understanding and support, knowing that this must be the last thing they wanted to spend their day doing. Well, maybe just Mason since Noah struck me as an intellect.

"Twin, why don't you see if you can find a computer so we can pull up the chat rooms that Senator Vaughan set up for bitten wolves," Noah suggested.

"This is why they say you're the brains and I'm the brawn," Mason said as he hopped off the couch and headed out on his mission.

Walking over to Noah, I wrapped my arms around his middle and rested my head on his chest. "Thank you, I'm sure you had better things to do today."

"That's the thing about mates, even unclaimed ones. Once we know who we're intended to be with, there's nothing we won't do for them,"

Noah explained. "Come on, let's grab some books and head back to your nest."

Zander's library was a wealth of information on all kinds of things—music, business, history of humans and supernaturals, and some fiction scattered throughout. Between Noah and I there were about ten books we thought would be helpful. Mason even found a laptop that we could use as well.

"You two head on up and get started. I'm gonna raid this kitchen for snacks. There's no way that you can have a study session like this without snacks," Mason explained.

Shaking my head, I left him to it and headed back up to the nest.

"Do you feel more relaxed with less of us around?" Noah asked as we climbed back onto the bean bag chair. "I only ask because you seem much less submissive if that makes any sense."

Taking a moment, I thought about that and checked in with my wolf. She was contentedly napping, feeling safe, secure, and looked after. "Do you think it has something to do with you and Mason being tied to my elven side?"

"It could be, or the fact that your omega nature isn't as on alert with the alphas being gone. You aren't just a werewolf. You're elf, too, so it might bring out some odd quirks in traits," Noah mused.

"Seems like everything just leads to more questions than answers," I grumbled.

Noah hummed and ran his finger through my hair. "Then I guess we better get reading so you can find some answers."

It didn't take Mason long to join us, arms full of snacks, and we dove into our research.

"Oh, here's something!" I exclaimed after finding nothing in the first two books. "This explains why I couldn't eat before you guys. Since omegas are at the bottom of the pecking order, we either have to go last or be given our food by an alpha."

Mason shifted to look up at me from where his head was laying on my stomach. "I guess we should have figured that one out based on how you acted after your first kill."

Hmm, he wasn't wrong on that. I had assumed it was because I was in wolf form.

"Listen to this," Noah cut in. "Empathic omegas used to be fairly common, but they've become more rare. Some can sense the mood of a pack member without touching them if they know each other. Otherwise, to get the best reading on someone, they have to touch them directly."

"Are elves empathic at all, do you think?" I wondered. "Before my first shift, I could feel some of your emotions, but now it's like I can't block them out. At least all six of you guys seem to have your emotions under control for the most part except when you get mad. Could that be why the alphas affect me so much? Because of the double hit of dominance and emotion?"

The twins muttered an agreement with my logic but didn't have much else to add on the matter.

"Ah, here! In this chat room, some omegas are talking about how stressful dealing with everyone's emotions can be and how nests are a major help in recharging," Mason said. "We might need to make you one in the pack house, so if things get too much, you can sneak away there."

I was beginning to see why omegas lived a very sheltered, coddled life. Everything about them was emotional, whether it was pouring into others or taking the brunt of emotions from them. This was how they created balance, by understanding the mental wellbeing of all the pack members as a means to help them. Colt kept saying how this pack was so healthy, and this made me hope I wouldn't have too much to deal with.

The trouble was going to come with the fact that I'd never been trained to deal with emotions. Feelings were something the Organization worked out of us, knowing the job would shatter us if we were emotionally invested. After all the research I did, sometimes I agreed with the hit and knew it was the right choice. Other times, it was someone standing in the way of a greedy person who just wanted to be richer. Either way, regardless of my agreement with the course of action, it wasn't my place to judge. It was my job to pull the trigger or press the plunger, and in order to do that, you had to be good at locking away the parts of yourself that were too human.

Somehow, I was going to have to deal with emotions, my own and others, which meant unlearning decades of conditioning. Let's hope these men were as understanding as they appeared to be as I figured this out because I could already feel my wolf starting to worry about messing up our job.

"Lane said something about a pack meal. What are those like?" I asked, setting my book down and grabbing some beef jerky.

Noah shifted behind me so he could see me better. "The alphas try to do them once a month so new members can be greeted and foster a better sense of community. See, packs live a little on the hippy side of life."

"What my twin is trying to say is that we're basically a commune. We share all the resources that we can amongst the pack. There is a giant ass garden, a school, daycare for working parents, patrol groups, cooks who make lunch for those working on property, and a few other odd jobs," Mason clarified. "Elias, Noah, and I are heads of the patrols that watch our borders. Our territory butts up to the mountains, and we sometimes get lost humans wandering in. They're mostly there to keep other packs or uninvited supers off our land."

"Is there trouble with the other supers in the area?" I questioned, not having considered that issue.

Mason and Noah exchanged a look before they decided on an answer.

"It's not that we have a problem with anyone, but having a successful, fast-growing pack draws attention these days. Some packs aren't as well managed, and people are going hungry, sneaking onto our land to steal from us. We help a lot of smaller packs in the area, but they have to go about it the proper way," Noah stated.

Mason sat up and turned to face me. "Like in anything, there is good and bad in all people or groups. Part of being in a pack is knowing you have protection from the bad in the world. Sometimes Colt will have Noah and me help out another pack if they need some strong enforcers. We don't mind, of course, since we tend to get paid, but sometimes we help a new alpha stabilize their pack just because it's the right thing to do."

"Sounds like I ended up with some very noble mates, now didn't I?" I said with a smile. "Alright, I think we've done a lot of research here today. Let's do something fun until the others get back."

"Oh, thank god," Mason sighed. "What do you say we go check out the movie situation? That TV looked pretty badass!"

One nod from me, and I was tossed over his shoulder, hauled out of my nest and into the living room. It didn't take us long to find out Zander had every streaming service known to man, plus tons of movies for us to select from.

"Oh, we are *so* watching *John Wick*!" Noah announced the moment he saw it.

"Nah, fuck that. The puppy gets killed! Why would we do that to snuggles?" Mason argued.

"Guys," I interjected, "I love those movies. Keanu Reeves is one of my favorite actors. He does his own stunts and is sexy to watch."

Noah and Mason gaped at me then gave each other a meaningful look. "Okay, *so* not gonna happen. What's your next pick? What about *Shrek? No* one's sexy in that movie," Mason offered.

"Yes, perfect choice, twin," Noah agreed.

"Are you jealous about me calling Keanu Reeves sexy?" I chuckled, feeling oddly flattered they would get so protective of me over a man I would never meet.

Ignoring my question, they arranged themselves on the couch with me draped over them, humming in contentment. Another thing I'd learned today was that only alphas could purr; humming was the closest betas could come to making the same noise. This was how the others found us when they returned from whatever they'd been doing—the three of us watching *Shrek 3* which I didn't know was a thing.

"Looks like you guys have had a productive day." Colt smiled as he brushed some hair out of my face before kissing my forehead, not caring that I was sprawled on Mason's chest.

"We spent most of the day researching omegas and what it's like to live in a pack," I shared, slipping off of Mason to greet Lane and Elias.

Lane pulled me in for a tight hug, resting his chin on top of my head, and purred. "Did you learn anything helpful?"

"It cleared a lot of things up for me, but every omega is so different as to how sensitive they are to things. I do think that I'm a very strong empathic omega though," I informed the others.

"That makes sense. Cory was always aware of everyone's feelings, but I wouldn't have said he was strong in that area. He was more adept at finding those in pain, emotional or physical, and soothing them. Other emotions he didn't pick up on as well," Colt mused.

"That's something we'll have to keep in mind when you're around the pack. We don't want to overwhelm you," Lane said, more to Colt than to me. "Come on. Zander won't be back tonight, so let's see what we can make for dinner in his giant kitchen."

TWENTY

FINLEY

The next day was fairly the same; we all got up and ate breakfast with each other before Lane, Colt, and Elias went about their days. I ended up back in my nest, reading, trying to gain all the knowledge I could about this new world that I was living in. Pack life was so much more complex than anyone gave it credit for, and I understood why Lane and Colt couldn't be with me right now. They hadn't been prepared for an omega, let alone a mate, to show up in their lives, so an adjustment period was bound to happen.

"Snuggles, are you really going to spend all day holed up here again?" Mason asked from the doorway.

Closing my book, I gave him my full attention. "Did you have something else in mind?"

The grin on his face told me he did indeed have a plan. "Remember how you said you wanted to get better at using your senses as a wolf?" I nodded. "What about a game of hide and seek? You could use all the skills you've learned as an assassin and whatever I'm sure you've learned from those books to see how long you can avoid being caught."

The idea was rather brilliant; it gave me a chance to figure things out *and* test the skills I already had. I'd been far too inactive the last few days, and even my wolf perked up at this idea. She wanted to get out and play too. If I wanted the chance to re-enter the world in hopes of finishing my mission, I needed to get a handle on my werewolf side.

Not to mention how to act like a normal person despite heightened senses and crazy emotions.

"Okay, what are the rules?" I asked, sliding out of my nest.

"Hey, Noah, she agreed to the game!" Mason called over his shoulder. Seconds later, Noah was standing beside him with an excited energy around him. "She wants to know the rules…"

"Don't get caught?" Noah suggested.

"Sounds perfect. Throw whatever you got at us, snuggles. I want to see just how badass you keep claiming to be," Mason challenged. "Now, I'm going to close my eyes and count to five. That should be more than enough time for you to get a head start."

They both stepped into the room and covered their eyes. "One…"

I flew out of the room and down the stairs, having to trust in my new enhanced abilities as I aimed for the sliding glass door. My wolf was hopping around in my head, excited that she was going to be let out to play. I didn't want to waste time stripping out of my clothes, so I hoped shifting in them wouldn't slow me down. The second I crossed over the threshold, my wolf leapt forward, and we shifted in mid air, clothes and all. Since I was much bigger as a wolf, my clothes shredded, but my bra got caught on my front leg, causing me to stumble. I snarled at it, yanking it off with my teeth before I darted into the underbrush.

Remembering what Elias had said about scent, I tuned into my surroundings, trying to find the best way to lose the twins. I could hear them barking and snapping at each other as they made their way into the woods, heading deeper, not thinking I would stop so soon. I hunkered low and let my black coat keep me hidden as I moved through the shadowy forest. Even though it was close to the middle of the day, the dense trees kept the forest dim, perfect for me to hide in. Tracking the twins was almost as much fun as being chased by them. It was more challenging to keep out of sight, but this was far more natural to me as an assassin, and my wolf seemed to enjoy not being the center of attention.

I, of course, had no idea how large the forest was or what borders the pack had, but the only rule was don't get caught. They seemed very much confused on how to find me as they caught my own scent intermixed with theirs telling me we walked in a large circle. Baring my teeth in a wolfish grin, I came up with an idea. Using more of my skills in evading capture, I started to make different scent trails, doubling back or intersecting them to throw the twins off. I could tell they knew that I was close by since they kept circling the same area, trying to follow my scent. It didn't take them long to understand the game I was playing, making them yip with excitement at my challenge. As I made a new trail, I came across a river, sniffing it to see if I could drink from it. The water was clear and crisp, fresh run-off from the mountains that still had snow on them. The sound of a twig snapping had my alert ears swiveling, trying to locate where the sound had come from. The sound was so quick that it was difficult to pinpoint the exact source. Lifting my nose, I tried to catch a scent, but nothing out of the normal wooded smell stood out to me.

Then a wolf I didn't know burst out of an outcropping of rocks on the other side of the river, barreling into me. I tried to dodge out of the way, but the slick stones under my paws didn't give me enough traction. Getting slammed to the ground, I let out a pained yelp as I landed on my leg funny. The wolf snarled at me, growling low as they snapped their teeth at my face, warning me not to move. I could feel his anger pouring off of him like a slap to the face, but I couldn't tell if I was the cause or if it was something else.

My wolf was petrified and didn't need any encouragement not to move. Mind racing, I tried to think of a way to handle this, but I was afraid that if I shifted back to human, he would just kill me more easily. Paralyzed by my distress, my wolf let out a long whining howl, desperate for someone to come help us. All the training I'd gone through, the techniques that had been beaten into me day after day, was stripped away within seconds as the realization of why omegas didn't live very long became abundantly clear.

The twins returned my call, tackling the unknown wolf into the river, splashing water everywhere. The face full of icy water shocked my wolf enough that I could coax her into moving away from the fight. To her, there was no fight or flight; it was just flat out run the fuck away from the scary thing. Diving under a bush, I hunkered down and curled up into a ball, trying to keep from running even further away from the two men trying to keep me safe. The fight didn't last long, and soon, three waterlogged naked men stood on the riverbank, yelling at each other.

"Who the fuck was that?" the unknown man asked.

He looked older than the twins. My guess would be late forties or early fifties. His hair was salt and pepper while his beard was just steel gray. He was smaller in stature than the twins, but they were huge in my opinion. Other than Zander, I couldn't picture anyone coming close.

"Don't worry about it. The alphas will explain everything at the pack dinner tonight, Craig. Just know that she isn't a threat. You better be fucking praying to whatever gods you believe in that she isn't hurt," Noah snarled.

I could tell right away that the two of them didn't like each other very much, but Noah was far more dominant than Craig. Thanks to that, there was a lower chance of the stranger trying to go after me again now that Noah was blatantly calling him on his behavior.

"There's a strange wolf on our land, and you're telling me not to worry about it?!" Craig snapped. "Is this what the federal marshals wanted? Are you harboring a fugitive?"

Mason stepped in, catching the man by his throat. "Are you questioning the rule of your alphas, gamma?"

Craig fought to pull Mason's hold off of him as he struggled to breath. Inside, I was at war. Part of me wanted to put a stop to this, but the other part was simply too terrified to make a move. Gritting my teeth, I crawled out of the bush and shifted, knowing I needed to have more control over my actions to deal with this. I couldn't stop myself from wincing when I stood, the weight of my body settling on my ankle and making me hiss. Mason and Noah's eyes snapped in my direction upon hearing my pain, and both of them started to growl.

"Stop, Mason, let him go," I demanded as I made my way over to them. The ankle hurt, but it wasn't anything I couldn't handle. Craig, on the other hand, was turning blue. "Mason, you're going to kill him! Let the man go... please."

"He hurt you," Mason growled, eyes lit with outrage. "No one gets to hurt you while I'm around."

"Craig didn't know who I was. He was doing the right thing by trying to protect his pack," I argued. "I would have done the same thing."

Noah stepped up and turned me to look at him. "He should have scented that you're an omega, so there was no need for him to act as he did. Not to mention your mates' scents are all over you, another warning that you were no threat to this pack."

I blinked up at him, not having considered that aspect to this situation. "At least let him breathe so he can talk. I'd like to hear what he has to say."

Mason dropped the wolf back into the river, causing the man to splutter at the frigid temperature. "There's no way that she's really an omega. They don't just show up out of thin air! What did you guys put on her? She's not acting like a scared shitless bottom feeder."

Whatever hope that man had of getting out of this unharmed had now flown out the window. Mason lunged at him, not caring that he was clueless as to what he'd just done. Noah picked me up and cradled me against his chest as Mason all but dragged the man out of the water and over the ground as we headed back into the forest.

"Noah, I can walk, and if I shift, it will be easier with all the extra legs," I said, wiggling for him to put me down, but at one look from him, I shut my mouth and sat still.

Up until this point, I had thought that Mason was the one to be worried about, but the rage that glowed in Noah's gaze told me Craig was lucky it was Mason dragging him around. Noah tucked me tighter against his chest, nuzzling my hair as we left the river. I had a guess as to where we were going, but I wasn't sure until I started to see the simple cabins scattered about the forest. The pack house was in the middle of the whole village, which was where Mason dropped Craig to hustle up the porch and into the house. Seconds later, he was back with a cell phone up to his ear.

"You want me to deal with him, or one of you?" Mason asked into the phone, eyes locked on Craig. At least he had the smarts to not move from where he'd been placed.

The pulse of angry energy that was coming off of Noah and Mason made me a little sick to my stomach, but I knew they were going to protect me. Noah seemed to be in an almost primal state, refusing to put me down, tightening his arms any time I tried moving.

My wolf still wanted nothing to do with this situation and begged for me to let us allow our mates to handle things. I, on the other hand, didn't want a man to die because he didn't know who I was, but as the twins had pointed out, Craig should have known better. So why risk their wrath?

"Finley, sit still," Noah instructed, flicking his eyes down to me for a moment before returning to Craig.

"Do you really think he would hurt me?" I questioned, feeling so confused as to what was really happening here.

The sound of a vehicle racing down the road caught my attention, and I could see a cloud of dust getting kicked up as a truck came flying up the drive. An extremely pissed off Colt was driving, with Lane looking not much better off in the passenger seat. An auburn wolf jumped out of the back when it slowed enough, then came charging over, flying by me to pounce on Craig. Elias bared his teeth, letting out a low, threatening growl as he loomed over the man under his paws.

Distracted by Elias, I didn't notice Lane until he was scooping me out of Noah's arms and cuddling me to his chest like a baby. "Are you alright, sweetheart?"

Nuzzling my face into his neck, I took a deep, calming breath of his clean scent to ground me despite the chaos of emotions. Before my shift, I could catch glimpses of their emotions, but now it was like getting blasted with one feeling after another. Lane was angry as well as worried, but his anger at seeing who'd caused the trouble outweighed the latter.

"You attacked my MATE!" Colt roared, causing me to peek out from Lane's neck. "Based on that fact alone, I could kill you for harming her, but add on the fact that she's an omega, and you have no hope for leniency from us."

Colt blazed with alpha energy, making me shrink into Lane's hold. I knew he wasn't mad at me, but it was oppressive to my omega nature, and I didn't know what to do to fix it. As if sensing my distress, Noah wrapped his hand around my ankle, offering his support and allowing me to take a deep, ragged breath.

"How was I to know you took a mate?!" Craig shot back. "You were gone for two, almost three days, without a word, and half that time you took the betas with you. Then, while I'm out on patrol, I find this strange wolf lurking about our forest, leading those two on a wild goose chase."

"Do you have a nose, or did that get lost with your brain?" Mason growled. "We were playing, you fucking moron. She's a new shifter, and learning how to be a wolf is essential to helping the bond grow between human and wolf. You were bitten. I'd think it would be easy for you, of all people, to understand that."

"Yes, and I was unlucky enough to be bitten by a gamma when I should have been an alpha! Do you know who I was before I was turned into this *abomination*?" Craig spluttered. "I ran a million-dollar company and had thousands of employees to look after, but it was all stripped away from me by a damn dog."

I gasped in shock when I felt his self-loathing and hatred for us and who he was. The intense anger that he felt about being a werewolf made my issues pale in comparison. It was almost as if he'd become toxic to himself; if left unchecked, it would spill out to others around him. If someone didn't do something, he would be too far lost with no hope of redemption.

TWENTY-ONE

FINLEY

Lifting a hand to Lane's face, his gaze instantly fell on me, giving me his full attention. "I need you to put me down." Lane's scowl told me that he was not a fan of this idea in the slightest, and he only clutched me tighter. "Please."

"Why?"

"He needs my help. Can't you feel how lost he is?" I questioned.

As I struggled to keep from being overwhelmed by Craig's emotions, I focused in on them more. I wanted to understand so I could find a way to help him, and if I could almost zero in on one of those feelings and trace it deeper, maybe I could do that.

Lane's eyes narrowed as he looked over at the man then back down to me. "No, all I feel is anger directed at you."

"Then you're going to need to trust me. This is what omegas do, right? Heal and nurture the pack..."

A low growl rumbled in Lane's chest, but he slowly set me down, then he yanked his t-shirt off and slipped it over my head. "If he tries to hurt you, there is nothing on this Earth that will save him from our wrath."

I nodded and slowly walked up to Elias. He was still standing on Craig's chest, keeping the irate man trapped. Running my hand over Elias's back, he stopped growling. He looked up at me questioningly before turning to Colt.

"What are you doing, Finley?!" Colt demanded, stepping forward, but Lane grabbed his arm, earning his attention. "I know what she wants, but it doesn't mean it's safe. Her need to heal is blinding her to danger."

Flinching at his disapproval, I closed my eyes and took a deep breath, trying to calm my own emotions so that I could withstand the ones I was receiving from others. "I'm this pack's omega, and he needs my help. Let me try, Colt."

Lane whispered something to Colt, but I was too focused on the man shooting hatred at me out of his eyes. I knelt down next to him, placing my hand on his arm, and I was promptly bombarded with his rage. Gasping, I dropped my head, trying to not let his feelings become my own. I might not love myself at the moment, but I certainly didn't want to die rather than live as a werewolf.

"Why so much hate?" I whispered to Craig, keeping my eyes closed to focus.

Not really understanding what I was trying to do, I leaned on my instincts. I pushed past the self-loathing and tried to find the root emotion fueling this hatred. There had to be a moment when or after he was changed that had made him feel this way. Once I found it, I would know how to fix it.

"You're alive, and even though you don't have your company anymore, you still have so much to offer this pack. I understand having everything taken from you in the blink of an eye; my whole life was ripped away from me in seconds. But I'm choosing to learn and make the most of this life I know I have to live." Finally catching on to the root problem, I opened my eyes and met his gaze. "Who are you truly mad at?"

Tears pooled in the man's eyes as he tried to shake off my hold on him. "Get away from me, you bitch. I don't need anything from the likes of you!" With that statement, he spat in my face, and in the next moment, I was covered in blood after Elias tore out his throat.

Sitting back on my heels, I watched the life drain out of Craig. There was still one emotion left to catch. In that last moment, with his final breath, I got one fleeting emotion—relief.

"Does anyone know his story?" I asked, looking up at the others.

They were all gathered around, looking at me as if I might start screaming or burst into tears. Didn't they understand that death meant nothing to me other than a job well done?

"That's what you want to ask?" Mason blurted out with a bark of laughter. "God, this woman is unlike any other."

Cocking my head to the side, I frowned. "Why wouldn't I ask that?"

"Oh, I don't know, snuggles, maybe because you're covered in this dick's blood, still kneeling next to his corpse like that's a typical Wednesday afternoon," Mason pointed out. "Any other woman would be screaming their head off or sobbing their eyes out."

"This isn't my first time seeing death..." I stated, unsure if they'd forgotten.

Turning back to the body, I closed Craig's eyes and stood, using the bottom of the t-shirt to wipe my face clean of blood. Catching the sound of a gasp, I whirled around and found a large group of people looking horrified to see me. *Well, this isn't how I pictured meeting the rest of the pack.* Lane pulled himself together first and stepped out in front of me as Noah grabbed my hand, pulling me toward the house.

"Everything is fine. Unfortunately, Craig crossed a line that gave us no choice but to end his life," Lane addressed. "As one of this pack's alphas, it is my job to keep everyone safe, and in some cases, that leads to a tragic event such as this. The pack meal will still happen tonight, and it's even more important to attend so that situations like this don't happen again. Trust in us and return to your duties." The crowd all murmured to themselves, but they did as was asked of them and wandered back to wherever they had come from.

Noah led me through the house and up the stairs, but instead of going to the room I'd been given, he entered a different one that smelled of fresh evergreen. *Colt.* While this house wasn't nearly as opulent as Zander's, it still had a feel to it that I liked. It emanated safety and warmth, like it was made to have people bustling around in it. Noah turned on the shower and pulled Lane's shirt off of me before ushering me in and closing the glass door after me.

"Get cleaned up while I grab you some clothes," Noah instructed as he slipped out of the bathroom.

I got the feeling that the guys didn't believe me when I said that I was fine, but that was a lesson they'd have to learn in their own time. Death was just another part of my job, so it was hard to freak out over it. Who would hire an assassin that broke down at the sight of a fresh kill? I couldn't even count the number of people who had died under my own hand or in my arms. Those assassins who carried their victims with them didn't last long in the business. They usually ended up killing themselves, unable to deal with the weight of it all.

The only kill that I remembered was my first one, but that wasn't unusual. At that point, most of us were only partly numb. It wasn't until the horror of that first death that you truly understood why you needed to disconnect your feelings from the job.

It happened the year I turned sixteen. I wasn't even supposed to be doing anything but observing a veteran assassin, but the job had gone south when the wife of our hit was home instead out like she should've been. I acted without thinking, knowing that we couldn't leave any witnesses. She didn't even know I was there when she got out of her bed to investigate the noise coming from her husband's study. There I was, lurking in the shadows as she gasped at the sight of her husband being strangled to death. Before she could bolt down the hall to the upstairs landline, I slit her throat. From that point on, I was one of the youngest trainees to be let out into the field. The Organization had seen no point in holding me back when I'd managed my first kill, clean and by the book.

Noah's return to the bathroom pulled me out of my head, and I realized I'd just been lingering under the hot water. Wringing out my hair, I stepped out, expecting Noah to hand me the towel, but instead, he proceeded to dry me himself.

"Are you sure you're alright?" Noah asked as he bent down to dry off my legs.

"Will you believe me if I tell you that I'm totally fine?" I countered.

He looked up at me seriously, contemplating his answer. "There are moments like this one that you're extremely hard to read. Having a stronger ability to gauge people's responses, I'm not used to dealing with something like that. Since you've shifted, you show a lot more emotion... but still less than most. Right now, you're a blank slate, giving me nothing to work off of to understand how you're doing."

There was something about the fact that he was so honest with me that made me want to be honest in return. "One of the only ways you can deal with killing as often as I have is to remove yourself from the situation. Craig is no longer Craig. That outside is the body of a man who wanted to die and goaded Elias into doing it. As I was showering, I tried to think of how many people I'd killed since I was sixteen, and I can't tell you. I know that it's over fifty, but that's only because after that point, you're awarded the title of elite assassin. That's who I am, Noah."

His eyes widened as he absorbed what I was saying. "You've killed over fifty people, and you started when you were *sixteen*? How have you still hung on to such a caring heart?"

"Oh, that's all the omega's doing," I snorted.

"No, I don't think so," Noah challenged. "Even if you're an elf or only part elf, you wouldn't have been turned by an omega if you didn't have an affinity for it. Omegas bind the pack together through caring for the pack on an emotional level. What you tried to do for Craig, for example. If he had let you, I know you would've tried to help him through his pain and hatred of being turned. Unfortunately, like you said, he wanted to die."

When he put it like that, it was hard to argue, but I wasn't convinced that it wasn't just the omega traits taking over my normal personality. This new venture into learning about emotional wellbeing was so foreign to me, but now I'd gotten a taste of how powerful it could be. Noah was right; Craig didn't want to be healed... but what if he had? Could a person who'd never acknowledged their own emotions help another? There was so much for me to learn, and I was discovering that I might actually want to delve into emotions more.

Noah held out a pair of sweatpants that smelled like Colt, and I stepped into them, enjoying being surrounded by his scent. The t-shirt was from Lane, and the hoodie that he bundled me up in was covered in his scent. In a way, I didn't understand why being wrapped up in their scents calmed me and set me at ease, but I was glad to have the comfort. My wolf was mourning the loss of a pack member, knowing that we could have helped. It was hard for her to understand the idea of someone wanting to die.

"Come on, let's head back downstairs. I'm sure the others will want to check in on you," Noah suggested as he coaxed me out of Colt's room.

We found the others in the living room in various stages of restlessness, but my attention was drawn right to Elias. He sat in one of the large leather armchairs, and he refused to look at me. His body was tensed as if he was ready to bolt at a moment's notice if the need arose, so I walked right up to him and curled up on his lap. My face pressed against his neck, I fisted his black Henley in my hands. It took him a few moments before he relaxed enough to wrap his arms around me, resting his cheek against the top of my head.

"I'm not upset you killed him; he left you no choice," I whispered. "You kept me safe."

At this, Elias took a deep breath, and it was like he deflated with the release of what must have been one of his worries. I couldn't tell you how I knew that was what had been bothering him, other than to blame it on the new empathic omega abilities. He let his hand run up and down my back as we sat in silence like we were the only ones in the room. "Little one," Colt ventured, causing me to crack an eye open and look up at him. "Come here, please."

I tried to pull out of Elias' hold, but he tightened his arms and released a low rumble at my movement.

Colt narrowed his eyes at his beta, putting some dominance behind it. "Let my mate go, Elias. I know you're just trying to keep her safe after Craig set off your protectiveness, but you are not the only one who is concerned. I let you hold her because you needed it, but I'm now telling you to let her go."

"She's my charge as well as soon-to-be mate," Elias muttered. "What will you do then?"

"This is all new to us, her elf nature pulling more than one mate to her, but it hasn't changed who we are. At this moment, my wolf wants to rip out your throat for keeping her from us since you are not yet mated. When I see her with Lane or Zander, I don't have the same need to kill them like I do you right now," Colt explained through gritted teeth.

Lane stepped up as if to be a buffer between the two of them. "Let her go for now, Elias. You know she's safe with Colt."

Elias grunted as he turned to look down at me. Lifting a hand, he trailed a finger down my cheek, then tucked under my chin, and lifted my face to him. Slowly, giving me time to pull away, he pressed a gentle kiss on my lips as if he were afraid to break me. Then he pulled away, nodding to Colt. I reached out a hand to my mate, giving him the lifeline he needed to pull me from Elias' lap and into his own arms. Colt showered my face in kisses before he nuzzled the crook my neck where his mate mark was, sending shivers of pleasure down my spine.

"What are we to do with you, mate of mine?" Colt murmured against my skin.

TWENTY-TWO

FINLEY

Lane chuckled. "Seems like we might need to keep you with us so you don't get into more trouble."

Colt looked up at him. "Then we'll never get anything done. Look how cute she is, not to mention how good she smells, totally distracting."

Never in all my life had I had someone talk about me like this. I felt my cheeks burn with the foreign sensation of blushing at how sincere they were being about this. "You guys, I'm very capable of handling myself. He just surprised me. I'm still working on all these new senses and how to use them to the best advantage. I'll be fine here with Noah and Mason. Go finish whatever I pulled you away from."

"Does that mean you're going to stay in the house?" Lane asked hopefully.

"Is that what needs to happen so you can relax?" I questioned, quirking a brow at him.

Lane tapped his chin as he thought. "Yes, I believe my wolf and I agree that knowing you're safe in our home would set us at ease."

"Alright, then that's what I'll do... for today," I offered. "Like Colt said, this is new to all of us, but I hope after meeting the rest of the pack, I won't have to be so locked down."

Lane and Colt gave each other a meaningful look, but eventually, they both agreed. Each of them gave me a searing kiss before they left, only this time Elias stayed.

"So what do you have around here to do for fun?" I asked, looking at my three babysitters.

Mason grinned at me and wagged his eyebrows. "You don't think we're really going to keep you cooped up in the house, do you?"

"We have a place we want to show you. It started off being something for the kids, but we changed our minds about that. It's close to the house," Noah added.

I glanced at Elias out of the corner of my eye, and he didn't seem all too bothered by the idea, so I shrugged. "Alright, but if you get in trouble with the alphas, I'm not gonna cover your asses."

"That's harsh, snuggles!" Mason whined, pushing out his full bottom lip in a pout. "Guess we'll just have to make it worth you changing your mind."

Mason led the way out the back door that butted right up to the forest, and I expected him to start shedding his clothes to shift, but he kept walking. I glanced down at my bare feet, but the soft grass felt so nice I decided not to worry about finding shoes. Mason led us deeper into the woods that I was sure I would soon find as a second home given enough time. My wolf was happy to be back out here in nature and particularly excited to have three of our pack members looking out for us. She liked them very much and felt safe knowing they were guarding us. Wanting to understand my own emotions better, I followed the connection I felt for them to its origin. The knowledge that they *belonged* to me was clear, but it wasn't attached to my wolf; it was connected to that something else. It was almost as if that part of me was awakening but still buried deep inside me, waiting to break free. Knowing that I was something else, and might have always been, was hard to wrap my head around, but it also made so much more sense. Nothing about my first shift and how I acted as an omega, let alone a typical werewolf, seemed to be normal. Or at least according to the guys. Who was I to know what was normal or not?

I was so lost in thought that I missed when Mason stopped walking. If Noah hadn't pulled me to a stop, I would have crashed into his broad back.

"Look up," Noah whispered.

Curious, I did as he asked, and my gasp of excitement echoed in the quiet forest. "Is that a tree house!?"

When I was younger, I'd heard about them from some of the older kids the Organization had brought into the fold; they'd lived out in the normal world longer than I had, and they'd shared stories about what "normal" childhoods were like. For whatever reason, tree houses were something that had always stuck in my mind. Something about them seemed so magical, like they were a portal to another world. Never did I think I would get to experience one in my life, especially now that I was grown.

"Yup," Mason said, popping the 'P' and grinning at me proudly. "Noah and I built it with our own two hands!"

Tucked away up in a massive oak tree was a small house with a wooden spiral staircase leading to the floor entrance. Unable to stop myself, I hustled up the stairs and shoved open the trap door to reveal the inside of this charming space. It was simple, with two woven hammocks hung up side by side under a loft area, but that only added to the magical rustic vibe it gave off. A rope ladder hung from the loft, giving access to the top space filled with blankets and pillows. A soft rug covered the floor in the open space, with large windows showing off the forest and letting in natural light. Suddenly, twinkle lights blazed into existence, making the small house light up with so much warmth and magic. A low bookshelf was along one wall filled with books and a few games that didn't look to be used much. More large pillows and blankets were stacked along the edge of the wall for someone to use in this common space. I spotted a small kitchen set-up that had a camping stove, a kettle, and some mugs, because I'd been told nothing said secret hideaway like having a steaming cup of hot cocoa.

"This place is like nothing I've ever seen before." I sighed, feeling at peace for the first time since I was sent to New York.

Turning back to face the three men who took up much of the small space, I had to smirk. The ceiling was definitely tall enough to accommodate their height, but there was still an unavoidable sense of them being far too large for this space.

"Why didn't you give it to the kids? I would think it's a perfect place for them to play," I asked as I started to snoop around the place.

Immediately, I could tell that question touched on a sore subject for the twins as they shifted uncomfortably where they stood. Elias, on the other hand, walked over to a space close to the windows and lounged against a pile of pillows.

"My brother and I are born wolves, and the biggest difference between a born werewolf and bitten one is that we can change our status in the pack. Mason and I could be alphas if given the chance to fight for that rank, but it just hasn't been the right time to do that. Honestly, I like being a strong beta, but Mason doesn't feel the same way I do," Noah explained.

Mason glared at his twin then looked over at me. "I just know that I'm meant for something more than being the support beta to a strong pack. I can do more. Our pack isn't big enough to support three alphas, so I haven't made my move yet. This place gives me somewhere that's away from it all. When I get too frustrated or I butt heads with Lane or Colt, this is the place I come to cool off. Here it's just me and Noah, but we both agreed that we wanted to share it with you so you have a place to go when things are too overwhelming."

I couldn't help myself. I leaped at both of them, and they caught me easily, wrapping themselves around me. "Thank you for being so thoughtful."

They held me for a few more moments, but the urge to make the space more comfortable kept nagging at me. Pulling away, I climbed up the ladder and tossed down all the blankets and pillows that were in the loft, then I shooed Elias out of the space so I could get to work. This was a good start, but it needed to be arranged right. I loved the feeling of being able to see the forest and the goings on of the wildlife around me, but it needed the right sort of set-up to experience it. Pulling the circular carpet closer to the window so it covered the wood floor was the first step, then I used the thickest blanket for the foundation. When I found that I'd used all the blankets and it still wasn't right, a frustrated growl slipped out.

"What's wrong, love?" Noah asked, coming up behind me and settling his hands on my hips.

"It's not right! There needs to be more blankets," I muttered, stepping out of his hold and kneeling in the pile. "The pillows will help, but it's missing something."

I started shoving pillows under some of the blankets, punching them to get the *feel* my body was pining for. Yet whatever driving force was behind this just wasn't satisfied with the outcome. The space was right, the window was perfect, and the late afternoon sun was warm, but it was still somehow empty.

"Elias, head back to the house and grab blankets from all our rooms. Do we have anything at the house that might smell like Zander?" Noah asked from somewhere behind me.

Yanking one of the pillows from the pile, I growled at it before I shoved it into another spot that worked better. The need to make this perfect was so strong I started to feel tears pricking in my eyes. *Why can't I do this right?*

"Okay, snuggles, hold on. We think we know what the problem is," Mason crooned as he wrapped me up in his arms.

"It has to be right, Mason." I nuzzled into his shirt. "You made this beautiful house, and I want to make it perfect, but I can't seem to figure it out."

"Oh, my dear sweet snuggles, you're just nesting. It's perfectly normal. Didn't you read about it in all those books?"

"Yes, but reading something and experiencing it are completely different. Who gets this upset when they can't make the perfect pillow fort?" I grumbled.

"I should have known showing you a space like this would trigger the need to nest. Elias is off to get what you need, then it will be perfect, just like you, I promise," Mason assured me, pulling me from his chest to wipe my tears away with his thumbs before kissing me on the lips. "Who would have guessed that you would be such a stickler for details? We can take you to Zander's house, and you can curl up in that nest if we can't get this one perfect."

"NO!" I shouted, surprising us both with my vehemence. "This is important. I have to finish this one first. The other one is already set up; this one is special."

Mason grinned at me like a kid who just found out Christmas came early and he was getting double the presents. "Yeah, I'm keeping you for sure after saying something like that. You turned down a curated omega nest for our janky treehouse as your first official nest. Not gonna lie, that is a major ego boost right there."

Noah joined Mason and me, coming up from behind so I was boxed in by them, and I hummed with pleasure at feeling them so close in this space they had built.

"I grabbed what I could," Elias stated as he returned. "I also made sure to tell the alphas where we were seeing as she won't leave until this is completed."

I perked up the moment I saw the pile of blankets. Flashing a grin at Elias, I wiggled out of the twins' hold, and they carefully removed themselves from my nest as I started work once again. Noah had been right; what had been missing this whole time was the sense of pack. Now that I had something from all my men, even a pillow from Zander, I made better progress. Then it was finished, and I was able to breathe a sigh of relief and curl right up into the center of my first ever nest in the setting sunlight. It was perfect. Everything about it was, right down to the number of pillows and how far I sank into the blankets.

"How long has she been working on this?" Lane whispered, drawing my attention enough to peek over a pillow.

Huddled up together in the limited space I'd left were my mates, all six of them. I paused a moment as I rolled that around my brain; this was the first time I had considered them all my mates. I knew Zander, Lane, and Colt were, my wolf had made it very clear they were ours, but the other three were more bonded to my elf side. It would seem that this nesting had been a combined draw from both parts of my nature, and it was pleased to have a space to share with them.

"Are you all just going to stand there and stare at me?" I asked, resting my chin on the pillow in front of me.

Zander's eyebrows shot to his hairline. "You want us to join you?"

"Why else would I make a nest?" I countered.

"Well, some omegas tend to keep their nests as a private place just for them to enjoy unless they're near their heat," Zander explained.

I sat up and looked at them all questioningly. "So you don't want to come cuddle with me in my nest after you've been gone for a whole day?"

Mason snorted and started to walk over to join me, but I spotted something and raised a hand to stop him. "No shoes or socks, please."

All the guys quickly obeyed before making their way over to my nest. I smiled at them, so excited to share this space and for us to take a much needed moment to just be. Our time together had been one big thing after another, and I *knew* that my mates needed to take a few moments to relax and take a few deep breaths. Zander reached me first, drawing me against his chest, while Mason was wrapping himself around my legs, his face nuzzling into my stomach.

The others joined in until we were a puppy pile in my new nest, and I was surrounded on all sides. I could feel the stress and tension they each held drifting away as they took deep breaths of my scent. My alphas started to purr, giving me a euphoric feeling as my whole body vibrated with their pleasure. My wolf let out a croon of happiness as she curled up and let out the biggest sigh. Once everything calmed down, their breathing became more even, telling me that some were on the verge of falling asleep. As I relaxed into their bodies, I caught a glimmer of something glowing deep within me.

Could this be my elf magic? Was being around my mates stirring this part of me into wakefulness? It seemed that only time would tell, but some instinct told me that this was the calm before the storm.

TWENTY-THREE

FINLEY

"Little dove, we need to head out for the pack dinner," Zander whispered in my ear as he pressed kisses along the side of my face. "The others have already left to get things set up. We hate to wake you, but we let you sleep as long as we could."

Letting out a grunt, I rolled onto my back and looked up at his silver gaze. He watched me with such tenderness that I couldn't help but smile at him. "How long have I been out?"

"Only two hours, but with how crazy things have been the last few days, we thought you needed whatever sleep you could get. If you want to change, I brought some clothes with me since I knew you didn't have any at the pack house," Zander offered.

Sitting up, I kissed him, marveling at how thoughtful and caring he was. Yeah, he's a bit possessive and growly, but I had a feeling I was seeing a side of him not many did. He was softer if you will.

"I missed you," I murmured, resting my forehead against his.

Zander started to purr at my words. "I missed you too, little dove."

He peppered my face with kisses until he reached my lips, leaning into the kiss and pressing me down amidst the blankets. Shifting, he straddled my hips and yanked the hoodie off of me so he could slide his hands under my t-shirt to cup my breasts. I arched into him, begging for him to touch me more, craving his attention and desire for me.

"You, little dove, are trouble on so many levels, you know that? How can they expect me to let you leave here when the scent of your need is so thick in the air?" Zander whispered along my neck as he moved lower.

I moaned when he shucked up my shirt and latched onto one of my nipples, rolling his tongue, encouraging them to peak. Reaching up, I grabbed hold of his hair, encouraging him to continue what he was doing, while his other hand snaked into my sweatpants. His fingers dipped between my legs, and it was now his turn to groan as he felt how wet I was for him.

"Please, Zander, don't tease me," I begged when he flicked a finger over my clit, making me jerk.

Zander nuzzled his face into my stomach. "Don't you fret. I'll make sure to take care of you, my mate."

Nipping on his way down, he pulled off my sweats and then shoved down his jeans, letting his proud cock free, hard and ready for action. I knew this wasn't going to be a slow and intimate moment. We were both hungering for each other, and the only way to handle it was to give in to the moment and revel in each other. He slid two fingers in me, checking whether I was ready, causing me to let out a shout. As quickly as the fingers came, they left, only to be replaced with his dick thrusting in to the hilt, making my back bow with the onslaught of pleasure.

"Oh god yes!" I cried, digging my nails into his shoulders as I held on.

He let himself enjoy the moment of being fully connected before he started to thrust into me earnestly. Never was I more thankful for the thick padding of blankets because this mate of mine was trying to fuck me through the floor. There was no holding back. He was taking what he wanted from me, and I was more than happy to give it to him, meeting him thrust for thrust. Growling, he captured my lips. The battle continued as we fought to take control of the kiss, but I met him head on. I could feel my orgasm building as his knot started to expand, hitting those places only the knot could. The sensation was easy to get addicted to, and I wondered how other women could survive if they never got a taste of this in their lives. Zander grunted, teeth sinking into my neck as he became fully locked to me, giving short thrusts that sent me right off the cliff, screaming out my pleasure. He poured his seed into me, adding to my climax in a way I never thought possible.

Rolling us to our sides, he brushed my hair out of my face, eyes full of wonder. "How the world decided that I should be so blessed with you I will never understand, but if they think they can ever take you from me, I will burn it all down."

I grinned at him, swirling my hips to send shockwaves through us both as I kissed along his chest and up his neck. "I might not be thrilled to be an omega, but if it gave me you and the others, I can't be too upset about it, now can I?"

"I know you still have so many questions, little dove, and I have some answers for you. But I would like to get through this pack meal first. We can all talk about it tomorrow after a good night's sleep," Zander said, kissing me on the nose. "That alright with you?"

"Yes, alpha," I whispered. With a purr, Zander started to thrust into me again. It would seem he liked being called alpha. I would have to store that away for later. Right now, my brain was taken over by yet another orgasm.

⸺⬦⸺

Twenty minutes later, I was cleaned up and dressed in the clothes that Zander had brought me. I had to admit his taste wasn't bad; he kept things functional, warm, and stylish, which was more than I could say for my previous wardrobe. Being an assassin meant going undercover so often I'd never quite figured out what *my* style was. Growing up, we had been given a uniform to wear for training, and many times we defaulted to black because it showed less of the stains we acquired during our jobs. Not to mention it made you less noticeable, which was the number one priority of an assassin.

"Is it normal for werewolves to heal this fast? My ankle is fully healed like nothing even happened," I shared as we walked hand in hand to the pack gathering.

Zander scowled at the mention of me being hurt, but he did answer my question. "Us shifters can heal incredibly fast, even more so if we shift. You have to add in the fact that you're an elf, too. That brings their healing abilities into the equation. Many elves have healing magic, which is likely why you feel so rested and rejuvenated after taking that nap."

"Is that something you learned from your meeting?" I pressed, hoping he would give me more.

"Yes and no," was the vague answer I received.

The night was cold enough that I could see my breath, but it was still pleasant. A massive bonfire lit up the space as we approached, adding its own heat along with the space heaters under the pavilion where the picnic tables were set up. Lane was working one of the grills while another person helped him with the burgers and hotdogs. Noah and Mason manned the table with all the condiments and sides, keeping the kids from stealing bags of chips. Colt was chatting with a few members of the pack, but when we caught his eye, he stopped talking, and a smile lit up his face. Excusing himself, he headed right over to us, scooped me up into his arms, and twirled me around.

"Little one, I don't know what magic you used during that nap we took, but I feel better than I've felt in ages!" he announced, kissing me soundly before setting me down. "Are you ready to meet everyone?"

I gave him a half-hearted smile. "Ready as I'll ever be, I guess. I've never been a fan of being the center of attention; it goes against everything I've been taught."

"Everything will be fine, I promise, and you have the six of us backing you up. You won't be doing this alone," Colt reassured as he took my hand and headed for the pavilion.

Jumping onto one of the tables, he released a shrill whistle that caught everyone's attention, bringing an immediate silence to the gathering. I stood next to the table with Zander at my back as my other mates and soon-to-be mates joined us.

"I know you've all been wondering what the occasion is for this pack dinner and about the events of earlier today. Well, now is the time you all get to be filled in. Questions will be answered, but first, I would like to introduce our newest pack member." Reaching down, Colt extended a hand to me, easily pulling me up, and Lane and Zander joined us as well. "This is Finley. Through a tragic turn of events, she was bitten by a lost wolf from our pack, making her ours to claim. When we left four days ago to retrieve her from New York, I also discovered that she's my mate, along with Lane and Zander's as well."

This caused the whole crowd to gasp before murmurs started to flutter throughout the silence.

"Believe me, I was just as shocked as you all when it happened. We're still investigating what has brought on this occurrence, but for now it doesn't really make a difference. Finley is also an omega. For those of you who don't know what that means, our pack is truly blessed to have such a gift. Omegas are the lynch pin of a pack, having the ability to *see* the pack in ways that an alpha or average wolf cannot. I hope you'll make Finley feel as welcome as you have every other new member that has come to our pack. Just know that anything less than the respect she deserves as mate to your alphas will not be tolerated," Colt stated, making sure he put alpha command behind those words. "Zander has been a lone alpha on our pack lands, and we have not yet determined how things will go with sharing a mate, but we ask that you respect his rank while we figure out what is best for this pack and the mate that we share."

The pack was divided in their reactions to all that Colt shared, but none seemed to be of the mindset of Craig, so that was a plus. I was helped off the table, and the gathering started up again as Colt led me into the crowd near the bonfire. Many of the pack members came up to greet me, shaking my hand or giving me a hug. Then three ladies approached us, and a smile grew on Colt's face.

"Good evening, Katie, Peggy, Milly," Colt greeted. "Allow me to personally introduce you to my mate Finley. As you heard, she is brand new to our pack."

They had to be sisters; the resemblance between them was too strong to not be related in some way. They all had the same blonde hair in different lengths and styles, along with similar face shapes. Milly seemed to be the oldest, with soft wrinkles around her hazel eyes, but I wouldn't say by much. Granted, when you could easily live to be two hundred, telling someone's age was tough. Katie had bright green eyes that watched me with excitement, a smile tugging at her lips, while Peggy narrowed her chocolate brown eyes at me with a slight frown.

"I hope that you three might show her the ropes of pack life while she adjusts?" Colt encouraged, turning to me to watch my reaction.

"Of course, alpha, it would be an honor to assist your mate in transitioning into pack life," Katie answered, giving in to the smile she'd been fighting. "Finley, would you like to join us so we can introduce you to a few other ladies?"

With her standing this close, I got a warm and friendly energy from her, while others got lost in the flurry of people, much like a bunch of conversations melding in a crowd. Even still, part of me hesitated at the idea of going off with them, but I knew this would be part of my life now. I needed to stand on my own two feet. Having my mates around me all the time wouldn't give me a chance to do that. "Sounds good to me."

"Don't worry, Alpha Colt. We'll make sure to keep an eye on her." Katie beamed as she took my arm in hers.

"I would expect nothing less from the McAlister sisters." Colt smiled and kissed my temple before giving my hand a squeeze. "You sure you're alright to hang with them without me?"

Nodding, I looked back at the sisters with a tentative smile. The life of an assassin didn't breed friendships, and I had always been one to prefer working alone, so the concept of 'girlfriends' was one I was not practiced in. Sure, I could fake it and play the role, but I'd never had the need to develop real friends.

"Go on, Alpha Colt. We'll look after her," Milly assured, waving him off when he lingered, not confident in my response.

He flicked his gaze over to the sister then back to me. "Elias is around if you need him."

"I'll be fine," I sighed, knowing he wouldn't leave until I gave him an answer.

After one more kiss and a nuzzle, he left to go help, leaving me to face off with three sisters whose attention was focused solely on me.

TWENTY-FOUR

FINLEY

"Come, let's find a spot by the bonfire. It's only going to get cooler as the night goes on," Milly said, waving for me to follow after them.

I could tell by their scent that Milly was a beta, while Katie and Peggy were both gammas or typical middle-of-the-pack wolves. Peggy might not be my biggest fan at the moment, but when her arm brushed up against me, I discovered it was more out of concern for the pack. It made me wonder what had happened in the past or what my mates might not know about going on under their noses. We found a table near the fire that was available, and when I tried to sit on the end, Milly coaxed me toward the middle.

"We aren't scary. I promise we don't bite," Milly assured me.

My brain whirled with the tug-of-war and how much to tell people about my life before getting bitten, knowing it would shock them even more. The need to have an exit was a requirement I had from my training. Plus, my wolf wasn't feeling safe with our new pack yet since our mates weren't with us. I took a deep breath and tried to ease both our fears, knowing that if it came down to it, I would be able to manage most things that came my way. I was not helpless, and I refused to ever be.

"So I know this is probably rude to ask, but what happened with Craig earlier today? None of the alphas or the lead betas will say anything other than it was deserved," Katie asked, looking at me hopefully.

I groaned in my head, frustrated at not knowing the rules about what I could say and what I shouldn't. Being their mate meant I would know things that weren't going to be common knowledge or ever shared with the pack. Diplomacy was not in my training. I took orders and fulfilled my mission—that was it.

"Katie!" Milly snapped. "If the alphas haven't told us anything, then we aren't supposed to know. Shame on you for trying to use her like that. You know omegas have a hard time not giving in to orders."

"Oh, like I have enough dominance to force her into telling me any-thing!" Katie huffed. "Tell her, Finley, do you feel the *need* to answer my request?"

Pausing to consider that a moment, I could feel my wolf's agitation, but it had nothing to do with Katie's request. More so with the fallout if I accidentally did something to anger my mates. "No, I don't feel compelled to answer her question," I mused. It was nice to know that I still had that ability away from dominant wolves.

There, that wasn't so hard. Keep it simple and to the point. That way, things can't get fucked up.

The sisters looked at me wide-eyed, a little shocked by my answer, and that sent my wolf into a tailspin. *Did we do it wrong?* I closed my eyes, trying to get control of my wolf and calm her down, giving me a chance to find out what had caused their reaction, but she was far too stressed for me to control.

I got up from the table. "Excuse me, I'm not feeling well at the mo-ment."

Rushing away, I searched the crowd, trying to find any of my mates, but as I moved, everyone kept reaching out to touch me. The over-whelming sense of their emotions, some good, some bad, pounded into my head until I couldn't escape it all.

Then the scent of a citrus-tinged ocean breeze filled my nose as a rough hand cradled my face. Elias had come to save me. Without opening my eyes, I reached out and wrapped my arms around his neck, letting him pull me against him.

"What is wrong, my heart?" he whispered into my ear.

I nuzzled into his neck, deeply breathing in his calming scent. "It's too much—so many emotions, people keep touching me—and I don't know the rules, Elias."

Elias hummed his understanding and picked me up, pulling my legs to wrap around his waist as he carried me away from the stunned people around me. I had forgotten that Noah told me Elias didn't like to be touched, but when it came to me, it was almost as if he craved it. My wolf wagged her tail in excitement, knowing that we were helping him and getting the grounding we needed at the same time.

"What's wrong?" Mason asked me as he appeared, brushing his hand along my cheek.

"Grab the others and tell them to meet me on the pack house porch. We need to clarify a few things," Elias instructed, his voice rough with held-back anger.

He carried me up the steps and settled us on the porch swing, curling me up on his lap, his arm tightly clasped around me as he started rocking. My wolf, now free from the social environment and wrapped up in our mate and protector, finally settled, allowing me to breathe easier.

"I'm sorry," I murmured, feeling a wave of guilt at causing a scene.

Elias shifted me so I could see the scowl on his face. "None of this is your fault. We should have prepared you better for this situation. This is on us, not on you, my heart."

Heavily sighing, I melted into his warm body and waited for the others to join us. Of course, it didn't take long for them to arrive, a worried expression on everyone's face as their gazes landed on me.

"What's wrong? What happened?" Lane asked, sliding in beside Elias and pulling my legs onto his lap.

"We didn't do our jobs is what happened," Elias snarled. "How could you just leave her out there to fend for herself with the pack? She's an omega, for fuck's sake, and we didn't give her any rules or guidelines to follow. I found her practically in a panic attack because she was so overwhelmed!"

The others looked a mix between shocked and pissed the fuck off with how Elias was talking to them, but I knew he was upset because he felt like he'd failed me.

"Fuck," Colt snapped, turning and gripping the porch railing until the sound of cracking wood was heard. "You're right, Elias. I should have thought that through better. I know better than to do that, goddamn it!"

"No," I spoke up. "I told Colt I was okay to be on my own. I didn't realize how much I didn't understand until it was already too late."

Noah knelt in front of me and grasped my hands, pulling them up so he could kiss the backs of them. "Okay, love, what can we do to help make you feel more comfortable going back out there?"

"There are a lot of things that I know from my job as an assassin, plus being your mate. I know far too many secrets in general... What am I allowed to say?" I inquired, trying to explain what it was that I was feeling even though I didn't fully understand it. "Katie asked me about Craig, but then she also mentioned you haven't given any details. My wolf panicked, and with everyone's emotions flying at me, I couldn't stop it."

Noah looked up at the others with a frown. "Elias is right; we should have taken her past into account, not to mention the omega nature. We put her out in the pack, expecting her to just figure it out like a normal pack member, but she can't. That's our fuck up." Turning back to me, Noah asked another question. "What is it that you're most worried about?"

"I don't want to get in trouble for saying something I shouldn't or have other people mad at me when I won't tell them things..."

Zander grunted from where he was leaning against the railing, watching me intently. "Elves can't lie. It hurts them, or their power, I think, but without someone to ask, we can't know for sure. Adding that to her fear of disappointing or angering one of us is a real double whammy, I'm sure."

Now that he said it, I realized that I wasn't a person that lied very often. Sure, I did it for work, but that was somehow different because I was under contract. It wasn't *me* doing the lying; it was the character I was playing. The fact that I would rather kill someone than tell a lie made far more sense to me. Now that I was thinking about it, I was noticing something else. I had a certain *evasiveness* that was just part of me, being able to answer a direct question in a way that naturally skirted around the full truth.

"Thank you, love, for explaining this to us so we can help you better," Noah reassured me. "Do one of the alphas need to tell you the rules, or can any of us do it?"

Pausing, I thought about that, checking in with my wolf and whatever elven magic was stirring. "Any of my mates can set rules and boundaries. Alphas are the only ones who can force me to answer or do something against my will."

The alphas snarled at that, looking offended that I would even think they would do such a thing.

"Little dove, the day I force you to do something against your will is the day that Colt or Lane should fucking kill me. There is no reason on this planet that I would ever need to do that," Zander declared, looking at the other two for their agreement.

Lane squeezed my ankle, drawing my attention to him. "I know we can be demanding and stubborn about certain things, but I don't want you to ever fear that we're going to do that to you. Sweetheart, you are everything to us, and some of us are learning all this right along with you. Just know that what hurts you hurts us."

My heart warmed with their concern, but I hadn't said that to make them think I was worried they would do it. "When I said alphas, I believe that applies to any alpha. At any point, an alpha could bark a command at me, and I'll have to obey."

They all looked angry at this revelation.

"Sweetheart, are you telling us that if you go to another pack or an alpha visits here, they can order you to tell them or do anything they want?" Lane demanded.

"From what little I know of myself, yes, there is a possibility that can happen," I explained. "I can fight it and try to work around the request, but if they know how to ask correctly, I'm screwed."

"That settles it. You are never leaving these pack lands," Zander grunted, crossing his arms over his chest.

Noah sighed as he rolled his eyes at me. "One issue at a time, let's get this settled before we put her on lockdown for a danger we don't know about yet. Finley, I leave it up to you to tell people about what your life was like before joining the pack. However, you are not to disclose any of your missions or the secrets that you might know about supernaturals or people of importance without addressing it with us first. Matters of the pack you might hear about or be involved in as the alphas' mate stay between the six of us unless we give you permission to share with others. Now, for the matter of you being an elf, that is not to be shared with anyone outside of your mates—ever. Elves, even when they were around, were highly sought after. For you to be one of the only ones left, it would make you a target of immense value."

I nodded, agreeing to his choices.

"Is there anything else he didn't cover that you need clarification on?" Lane asked.

"Am I allowed to tell people that I won't talk about it even if they press me about it?" I added.

Lane gave me a confused look before answering. "Yes, I give you permission to blame us for why you can't answer something if they press you about it. Why would that need to be addressed?"

"My wolf can't stand the thought of you all being mad at me for upsetting another pack member. The concept of disappointing you sends her into a panic," I answered.

Hearing this, Lane gave me a soft smile and leaned forward to kiss me on the forehead. "I know this must be so hard to wrap your brain around after being so independent up until this point. We'll do better, I promise, so you don't end up in a situation like this again. Forgive us?"

Lifting my face, Lane gave in to my silent request, kissing me to give me that last bit of reassurance I needed. Then my stomach made it known that the scent of food in the air was teasing us. Lane stood and pulled me to my feet, grinning. "Sounds like we need to feed you. Good thing I'm a grill master. My burgers are the best in the state."

Someone behind me scoffed as if they were trying to cover up laughter.

"Only took him a few years of burnt hockey pucks to get there," Mason shared, dodging the kick that Lane aimed at him. "What, you gonna tell me I'm wrong? You make a bomb ass burger now, but it wasn't always that way."

"Twin, that's just wrong to make a man look bad in front of his mate," Noah scolded.

We all laughed as we made our way back to the party where Lane fixed me a plate and found me a seat at one of the picnic tables. The betas and Zander joined me with their meals as Colt and Lane went off to do whatever alphas do. The burger was amazing, as well as the other homemade sides. I could get used to this kind of life where I got to eat whatever I wanted without worrying about gaining weight.

"Um, Finley," Katie's soft voice sounded from beside me.

I'd been so intent on my meal that I didn't hear her walk up; the downside to being with my mates was I felt safe enough not to be on alert all the time. Turning, I looked up to see her wringing her hands and nervously staring at her feet. I reached out and took her hand, feeling her anxiety and needing to help ease her worries in any way that I could. The whiplash I was getting from tonight was wearing on me, but now that I knew where I stood with my mates and pack leaders, I was far more at ease.

"What's wrong?" I questioned when she just gaped at me.

Her cheeks blushed with embarrassment. "Oh, right, well, that's what I was coming to ask you. I'm sorry if I did something to upset you. That wasn't my intention. My sisters are always telling me that I'm nosy and impulsive. I shouldn't have pressed you about what happened with Craig; if our alphas didn't think we needed to know, then I should trust that."

I could feel the men around me watching her, coming to an understanding as to what had set me off. "The learning curve of being an omega has been a little rough, and I learned tonight that I have to have some ground rules about interacting with the pack. I'm also not very good at talking with people. In my life before this, I didn't have friends or much control over my life, so it all just got a little overwhelming."

"Ah, I see..." Katie offered with a nod. "Well, enjoy the rest of your night."

Watching her walk away, I groaned. "I suck at people-ing."

TWENTY-FIVE

ZANDER

Thankfully, the rest of the night was uneventful, and we managed to mingle with the pack, introducing Finley to a few people without overwhelming her. Everything in me wanted to toss her over my shoulder and take her back to my house where she wouldn't be so stressed. I'd always been possessive over my things, but the level of caveman that I had to fight when it came to Finley was extreme. When it reached the point that I could tell she had reached her limit, I decided I didn't care what the others thought. I was taking her home.

Bending down, I pulled her onto my hip like a child and nodded to the couple we had been chit chatting with. "I'm sorry to cut the night short, but Finley has had a full day and is still adjusting after her first shift."

"Of course, alpha," the female whose name I couldn't remember said with a smile. "We hope to see you around more, Finley."

I nodded to her mate and headed off into the woods. It was the first time I regretted not living closer, but I was enjoying the fact that I would get to hold my beautiful mate in my arms.

"Thank you," Finley whispered as she wrapped her arms around my neck and rested her head on my shoulder. "I had no idea being around people would take so much energy. There has to be a way to tone down my empathic abilities."

Frowning, I glanced down at her from the corner of my eye. "Wait, you could feel *everyone's* emotions the whole time? I thought it was only in extreme cases when emotions ran high. We knew that was something omegas might be able to do if they were sensitive enough, but not all are. I've heard some are more gifted toward healing or at least relieving pain."

"It wasn't this bad before the shift, but up until today I've only been with you six. That made me think it was because you guys are my mates and whatever elf voodoo I have going on, but after that gathering, it's clear that I can pick up on anyone if I try. It's worse when there's contact, almost like a direct link right to whatever they're feeling," she explained.

The thought of other people freely touching my mate made me see red. Who gave them the right to touch what wasn't theirs?

"Do people touch you often?" I asked, trying to keep my cool, but the growl in my voice told me I wasn't hiding anything.

I could feel her smiling against my neck where she'd nuzzled into me. "Am I sensing you're jealous?"

"It's not jealousy when you're mine, little dove," I stated.

She chuckled and kissed me on the neck before pulling back to look at me. "Hmm, possessive is a good look on you."

Unable to deny myself, I caught her lips with my own, releasing the growl I'd been holding back. "Glad you like it because it's not going to change any time soon. Now, answer the question. Are people touching you when they shouldn't be?" I pressed, trying not to make it a forced order no matter how badly I wanted to.

"No, it's more innocent than that," she assured me. "The brush of an arm passing by, reaching for the same thing and touching hands, or even a simple handshake in greeting."

I thought back to how many people she'd met and how shifters were naturally more touchy feely than normal humans. This was another thing we were going to need to pay attention to. *Fuck, there has to be some tutorial or guide on how to deal with this.* Omegas were becoming more rare, but there were still plenty around to ask about such a thing. I had already started pulling books from the library that might be helpful, but it seemed I was going to be even more in debt to my Senate contact.

"Do we overwhelm you?" I inquired, hoping that holding her like this wasn't draining her. I knew my anxiety was high right now, trying to figure all this out. I didn't want her to have that kind of turmoil bombarding her.

She shook her head and sighed. "No, if I look for it, I can feel it, but our bond seems to give me more control over what I glean from you. Almost as if there is a built-in filter unless your emotions are super strong or I look for them. Plus, all of you seem to have more of a handle on your emotions than the rest of the pack."

"Good thing you have two nests that you can hide away in when things get too overwhelming."

"Can we all sleep together tonight?" Finley requested, looking at me with her stunning cobalt gaze. "It was so comforting when we were in my nest, and it seemed to help you guys as well."

On that, she wasn't wrong. Never had I woken up from a nap feeling more rested and ready to deal with the world than that moment. I had just come off of a six-month international tour for my latest album and still hadn't recovered from my jet lag until that nap. Part of me didn't want to go to sleep yet, but knowing I could snuggle up with her made the decision for me.

"If that's what you want, I'm sure no one will argue," I answered.

Once we entered my home, I set her down, taking a deep breath now that I was finally back in my space for the night. It had been an extremely long time since I'd been part of a pack. Once I'd left the one I grew up in, I'd been on my own. My wolf and I didn't feel the same need to be surrounded by others—unless they were fans. My true passion was wanting to enlighten the world to the fact that just because someone was or became a super, they didn't stop being human.

Yes, in the literal sense, they did, but we still wanted to enjoy the world the way everyone else did. Sure, we were all out in the 'open,' if you will, but our lives weren't equal. There were still so many ways that we were kept separate, with supers being looked down on just because we were something *extra*. Now, if a doctor or teacher was outed as a super, they would lose their jobs. Despite many supers' attempts to educate the public, many people still believed they could be changed by a simple touch. If that wasn't the case, then they feared us, thinking we couldn't be trusted with vulnerable populations because we were "monsters." So, supers either lived in a supernatural community or lived among the humans while fiercely guarding their secret. There was no in between despite the fact that we'd been coexisting for centuries. The only difference now was that we announced ourselves. We'd been around as long as humanity had; we were just more patient, living in the shadows while keeping our true natures hidden.

"Hey, you okay?" Finley asked, slipping her hand into mine. The contact was a reminder that although there were still all these problems out in the world, I had something more pressing to be thinking about right here.

I looked down at her and smiled. "Fine, just lost in thought is all. Do you need anything to drink or eat, or are you just ready for bed?"

She stilled, and I could tell she was mulling over my question. I noticed she did this a lot, but I wasn't sure if it was some kind of conflict between what she wanted and what her wolf desired, or if it was something she'd always done. I had to admit it was cute when she got the little wrinkle in between her brows.

"No, I'm fine, but I would like to know how things went today with your Senate contact. I know you wanted to wait until tomorrow, but who knows what tomorrow will bring," she pointed out.

I hummed my agreement, wandered over to the couch, and pulled her onto my lap. "The others should be here in a moment. Let's wait for them so I don't have to explain it all again. In the meantime, is anything else on your mind?"

"It's taking effort to remember to use all of my heightened senses. I keep trying to focus on one of them, but then I lose the others."

"That's because you keep pushing your wolf to the side. If you let her co-exist with you, then you won't need to call on her because she'll already be there," I explained.

Finley tilted her head, giving me a look that told me she didn't understand what I was saying at all. "Okay, so you can feel your wolf in your mind, right? Where is she, and what is she doing?"

"She's curled up, taking a nap off to the side. Being on alert all night wore her out," Finley shared.

"Now, if you needed her, you would have to wake her up to get her attention because she's completely removed from your human consciousness. If you let her linger in your mind without shutting the door on her, then she would share your state of mind without taking over. She'd be there as support, picking up on things your human side can't," I said, educating her the best I could.

Being a born wolf, I'd always had to share space with my wolf, and being over a hundred years old, I couldn't comprehend how to live any other way.

"Will sharing space with her increase her omega influence over me?"

Ah, *that* was the real problem. "Little dove, no matter what you do or how you interact with your wolf, you will forever be an omega. Even when your elf nature manifests, that won't remove your status as an omega. It might help level things off, or possibly make it worse, but we don't know. Being a born wolf, I don't understand the struggle of fighting against one's nature, but I do understand not loving being a werewolf. As hard as it seems, learning to accept where you're at now is the only way to survive this life. You'll live half blind and deaf if you keep your wolf locked away like this." I reached up and tucked a flyaway hair behind her ear before stroking her cheek, willing her to hear what I was trying to say. "Don't let your frustration and anger at being made an omega ruin you like it did Craig. Sadly, I've seen too many lost because they couldn't accept who they became after getting bitten."

"I hear you, but it's hard," she answered honestly, leaning into my hand for comfort.

Even without an empathic gift, I could see how tough it was on my mate; she was such a strong, confident woman who was so capable. The glimpse I'd gotten of who she was before her first shift was astounding, but there was a different power in her now. She just couldn't see it yet. All I knew was that I was going to make sure she understood how amazing she was now, and once she matured into her elf abilities, she would be spectacular.

TWENTY-SIX

FINLEY

I was enjoying the peace and quiet of Zander's home, but it didn't take long for the others to join us. Mason pulled me from Zander's arm, ignoring the growl that came from him, and curled us both up in the large overstuffed armchair.

"You know, snuggles, you are hard to get ahold of with all the others around," Mason murmured against my ear. "I had to brave the dangers of pulling you right out of an alpha's arms!"

I rolled my eyes at how dramatic he was being while the others found their spot. "Zander has news to share with us from his meeting today," I announced.

Hearing this, everyone turned their attention to the alpha in question.

"I wanted to wait until tomorrow, but my wise mate warned me that we have no idea what tomorrow might hold if today was anything to go by," Zander muttered. "My contact is old enough that they were around before the war between the elves happened. As far as they know, there has never been an elf that's been turned by a werewolf. By vampires, yes, but nothing else has been recorded or shared in the materials we have access to. They're sending me books on the Light Elves' history since the Senate collected them all, safeguarding them in the vaults."

"Holy shit, how close are you to the Senate for them to allow such a thing?" Lane asked.

I watched Zander, feeling his internal struggle as he made the choice on how to answer. "It's my mother... Senator Morwyn Vaughan is my mother," Zander announced.

The others shifted in their seats and looked at one another in surprise.

"That certainly explains a lot," Colt responded, running his hands through his hair. "I always wondered why you were allowed to do what you do, proclaiming you're a werewolf all over the world with your music. It always seemed odd that while the Senate wanted us to be integrated, they didn't want all our secrets told."

"You're right on that. I have to get approval on everything I want to say, especially if it's on live TV or the radio, but I've been known to deviate if there's something that needs to be corrected," Zander shared with a grin. "As much as it has been a ball and chain in my life, it's moments like this where it's helpful. Mother was able to get me what I needed and shared something that will be somewhat helpful when Finley comes into her power. Oh, she also handled the issue with the Marshals as well, so they won't be bothering us any further."

Perking up at the idea of getting some answers, I leaned forward. "What did she tell you?"

"If you're a full elf, which I do believe you are, then even though you're soon-to-be thirty, you are still considered an adolescent. This means that until you come into your powers, you are unable to reproduce. Even if you've gone into heat, your body isn't ready to host a child, so it won't allow it to take root," Zander informed.

My jaw dropped at this; the thought of children hadn't even crossed my mind since I'd never planned on having any. I'd been given an implant by the Organization to stop pregnancies from happening; pregnant assassins just were not a thing, so while that was still my job, children would never be an option.

"So does that mean the birth control I'm on isn't needed until after I've 'matured'?" I questioned.

"The moment you had your first shift that stopped being effective. Werewolves don't process medicine the way humans do; our bodies burn off their benefits too fast. We also don't get sick or contract viruses like humans do. We run too hot for it to survive," Lane interjected. "That's what our company is working on—medication that can be used on supers when needed. If a wolf, or any shifter for that matter, gets so wounded that they can't shift to accelerate their healing, there's nothing we can do for the pain. Even the strongest drug only lasts for a half hour at the most."

I thought back to our training and the education the Organization had given us on dealing with supers. Poison wouldn't work like it did on humans; we'd been taught to always take off the head, hit the heart, or burn them so they didn't come back. With what Zander just explained, this made more sense; the poison or toxin would get burned off too fast to kill, so it wouldn't finish the job.

"Mother believes that your elf heritage is why you could be turned into an omega," Zander continued. "Being a born super made you more compatible with the werewolf mutation. Something about elves' natural disposition being peacekeepers and nurturers helped to make the omega designation possible, in particular. But many elves were more than that, with some even being fierce warriors, and this might be why you feel so divided in your nature. So far, you've lived your life like an elf warrior, but the omega nature is now pulling on that gentler side of you. Both are true, but one outweighs the other at the moment. Hopefully, once you've matured into your elf nature, it will help to equalize the omega side of things."

Even though what he said made sense, it still meant I was going to be dealing with this for the foreseeable future since I had no clue when my birthday was.

"Did your mother have anything to say in regards to any other known elves?" Lane asked.

Before Zander could speak, Elias cut in from where he had been pacing behind the couch. "Isn't anyone worried that the Senate now knows about Finley? Didn't we just say that people shouldn't know about her being an elf? Hell, her being an omega makes her enough of a target," he snarled.

It was becoming exponentially clear to me why Elias had become one of my Sentinels; my safety was always his first thought no matter how it might affect the alphas.

"Do you think my mother would cause harm to my mate? I'm her only child, so the chance of having any grandchildren or carrying on our family line rests with me!" Zander snapped as he leaped to his feet. "There is no way that I would allow anyone to take Finley from me no matter who they are. You aren't the only one who's concerned about her safety!"

"Really, if that were true, why didn't you tell us about your mother from the start? Seems like you don't trust us enough to share when it involves *our* mate!" Elias challenged.

Zander growled in warning. "She isn't your mate yet, beta."

Shoving out of Mason's arms, I shot to my feet. "Stop it!" The room stilled, and they all turned to look at me, taken aback at my outburst. "All of you in this room are mine—regardless of whether I bear your mark. I refuse to let you fight over your place beside me when I need *all* of you. Elias is one of my Sentinels. It's his job to always think of the worst case and voice his concerns, just like Noah will always be the first to pick up on what I need without having to ask me. Each of you has a role to play in my life as well as a spot in my heart. We're new to each other and this dynamic, but I already know that I won't be able to survive this new life and the supernatural world without *all* of you. As for Zander's mother, I trust my mate to look after me and all of us, so if he trusts her, I'm supporting his decision."

Looking thoroughly chastised, Zander and Elias calmed down and backed off each other. I was glad even though I knew it wouldn't be the last battle between these two men. They were too similar for friction not to happen every so often.

"Snuggles is right," Mason spoke up. "I'm still not sure what role I fill in this group, but I do know that I trust each of you to watch her back if I'm not there. If the Senate comes for Finley, we'll deal with that together, but I choose to believe that Zander reached out to his *mother, not the Senate,* who wants the best for her son and his new mate."

I smiled at Mason, pleased that he'd spoken up on this matter and saw my logic. "I think it's best if we all head to bed; it's been a crazy day. If I could impose a request, I would love to have us all sleep together like we did in my nest." Everyone nodded or murmured their agreement, making me smile even bigger.

"Like we could ever say no when it makes you that excited." Noah snorted as he stood and held out his hand to me. "Come on, love, let's turn in for the night."

Between the stocked closet and the bathroom, I found everything I might need for daily life. Zander wasn't kidding when he said that he wanted this to be my home as well. Curling up in the middle of the bed, the others joined, finding whatever space they could to get close to me or at least touch some part of my body. It might not be the most comfortable for them in the long run, but now that I knew what this felt like, I wasn't sure I could sleep any other way.

Soft kisses along my skin woke me up with a smile. I rolled into the body behind me, breathing in the bright evergreen scent. "Good morning," I murmured.

"Good morning, little one, did you sleep well?" Colt asked as he kissed his mate mark on my neck.

I stretched out and rubbed my eyes before opening them, not feeling ready to start my day just yet. "Mmm, I slept like the dead."

The scent of something sweet drifted its way over to me from somewhere in the house, making my stomach announce its desire to enjoy whatever it might be.

"Little one, I know that it's going to take some time to adjust, but you need to eat more and more often. If you've reached the point that your stomach is begging for food, you've gone too long," Colt scolded me.

Sitting up, I scowled down at him. "What, you want me to set a timer and eat every two hours or something?"

Colt nodded. "That's actually a really good idea."

"I was joking, you know."

Colt grinned and booped me on the nose with a finger. "I figured, but that doesn't make it any less of a good idea. Come on, smells like whatever Lane and Zander were cooking up for breakfast is done. Time to fatten you up a bit."

"Are you saying I'm too skinny?" I demanded.

The look of panic on Colt's face as he tried to find a way to answer me was priceless. Leaning forward, I gave him a quick peck on the lips before I slid out of bed and headed to the bathroom. "Kidding!" I called over my shoulders.

"Looks like someone woke up with a little extra pep in their step," Colt chuckled. "Come down when you're ready. We need to make some plans for today."

I piled my hair up and hopped into the shower, scrubbed my body, and called it good. Starting off the day fresh and clean was the best feeling as well as a necessity for starting the day off right. I wandered through the options that Zander had bought me, quickly discovering that our idea of buying a *few* things was vastly different. I had a full wardrobe of everyday clothes, workout gear, business professional, and dresses for something more formal. Feeling the need to get a workout in, I slipped on leggings, a sports bra, and a workout tank with a sweatshirt. Along the bottom of the closet, I found a shoe rack full of options that were exactly my size. How Zander had managed to learn all this information was something I would love to know.

Ready for the day, I headed downstairs and found another feast of breakfast items laid out on the kitchen counter. What I'd been smelling was the giant icing-drowned cinnamon rolls that were making my mouth water at the sight.

"Snugg-le-s!" Mason called out from his spot at the table, mouth stuffed full of food, which he promptly started to choke on.

Noah slapped him on the back with a loud thump, sending whatever he'd been choking on out of his mouth and onto the plate. "Don't fucking talk with your mouth full, you barbarian."

"Holy shit, you saved my life, twin!" Mason gasped in between coughing fits.

"Isn't the first time and definitely won't be the last," Noah muttered. "Good morning, love, fill up a plate. We've all gotten ours."

Looking over the table, I saw that all of them had full plates in front of them even if they weren't really eating yet. They were doing this for me, that way I could easily grab my own meal without needing one of them to serve me. I grabbed the plate left for me and started with the cinnamon roll, working from there until the plate matched theirs in size. I took an open seat at the head of the table so I could see them all as they talked.

"So, unfortunately, sweetheart, all of us have things that we need to deal with today," Lane started. "Would you like to stay here for the day or have us drop you off with some of the pack that work around the property? It's up to you."

The idea of being stuck in this house didn't sit right with me, no matter how beautiful it was, but I wasn't sure I was so keen on spending solo time with the pack. "Are you guys leaving the pack lands?"

"I will be. Mother asked for me to meet her so she could introduce me to someone who spent most of their life living among the Light Elves. This kind of opportunity is too good to pass up," Zander shared, giving me an apologetic look.

"Colt and I will be close, but we have some meetings and new super-natural paramedics to train for the next two days. I know this came at the worst time, but the faster we get them on board and good to go, the freer we are to be around," Lane explained.

Elias reached over and took my hand, drawing my attention. "I will be on the pack lands, but being the only beta available to the whole pack, I can't stay with you."

"Oh, and where will you both be?" I asked, looking at the twins.

Mason scratched the back of his head as if nervous to tell me. "Ah, you see, snuggles, we got asked to be security at this shifter club last week in another town. We wanted to call them and tell them we had to cancel, but Colt said we couldn't."

"Little one, it's more complicated than that. We're the healthiest and largest pack on this side of Tennessee; if a smaller pack asks for our help, I feel it's our duty to help them," Colt added. "There may come a day that we need their help, so fostering a mindset of give and take is helpful to us all as a pack."

I nodded, agreeing with him on that logic. "Well, I can't plan on you guys being around me all the time, now can I? The goal is to get me more integrated with the pack anyway, right? So, no time like the present."

Colt cupped my face in his hands and kissed me soundly. "You are the most amazing mate I could have ever been blessed with. We'll make it up to you, I promise."

TWENTY-SEVEN

FINLEY

"Where would you like me to take you?" Elias asked as we walked down the road to the main pack area. "There are groups who work in the gardens, kitchen, and with the pack's children."

"With my skills, I could be of help on patrol," I ventured.

Elias growled at the idea and tightened his grip on my hand. "There's no way I'm going to let you do that, not to mention if your mates found out, I might get my throat ripped out—Sentinel or not."

That had me stopping in my tracks, scowling. "So I'm never going to be able to help this pack if it puts me in danger? Elias, I'm one of the best assassins the Organization had, not to mention I've killed more people in my life than all of you combined."

"Yes, but that was *before* you became an omega and mated three possessive, overprotective, dominating alphas," Elias countered. "I can't say that I like the idea of you being put in any kind of danger either. We have no idea how you will react. Mason and Noah said you froze when Craig attacked. You could have been mauled or even killed if the twins hadn't been there!"

My anger spiked at this; I'd always exceeded expectations in what was asked of me, pushing myself to be the best. I'd endured decades of training that would be considered torture by most people only to have him fault me for freezing one time!

My chest rumbled with a growl as I narrowed my eyes at him. "That's not fair. I have no idea how to fight as a wolf. That's like handing a gun to someone who's never shot one before then being pissed they missed the target. All I need is someone to teach me, show me how to use my body to the best advantage as a wolf, and believe me, that will never happen to me again."

Elias' eyes widened ever so slightly at my outburst, letting me know that I'd caught him off guard. "Be that as it may, it doesn't change what the others would think."

Even though he was the most emotionally locked down of my mates, I still caught a hint of something that told me he might not agree with the others on this matter.

"You're really telling me that my choices are no longer valid now that I have mates?" I snapped, pushing to see if he might back me up on this.

"Welcome to being part of the pack. The alpha is judge and jury when it comes to all things, especially when they're the alpha's mate. Add that detail as the cherry on top of the cake, and you, Finley, are now going to be living in a protective bubble."

Snarling, I twisted my hold on his hand to grab around his wrist. I jerked him to me, pitching him off balance so I could sweep out a foot in front of him, knocking him to his knees. "I might be forced to be labeled as omega, mated to the pack leaders, but I will *never* be placed aside to be coddled and protected from the dangers of this world."

The pain of betrayal burned in my chest, and it was then I noticed that wasn't the only thing that was scorching through my veins. There was a throb of power that pushed against my skin as if trying to break free, but it wasn't strong enough to manage it yet. The power built, causing me to gasp when it eventually had nowhere to go. I dropped to my knees, slumping into Elias' hold. He started to murmur something in my ear as he stroked my head, trying to get me to calm down. This feeling reminded me of the battle my body had gone through with that first shift. Could it be that I was closer to my birthday than any of us imagined?

"Breathe, my heart, just breathe," Elias whispered into my ear. "That's it, deep, even breaths. You need to slow your heart rate down."

It was hard to take deep, even breaths. My lungs refused to listen, making me gasp for air instead. Elias shifted me so my ear was on his chest over his heart. "Listen to mine and try to slow yours down to match. Breathe in through the nose and out through the mouth... Good, now do it again."

Once I stopped trying to force my body to listen to me and relaxed into Elias' hold, I managed to do as he asked. After I did it once, it was easier to do it again and again until I was breathing normally once more. I wrapped my arms around his chest and snuggled into his arms, more than a little freaked out at what my body had just gone through.

"What just happened?" I mumbled into his shirt.

He didn't answer right away, letting his hand rub up and down my back. "My best guess is that your elven nature peeked its head out of where it's been hiding in response to your emotions. It was clear that you were angry, but was that all that was going on in that beautiful mind?"

"I'm not a pretty bird to be put in a cage, looked at and only taken out when you feel like it. I'm a hawk, meant to fly free and hunt. Part of me is omega, but that isn't all that I am. There's a reason that I was *so* good at my job, Elias. It was the elven part of me—the warrior. I can't be kept in a bubble to make them feel better; it will crush me." I sobbed as I came to the realization.

We sat there for a while as I let my emotions run wild for the first time in a long time, and it felt amazing if I was being honest with myself. Elias shifted me so he could see my face, wiping my tears from my cheeks and giving me a sad smile.

"You, my heart, are one of the most complex creatures I have ever encountered," Elias said, placing a soft kiss on my forehead. "What if you and I do some training on how to fight as a wolf? We'll work on honing your senses and becoming one with your wolf nature. If I feel like you can manage fine with me, we'll broach the subject with the others."

My spirits soared at this. "I can work with that as long as there's hope I don't have to learn to knit or something else equally ridiculous."

Elias laughed, surprising the shit out of me. I'd gotten the impression he wasn't one to laugh at anything. "No, my heart, we won't make you learn how to knit... needlepoint maybe, but no knitting." Standing up, he reached out a hand and pulled me to my feet. "Come on, I think working in the gardens might be the thing for you today. Fresh air and sunshine always helps when I've had a rough night."

As much as I wanted to ask him what he meant by rough nights, I didn't feel that he would tell me until he was ready. Comfortable silence hung between us as we reached the main pack area and headed further north past most of the houses to an open plot of land with one of the largest gardens I'd ever seen. There were already people hard at work, preparing the land for spring, as well as others in the green house which Elias led me to. At first glance, the structure didn't look all that impressive, but once I entered, it was clear that the outside was deceiving.

"Peggy," Elias called out.

The woman in question looked up from where she was transferring a plant from a pot to the raised bed. Seeing Elias waving at her, she dusted off her hands with a slight frown and made her way over.

"What can I do for you, Beta Elias?" Peggy asked, her tone respectful but cold.

"Finley is here to work," Elias stated.

"I see. Do you have much experience working in a garden?" Peggy inquired as she looked me up and down.

My wolf whimpered, feeling as if she'd already failed our pack since I knew absolutely nothing about that. "No, I never had the chance to learn, but I catch on quickly."

"Hmph," Peggy grunted as she turned on her heel. "Come on, let's see if we can find you something simple enough to do."

I glanced over at Elias, who looked like he was about to bite her head off, and gripped his arm. He looked at me, and I gave a slight shake *no* as I headed off to follow Peggy. There was no way the pack would accept me or get to know me if I always had one of the leaders glued to my side, scaring everyone off. When I'd touched Peggy the other night, I could feel worry rooted in her concern that I would somehow harm the pack, so I had to trust that she might warm up after she saw I wasn't looking for trouble.

"We have a new addition to the greenhouse, but we haven't had the extra help to finish off these new raised beds since people have had to get jobs further away from pack lands," Peggy informed me as she stopped in front of ten twelve-by-twelve wooden squares made out of what looked like old railroad ties. "There's planting soil and other additives that need to be mixed together before we can fill the boxes. The supply room is over there." She pointed to a set of rolling barn doors. "Near the bag of soil is a list of all that needs to go in the mix, along with wheelbarrows and anything else you might need. Any questions?"

I shook my head no because I knew better than to think she really meant it.

"Don't pick anything unless expressly asked by myself or Daniel. This food is for the pack. We had a rough winter and lost a bunch of the winter crops, so what we have is precious. The pack is growing faster than we can support, which is why so many have left to work. I'm glad to see the alphas aren't playing favorites and having you pull your weight. I know omegas like to be spoiled, but you came to the wrong pack for that." Peggy sniffed as she turned on her heel and went back to what she was doing.

Oh boy, today was going to be delightful...

Three hours later, I was covered in dirt from head to toe and smelled like shit—literally. I'd gotten more than half the raised beds done when Katie appeared with a huge grin on her face. "I heard you got dropped off here this morning. God, you poor thing, Peggy's working you to the bone. I don't know why she has you doing this; we don't need to plant them for another few weeks, and it's not even April yet."

I had to bite my tongue not to say something rude about her sister. Luckily, I knew my face wouldn't show my irritation thanks to my years of training not to show my emotions.

"Come on, it's lunch time. We all gather at the pavilion to eat," Katie announced, grabbing my arm, dragging me away.

"Is there somewhere I can clean up?" I asked as I followed along.

Katie paused and looked at me again before blushing a little. "Right, of course you would want to scrape some of that mud off of you. Milly is always telling me to use my brain, but I just get so excited about meeting new people and all that. There's a washing station outside the greenhouse."

Sure enough, there was a row of sinks with bars of soap ready to use. Quickly as I could, using the frigid water, I scoured the dirt from my hands and arms, feeling better about joining the others for a meal. The sun was shining high in the sky, warming us as we stood in line to get our meal from the head table. I assumed this was run by the people who worked in the kitchens. Seeing the massive amounts of food they provided made me glad I wasn't placed there.

Our assassin training only included basic cooking skills so we didn't starve, so I was definitely not a chef. Grabbing a tray, I was given a bowl of hardy beef stew, fresh bread, and a cookie. This made me feel like I was once again back in basic training, life was much simpler back then and in some small ways I missed that.

"Oh look, there's Milly and a few of the other single ladies. You'll like them, I promise. Don't worry, Peggy takes her lunch back to the greenhouse. She isn't much for interacting with others," Katie rambled as she led the way.

I could tell that Katie meant well; she just had a larger than life personality that you either loved or hated. Being that I was far from impulsive, it was interesting to watch her interact with life around her, never knowing what she'd do next. It made me relax a little, knowing that Katie would be able to carry the conversation with the others, making it far less awkward than the silence I would provide.

"Oh, Finley, it's so nice to see you joining us," Milly greeted with a bright smile. "Grace, Sarah, and Barb, you remember meeting Finley last night?"

"Yes, it's nice to see you out and about with the pack," Barb said, nodding her head as I sat beside her.

Smiling at the new faces, I gave a little wave. "It's nice to meet all of you as well. I didn't know what to expect from pack life, but I'm impressed with what I've seen so far."

"Milly, we can't let her go back to the greenhouse. Peggy has her doing all the awful jobs for some reason," Katie muttered.

Her sister frowned at this. "Why, for heaven's sake, would she be doing that? They need a lot of help in the gardens, with planting the crops for spring and harvesting the last of the winter produce."

"It might have something to do with the fact that I have zero idea what I'm doing," I offered, not wanting to upset anyone when I didn't mind the hard labor. After so many years of pushing my body to its physical limit, having spent the last six days not doing much was odd.

"There are plenty of newcomers that have no idea what they're doing. I'm going to pair you up with one of the others who can show you the ropes and help us where we need it more." I started to argue, but she raised her hand to stop me. "Peggy might be in charge of the greenhouse, but I'm in charge of making sure we have help in the areas we need it. Someone's always claiming they need more people than they really do, so I keep it all as even as possible."

"See? Problem solved!" Katie said, clapping her hands before digging into her meal.

TWENTY-EIGHT

FINLEY

After lunch, Milly walked back to the greenhouse with me and marched right up to her sister. "What are you thinking, Peggy? Finley is being wasted on filling those planter boxes when we don't even need them yet. You have Mike and Kelly working overtime, trying to keep up with the spring planting. Why on earth are you not letting Finley help?"

"She has no idea what she's doing, and we can't afford to waste what the alphas have worked so hard to provide for us," Peggy snapped back.

When she brought up the alphas, I could feel jealousy and longing, making me think she had feelings for one of them. This might explain why she was so angry with me. From her perspective, I could understand it; to the female wolves in the pack, it probably felt like I'd snatched away all the powerful men, but it wasn't like I could help it.

Milly tossed up her hand and groaned. "We're fine! I don't understand why you keep thinking this pack is struggling. We've grown leaps and bounds over the past two years—for the better. Our alphas' business is booming. They are right now, as we speak, training more people to expand their reach. So please enlighten me as to your issues here."

"I don't need to explain myself to you, Milly. You may be my older sister, but you are *not* in charge of me or what I do in this greenhouse!" Peggy snarled, making me flinch at the sudden outburst.

Milly was having none of it, staring her sister down as they went head to head. "I still outrank you in every way that counts, so back down before I have to bring in someone else on this matter."

I could see that Peggy wanted to fight her sister, but the fact that she was less dominant left her with no leg to stand on. "Fine, I'll place her with Mike and Kelly, but I don't want her back in this greenhouse ever again."

"Ha!" Milly laughed. "I'd like to see you tell that to her mates. I'm sure they would love to know that you're treating her like crap because you had your eyes set on Lane. That was never going to happen no matter how much you mooned over him. Finley is his true mate even if it's slightly unorthodox for a wolf to share with others. It just shows how special Finley really is to them *and* to our pack, so suck it up and move on."

The vast amount of information that I'd just learned made me slightly uncomfortable, and all my wolf wanted was to slink away, but my training had me collecting every tidbit I could, knowing I might need it later. There was something about Peggy that was throwing me off, but I just couldn't put my finger on it. Hearing that she had a thing for Lane, it made more sense, accounting for her instant dislike of me. But that didn't make the reasons behind her worry about the pack's size and resources any clearer.

"If you'll follow me, Finley, I'll introduce you to Mike and Kelly. They're a mated pair and ever so delightful to spend time with... unlike some people here," Milly said, glaring at her sister as she waved for me to follow.

I was more than happy to remove myself from the situation and the rollercoaster ride of emotions that were flying around. It was over-whelming to filter through them, but it didn't wear me out like the pack gathering had. It seemed that smaller groups, like just the two sisters, were within my tolerance.

We entered another section of the greenhouse that opened up into a wide warehouse with a glass roof and misters hanging from the ceiling. Four people were hunched over planter boxes with various gardening tools around them, but upon hearing us enter, they looked up, watching us approach.

"Hello, you two, I'm sure you know who Finley is," Milly said by way of introduction. "It seems she got a little lost in the mix, but she'll be helping you guys out with planting for the rest of the day."

"Oh, that's lovely!" Kelly exclaimed, smiling at me. "With just a few of us in here, we need all the help we can muster. Most new people want to work with the kids or in the kitchen, but what's more fulfilling than growing what we can to feed the pack? You know, the alphas are trying to make it so that we can provide most of the food needs instead of having to order in supplies. I think by next year we might be able to, don't you think, dear?"

"Seeing as how last year we did about half and with how mild the winter has been, we have a good chance of it," Mike answered, kissing his wife's cheek.

"Don't mind the lovebirds. They've only been mated for a short while," Milly teased. "Alright, I'll leave you to it."

Mike was a small man, in both height and stature, but he had a kind face that set me at ease. Kelly was taller, and I could see she was already pregnant as she absently rubbed the baby bump. By their emotions alone, I could tell they were warm, kind people, and I was finally able to relax after the whole thing with Peggy. Those sisters were a force to be reckoned with, and the emotions they gave off were overwhelming and chaotic.

"So, Finley, what do you know about gardening?" Kelly asked.

"How to mix soil for the planter boxes..." I admitted.

This seemed to delight Kelly. "Oh, I love being able to teach new people such a valuable skill! Those who know how to plant and garden will never go hungry."

"Take it easy, honey. You don't want to scare her off with your exuberance," Mike chided gently.

"Yes, yes." Kelly rolled her eyes and patted her husband's shoulder before waving for me to follow her. "Come, let's get you some tools, gloves, and seeds!"

To say that the later part of my day was far more enjoyable than the beginning was an understatement. Kelly was easy to be around, chatting on while she worked, teaching me as she went. She was a born wolf, but Mike wasn't; he'd joined the pack two years ago. He and Kelly had bonded over their love of gardening, and their romance grew from there. It was interesting to hear how they fell in love the old-fashioned way. Now they were mated and expecting their first child.

"You know, I never knew how hard it would be to not shift for nine months," Kelly sighed as she took a break. "Having always been able to do so, it's almost like torture, but this little one will be worth it after it's all said and done."

"What happens if you shift?" I asked.

"Goodness, I'm sorry. I swear this baby is stealing brain cells every day. The shift will cause your baby to be terminated; the mutation in us does pass to our children but not while it's still being formed. If I were to shift, I would lose the child instantly," Kelly explained. "Typically, your wolf nature understands this and doesn't encourage it, but situations happen. It's tragic, but all you can do is try your best. This is why we as a pack treasure all children born. They are a labor of love. Some do end up deciding that it's not worth the pain or anxiety if they fail and lose the baby, but I've always wanted to be a mother, so I'm willing to do whatever it takes to see this child join the world."

That all made sense to me, but it had me thinking back to the fact that I couldn't have children yet... not that I wanted any right now—or ever. It was something I'd need to really reflect on for myself and my future. During their rut, my mates had already shown they wouldn't mind me having a baby, so I wouldn't put it past them to try to change my mind on the matter.

"Are you planning on having kids now that you're mated? I feel like it would be impossible to prevent it with three mates; one is hard enough for me to manage," Kelly admitted, giving me a meaningful look.

I couldn't help but laugh at that. "So far they have been very respectful in letting me adjust to everything going on, like the fact that I was instantly bonded to all three of them. To be honest, I think they're having a harder time wrapping their heads around the sharing part more than I am. I get all the benefits of the deal, minus the fact that they're all so busy right now. My wolf is trying to be understanding about them needing to be gone while they take care of pack matters."

"Oh, but isn't Alpha Zander on a break after his last tour? That's what the pack gossip was saying, but you can never trust those rumors," Kelly huffed. "All some women see are the dollar signs around him—a bunch of hussies, I say."

"Well then, it's a good thing I landed a mate who has absolutely no interest in my wealth," Zander interjected as he walked over to us.

I couldn't help the smile that instantly showed up when I saw him. "You're back."

"Indeed, little dove," Zander answered, smiling down at me. "I've come to pick you up and take you home with me... unless you're enjoying yourself here too much."

Before I answered, I looked over at Kelly and Mike, wanting to make sure that was okay with them. "Go, on. Honestly, when a man takes the time to escort you home, you don't dawdle. Now, get," Kelly shooed me away. "Leave your things. We'll take care of it. Have a good night and we'll see you soon."

It was hard not to like Kelly, so I impulsively reached out and gave her a hug, surprising myself. "Thanks for everything today."

Kelly blushed as she waved me off, tears welling up in her eyes. "This darn baby makes me cry over the silliest things!" Mike wrapped his arms around her and kissed her cheek as he waved goodbye to me.

Feeling much better about my day and interacting with the pack as a whole, I returned the wave as Zander and I walked out of the greenhouse.

"How did you know where I was?" I asked as he opened the door to a sleek white Land Rover.

"Do you really think we didn't all know what you were up to today? Elias made sure that everyone was kept in the loop," Zander informed me as he buckled me in. "I know you can protect yourself, but I like to know you're safe," he stated before catching me in a toe-curling kiss.

"If I get a kiss like that every time, I suddenly don't mind being apart all that much," I purred, giving him a wink.

Zander flashed me a sultry grin as he shut the door and made his way to the driver's side. "I should warn you though... Colt was not happy about how Peggy was treating you today."

"If Elias knew about that, I'm surprised she's still in one piece," I commented.

"That would be information we got from Milly. Apparently, she called Lane and Colt right after she dropped you off after lunch."

I glanced at Zander as we headed out to the main road. "What, did they call you right after to chat about it like a bunch of worried hens?"

"The three of us are your mates, Finley. Anything that happens with you is our business. It was only right that they called me to fill me in, which is also why I came to check on you. I needed to make sure things were going better this afternoon. Since there was only an hour left before five o'clock, I selfishly decided to just bring you home instead of leaving you to finish."

Even though he didn't say it outright, knowing that he missed me made me feel all warm inside. Truth be told, I'd missed all of them as well. It was crazy to think it had been only a few short days since I'd picked up the phone and called Colt. Now I was here, mated, an omega and elf, working with the pack to provide for our needs. The lone assassin had turned into a housewife, and it was as oddly wonderful as it was terrifying. Seeing Kelly and her mate, the love and respect that they shared with each other, gave me hope that I might be able to give that to my men. All my life I'd been told to be aloof and to keep relationships short because you couldn't be vulnerable. Maybe they were wrong... Maybe life could be better if I gave all of that a chance... *maybe.*

"How do you feel about going out tonight?" Zander asked, pulling me out of my thoughts. "Colt and Lane will be back around six, same with Elias, although the twins might not be back until tomorrow depending on how late the concert goes."

"That actually sounds like fun. I don't know the area at all, so it will be nice to get a feel for where I'm at. I'm so used to doing so much research on the location I end up in. It's odd to have no clue what's around me," I shared.

Zander took my dirt-covered hand in his and intertwined our fingers. "Do you think you can be happy here?"

His question caught me completely off guard. "What?"

"None of this was what you planned for your life, so it doesn't surprise me that this is going to take some adjusting. But do you think you could be happy living here in the woods of Tennessee with the pack and the six of us learning how to create a life together?"

The question he asked was something I'd been wrestling with all day, working without them to buffer how different my world really was now. "I'd like to try. You and the others mean a lot more to me than I would've imagined in such a short time. I don't know if that's because of the mate bond or whatever the elves call it, but I've never felt so cared for and protected in my life. There are aspects that I think we need to work through as we get to know each other, but I *want* to work through them if that makes sense?"

"Guess that's as good of an honest answer as I could ask for," he murmured, kissing the back of my hand. "Take your time cleaning up. I also brought home some magazines with design ideas for your nesting room if you're not sure what to do with it. I put them in there if you want some time to decompress after such a social day."

Now that he'd offered the option, it sounded heavenly to me. "Could I read one of the books your mother loaned you instead?"

"Absolutely, little dove."

TWENTY-NINE

FINLEY

When the others returned, they found me snuggled up in my giant bean bag pillow, reading, with Zander working next to me on his laptop. The book had good information on omegas, and researching new situations or unknown topics had always helped me feel more grounded.

"Don't you look comfortable, sweetheart," Lane said as he leaned down to kiss me on the forehead. "Did your day end up getting better once you got put with Mike and Kelly?"

"Yeah, they're both too sweet to ever upset anyone," I answered, sitting up. "Did you guys have a good day?"

"The batch of trainees that we have are looking very promising, which is a pleasant surprise. Sometimes we never know what we're going to get," Colt shared, then kissed me. "Zander mentioned something about going out tonight?"

"If you guys are up for it." I hesitated before saying more, my wolf worrying they might be too tired.

Colt's expression softened as if he could read my hesitation. "I think a night out is exactly what we need. Plus, this town will be your home now, so you should explore it. Let us get cleaned up. Elias should be back soon, and then we can head out. Sound good?"

"Sounds awesome," I assured him.

Another quick kiss from them both, then they headed off to get ready.

"Zander," I ventured.

"Yes, little dove?"

"Is everyone going to move in here? Or are they still going to live in the pack house?"

Zander wrapped an arm around my waist and pulled me onto his lap. "We haven't really had a chance to talk about it much. What do you think we should do?"

"Your house is bigger, giving everyone more space, but it's farther away from the core of the pack," I mused. "It's hard because both locations make sense, but living between both doesn't. If I had to pick, I'd vote for making your house our main living environment while still keeping things at the pack house in case we need it. I know I should want to be around the pack, but I like that we're set apart from them. And if they need something, it's not hard to get here, especially in shifted form."

"Selfishly, I agree with you," Zander shared, his lips ghosting along my neck. "Knowing that I have you safe in my home makes me feel better, and I have to agree with your want for privacy. Being a celebrity, it's nice to be out of the watchful eye of others. For you, though, I think it has to do with your elf nature. They lived in communities with each other, but they weren't as crammed together like werewolves prefer. Elves like to be near enough that if they needed help, they would get it, but not close enough that you'd see the others all the time. With your empathic abilities, I would think that it'd be healthy for you to get some more physical distance from the pack."

I hummed my agreement to that. Having the six of them home and safe with me was one thing, but knowing that the pack was surrounding us put me on edge. "How do you think Colt and Lane will feel about it?"

"You're not worried about the twins or Elias?" Zander questioned.

I shook my head. "They'll be wherever I am; they can't help it. Even though we aren't fully bonded yet, the connection is still there. To be honest, I'm surprised the twins could be gone from me this long without feeling a pull."

"How do you know that?" Zander asked, his voice awed. "That was something the man I spoke with today warned us about."

"Oh? What else did you learn?" I inquired, shifting so I was sitting sideways on his lap.

Zander grinned at me. "You're not going to like my answer on this one."

"When you put it that way, how could I?" I grumbled.

"He said the best thing to do is not to tell you anything more until we discover what happens once you've matured into your elven powers. There are many different branches of magic, and it's better to not influence you in one direction or another. Some things will be instinctual, like you just proved, and others we will tackle together with the information I've gathered. This man offered to come out and meet you if need be, but he's overseas at the moment, so it won't be soon," Zander explained.

I sighed and relaxed into him, not having the energy to stress about such things right now. I'd rather focus on the evening's agenda instead. "When you say going into town, what kind of town are we talking about?"

"Well, we back up to the Great Smoky Mountains, so we have a lot of small towns around us and a few tourist trap areas with shopping and restaurants. For tonight, though, I think we need to make the journey to one of the bigger towns with more to offer."

"Are we that out in the middle of nowhere that it's a journey to get to a substantial town?" I chuckled.

Zander just winked at me. "Let's keep some things a surprise, hmm."

"Do I need to change, or will what I'm wearing work for going out?" I questioned, looking down at my jeans and off-the-shoulder sweater.

"Like we would allow you to show any more skin to others," Elias growled from the doorway. "It's already questionable if I need to remove someone's eyes for staring at your sexy ass in those jeans."

Grinning at my surly protector, I winked. "You think my ass is sexy?"

"Yes," both Zander and Elias answered at the same time.

"Thanks for the confirmation there, boys." I laughed as I wiggled out of Zander's lap. "I'm gonna go find some shoes."

When I reached the door, Elias stepped in my way, his face dark with emotion. "Do I need to deal with Peggy? At the pack dinner, we warned the pack that we wouldn't allow any kind of disrespect like that."

"No, Milly laid into her already," I answered, resting a hand on his chest. "I don't want to cause even more trouble between us by having one of you scold her further. If she doesn't want me working in the greenhouse, I'm sure there are plenty of other places that would like my help."

"Just know that it's by your mercy that she lives. No one gets to talk to or treat you that way, my heart. Do you hear me?" Elias demanded, giving me a look that brokered no argument.

I cupped his cheek with my hand and stepped in closer. "I hear you, my protector."

Raising my face, he bent down and kissed me, gripping my hips in a hold that would bruise. Maybe I should have cared about that, but I loved the idea of having his mark on me, claiming me. Our connection hummed, but I knew it wasn't time to make him mine just yet. He pulled back and swatted me on the ass. "Go get your shoes on. The others are just about ready to head out; we'll meet you in the kitchen."

Far too pleased with his dark possessiveness, I couldn't help smiling as I jogged up the stairs to Zander's room.

Without the twins present, we could all fit in Zander's Land Rover, with me wedged between Colt and Lane in the backseat. The sun was setting, but there was still enough light to see my surroundings and take in the dense forest that our pack lived in. Soon, we were on the highway, and the forest fell away, exposing the mountains and the open areas that towns now filled. We drove for about forty-five minutes until we got to the town Zander had made dinner reservations at. I was a little nervous about being around the normal population, unsure of how my wolf would handle things, but I knew I was safe with my mates. The world knew about supers; it was just me adjusting to being one of them. Plus, it wasn't like we were going to announce our status as non-humans.

The restaurant's parking lot was full, and the sign outside boasted of having the best BBQ in the state. Colt took my hand as we headed to the entrance while Lane tried to keep people from running into me as we passed through the waiting crowd.

"If you would follow me, I have your table set up for you. We have your party placed in the back dining area," the hostess informed us as she led us away from the booming country music.

The space she brought us to was slightly more upscale than the rest of the restaurant, and only five other tables were set up with plenty of space in between. Another small group was enjoying their meal, but with the way the room was arranged, we had a fair amount of privacy.

"Can I just say that I *love* your music, Zander. Your newest album has been on repeat for weeks," the hostess gushed as she clutched the menus and gazed up at him with wide-eyed wonder.

My hackles rose as it was clear that she was making a pass at my mate. A growl rumbled in my chest, but before I could do anything about it, Colt turned me to face him, breaking my fixation on the woman.

"Easy there, little one," Colt chuckled. "Zander has no interest in her, but he has to play nice with fans unless they do something to warrant getting upset."

This didn't make me feel any better, but I allowed him to pull out a chair for me. Zander, however, had other thoughts about the situation. He walked right up to me, catching me around my waist, and kissed the hell out of me, staking his claim for all to see. He purred as he pulled back and looked down at me, possessiveness shining bright in his eyes.

"Don't ever doubt that I only have eyes for you, my little dove. Wolves mate for life, remember?" Zander chided as he winked and slid my chair in for me.

The hostess and the guests at the other table gawked at our PDA, but that just made me all the happier.

Colt grinned. "Your other side must be getting stronger in nature because I don't think an omega could have pulled that off."

"Oh, my wolf wasn't pleased with it happening. She was just too scared to do anything about it," I explained. "You are all mine, and no one gets to covet what's mine. If she'd tried to touch him, I'm not sure how things would have gone down, to be honest."

"Sweetheart, life is never going to be dull with you around, is it?" Lane said with a smile as he handed me a menu.

The waiter came out and took our orders without further incident, leaving us to chat as we waited for our food and drinks. The conversation flowed as we talked about our day and other happenings with the pack. Zander shared a few crazy tour stories with us, making me glad he wasn't on tour. Otherwise, I'd be leaving a trail of bodies everywhere he went. The atmosphere was so easy and wonderful that I thought now was as good a time as any to bring up my request.

"Elias and I were talking this morning," I ventured, knowing I might upset Elias since we'd already come to an agreement. My fear was that he wouldn't think I would ever be ready enough to talk about it with the others. Maybe I shouldn't push, but the human side of me was more afraid of being locked away than it was about making him angry with me. And right now, the human was calling the shots, not the wolf.

"Finley," Elias warned as the others gave me their full attention.

Ignoring him, I pressed on. "I know this isn't going to be the popular opinion, but I would like to work on training to fight as a wolf." My mates tensed at my words, and I could tell their gut response was to tell me no. "Please hear me out. As the past few days have shown, you can't be around me all the time, which makes sense. You all had lives and jobs before I entered the picture, and you still have those; I'm the one who's adrift without a true purpose. Working with the Organization, I spent all my life training, being tested, drilled, aiming for perfection. Now, I'm not using my body much at all, and I think that's part of the problem with my wolf."

"Explain," Lane asked, watching me with a calculating eye.

"I know everything about my human body. I know how far I can push myself when I'm working or hurt. I know nothing about my wolf other than the fact that the voice takes up space in my head. Zander was trying to help me share space with her instead of shutting her out. What if training and working with Elias or one of the other betas helps me bond with her better?" I challenged.

Colt leaned in, resting his elbows on the table. "Why one of the betas? Alphas are the strongest and better fighters."

"No, it won't work that way," I answered, shaking my head. "I've been finding that I do far better at managing my emotions when I'm around lower-ranked wolves. Elias, Noah, and Mason are drawn to me by my other nature, and that seems to make a difference in how I react to them. When you or the other alphas get too intense or your dominance comes into play, my omega side gets pulled to the forefront."

We had to pause the conversation as our food was brought out. I was salivating over the smell of smoky BBQ chicken and the sweet hint of honey in the corn muffin. Each of us being more hungry than we'd like to admit, we let the topic drop as we stuffed our faces, and I moaned at the taste of the food. Thankfully, Zander had doubled up our orders because one of the normal portions would not have been enough. After working all day, I was finally understanding how the guys could eat so much in one sitting.

"Let's say we agree that training would be the best thing for you," Zander started, bringing us back to our previous conversation. "Are you thinking this will mean you can start working for the Organization again?"

I could tell the others hadn't thought of this direction, and by the looks on their faces, they were *not* happy with the idea. "No, the woman who runs operations—my mentor, actually—told me that I was dead to the Organization. I was hoping to do more meaningful work like helping on patrol."

"What if another alpha comes across you? They could just order you to let them pass," Lane argued. "No, I don't think that would be wise until we know what developments your secondary nature will bring to the table."

"So, you're agreeing to the training though," I clarified.

The alphas all met each other's gazes before Colt sighed. "Yes, I can't stand the thought of you ending up in a situation like my brother and getting killed. Hopefully, with this added training, you won't freeze again."

Even though it was begrudging acceptance, I would take it and prove they didn't have anything to fear.

THIRTY

FINLEY

Once we were finished with dinner, we wandered through the downtown area because Zander had an obsession with picking up more things that he thought I needed.

"Little dove, you only have clothes and shoes to your name right now. A cellphone is a must. I want you to be able to call us at any time, day or night, in case something is wrong," Zander pointed out as he handed me a brand new phone.

"What about if I miss you? Can I call you then too?" I asked, being cheeky.

Zander caught my chin in his hand and kissed me with a growl on his lips. "*Especially* if you miss me. Better yet, you can video call me. Now, I think we need to get a laptop, swing by a bookstore—I've seen how much you like to read—and anything else you can think of."

"You don't have to rebuild my whole life in one night!" I protested, laughing when the others seemed to turn green at the idea of more shopping. "You three better send me your phone numbers, oh, and the twins too. Will they be back tonight, do you think?"

"Noah texted me saying it looked like they would be back early in the morning. They didn't want to drive back while tired," Colt answered.

I instantly pouted at the idea of my twins not coming home tonight. It was scary how quickly I was becoming attached to all these men, and on a much deeper level than I'd cared for anyone. Zander dragged us to a few more places before the others put down their foot and demanded to go home. With the trunk full of supplies for my new life, I grinned, snuggling up between my two grumpy alphas as we made our trip back home. Now that I had my new phone, I decided to text the twins.

Finley: Hey, it's Finley. Zander got me a phone.

Mason: SNUGGLES!!! I miss you like crazy!

Noah: Hey love, about time he gave us a way to talk to you when we're gone.

Finley: We drove into town for dinner, and Zander forced everyone to do some shopping.

Mason: Wait, don't tell me you went to Belly Up BBQ for dinner?! I fucking love that place!

Finley: That's the one. The food was amazing.

Noah: Did they tell you we'll be back bright and early in the morning?

Finley: Yeah, Colt told me right after you texted him. I'm gonna miss you in our snuggle pile.

Noah: Love, you have no idea how much we miss you right now. I'm almost crawling out of my skin with the need to hold you.

Mason: Yeah, what he said. I told him we should just drive back now.

Finley: No, be safe! I don't want you guys getting in an accident just to get back to me.

Mason: I can't believe you're siding with him!

Noah: See? Just like I said.

Finley: Goodnight, and I'll see you in the morning.

Noah: Night, sweet dreams!

Mason: Don't get too snuggly without us, snuggles. Sleep well. When I get there in the morning, you're all mine!

Mason: and Noah's too...

Laughing to myself, I tucked my phone into my back pocket and realized that something else was folded up there. The urge to take it out and look at it was strong, but I knew it would be better for me to look at it alone. Something in my gut told me that if someone could get past my defenses to place a note in my pocket, they must be from the Organization or one of its international sister companies. Thankfully, the guys were tired, content to just listen to music on the way back, because my mind was racing. When we got back to the pack lands, I could sense the difference in the way my body relaxed with the knowledge that we were on home turf. After we pulled up to Zander's house, the others took their truck to the pack house to get more clothes and things to spend the night.

"We really need to talk about consolidating down to one house," Zander muttered as he flopped onto the couch.

"What if that's what they're doing, packing up things to bring over a few loads at a time?" I countered.

Zander cracked open an eye at me. "What makes you think that?"

"Just a hunch," I answered with a shrug of my shoulders. "I'm gonna get ready for bed and look over these new books we got tonight."

"Sounds like a brilliant plan. I'll be up in a bit, just want to check in on a few things before heading up," Zander shared as he turned on a sports channel.

Grinning, I headed upstairs. I never would have pegged Zander for a sports fan, but it was March Madness according to what I was overhearing. I might not know much about sports, but I knew enough to fake it with the best of them. Assassins could never predict what information might be necessary to maintain a cover.

Alone in the master bathroom, I paused to listen, making sure no one else was lurking in the house. I quickly took my phone from my pocket, and the paper fluttered out to the floor where I snatched it up. Unfolding it, I saw it was written in the code all of us had been practicing since the day we started training.

The Dark Ring knows, and they're coming.

We have someone to get you out.

Be ready tonight.

You'll know the signal.

My whole body froze. That couldn't be what it said. Why would the Organization be sending anyone to come get me? Margaret told me that I was obsolete, so Finley the assassin was no longer in their records... but she had *also* said she would have my back. Had she sent someone to give me this note? How would the Dark Ring know about me unless someone told them? I'd killed everyone besides Delilah and her guard. Even then, they didn't know what I really looked like or that I had been bit.

Oh, fuck!

Dashing out of the bathroom, I raced to the nest and grabbed the laptop Mason had been using the other day. I didn't want to risk going downstairs to get the new one they'd got me. Better to do this quickly while they were distracted. My first thought was to pull up the news for New York. Sure enough, there I was being carried out in the arms of an international superstar on NBC's website. Motherfucker! With the matter being handled by the Senate, I had thought the video would have disappeared as well. If the Dark Ring knew I was with Zander, then they'd be coming after me, meaning everyone in the pack was at risk. *This leaves me no choice but to leave.*

My head sunk into my hands as my mind whirled with possibilities of what could happen. It had been five days since I blew up the house and fled, so they must have sent the federal marshals after me right away. Then Zander got his mother involved, so the Dark Ring couldn't use that move anymore. Speaking of his mother... I could go to Zander right now, tell him what was going on, and bring the Senate into this. Then again, I'd been sent to deal with this situation, and the only reason this was happening was because I had failed the job I was given. No—it was better to finish this myself.

While I came to that conclusion and found peace in that choice, my wolf was not at all on the same page. The thought of our mates or pack being in danger sent her into a tail-spin of panic. Her plan would have been for me to tell my mates so they could keep us safe. She'd much rather us shift so we could run and find a safe place to hide rather than head into the heart of danger.

"Sweetheart, what's wrong?" Lane asked from the doorway.

I kicked myself for not staying more alert. *If this is how I'm going to act, I might as well just hand myself over to the Dark Ring.* "Oh, I was just looking something up, but it wasn't the news I wanted to get."

Giving answers like this made me realize how instinctive the art of skirting the truth was to me. Everything I'd just said was true—but not at all what Lane really wanted to know. I couldn't let them know. If anything happened to them, I didn't know how I would live with myself. They were everything good and wonderful in my life, and there was no way I was going to let the Dark Ring steal a loved one from Colt again.

Lane frowned at me but didn't push the matter, holding his hand out to me instead. "Come to bed. If there's a solution to your problem, I'm sure you'll find it after getting some sleep."

"It's just hard when things from my past life didn't get resolved like I wanted them to." I sighed, walking up to Lane and taking his hand.

"There wasn't any closure, you know? I just got the rug ripped out from under me and was told to move on."

Lane tucked me against his side as we walked upstairs where I found Colt sorting through a suitcase full of things. He looked up and must have seen something in Lane's expression because he immediately paused.

"Everything okay?" he questioned.

"She's just feeling a little displaced between her new life and the one she was forced to leave," Lane answered.

Colt made his way over to me and cupped my face in his hands. "I know it's rough when life throws you curveballs and you're not ready for it. If you ask anyone, they've gone through something unexpected, but not all are as easy to adjust to afterward. Did you know that I was the one who bit Lane? All he was trying to do was save me after Cory had been taken from us. I had gotten severely wounded in the fight, and I was so out of my mind with anger and pain, that when he reached out to me, I cut him up with my claws and changed his life forever."

Shocked, I pulled out of Colt's hold to look at Lane, reading the sadness and understanding in his eyes. They drew me over to the bed and sat with me in the middle, each holding one of my hands as they talked.

"I was a human EMT at that point, fresh out of training and raring to save anyone I could. I was on my way home from a shift when I saw a naked, bloody man on the side of the road. My guess was a mugging or something else. When I turned him over to check his pulse, he lashed out, but I refused to leave. The damage had already been done at that point. I brought him to my place and nursed him back to health, and in return, Colt took me under his wing and guided me through my first shift. I was lucky to have him. Unfortunately, my parents couldn't handle my new life. They called me an 'abomination,' so Colt is really all I have now. Well, Colt and the rest of the pack," Lane shared, giving me a smile that didn't quite reach his eyes. He might make it sound like his parents rejecting him didn't hurt anymore, but I wasn't convinced.

Colt scoffed at that. "If I hadn't had Lane around when I lost Cory, I don't know that I would still be alive today. The universe decided that I wasn't a total failure as a brother and gave me a second shot while we both looked for Cory."

It was kind of adorable to see the relationship these guys had, and it made sense why they would be amazing co-alphas to the pack. "I'm sorry you didn't get a chance to see Cory again," I whispered, feeling awful for having been the one to end his life.

"Finley, from what you told me, there was no way for him to survive what he'd been through. As much as it hurts to know that he's dead, at least I don't have to wonder what hell he's living through," Colt assured me, pulling me onto his lap and hugging me tightly.

I tilted my head back and pressed my lips to his, snaking my arms around his neck and curling my fingers into his hair. Colt moaned at the contact and slid his hands under my sweater to run them up my sides, his fingers splayed along my ribs. Lane moved closer behind me, brushing my hair over my shoulder so he could kiss up the side of my neck. When he reached the spot he'd marked on the back of my neck, I broke from my kiss with Colt and cried out as pleasure shot through my body. Why were those marks so sensitive?

"Would you like us to take your mind off of things, little one?" Colt murmured against my lips before kissing along my jaw.

Lane bit down ever so slightly on his mark, making me jolt and rub myself against Colt's hardening cock. "Oh god, yes, make me forget everything but what's happening right now."

"Your wish is our command," Lane purred.

THIRTY-ONE

FINLEY

Between the two of them, I was quickly stripped and laid out on the bed for them to feast on. One thing I would say for this new omega nature was that my libido was now sky high, demanding orgasms from my mates. Seeing these two naked, hungry eyes directed at me, made me far wetter than I could have thought possible. Colt crawled up between my legs, tossing them over his shoulders so he had the best access to my pussy. Lane came up to my side and pulled me into a kiss that had me curling my toes as much as Colt's tongue against my clit. I moaned as they built the flames of need inside me until I was ready to beg for one of them to thrust into my needy cunt.

"Don't torture me tonight. I need you both to fuck my brains out," I pleaded as I grasped Lane's hard cock in my hand, pumping it to prove my point.

Lane hissed at my touch while Colt nipped the inside of my thigh before he sat up. "Are you saying we've left you so deprived that you're starved for our dicks?"

"If that's what you want to call it, I am in full support of your judgment," I answered with a smirk.

"Would you look at that? Someone is getting sassy tonight," Lane chuckled as he spoke to Colt.

Colt thrust my legs wide and flat to the bed, spread out for all to see. Good thing I was flexible. "Sounds to me like we might need to keep her mouth otherwise occupied, doesn't it?"

Lane grinned as he moved up closer. I sucked his cock all the way down, kissing his balls for good measure. "Holy fucking hell!"

"That's an omega for you, meant to take an alpha wherever he might like to give it." With those words, Colt thrust into me without warning.

They worked in tandem so that when Colt thrust, I went down on Lane, the two of them filling me at a savage pace. There was nothing I could do but hold on to Colt's arms as he pistoned into me and Lane made my eyes water. They had done just what I'd asked because in this moment I couldn't think of anything but my two mates fulfilling every need my body had at this moment. Lane pulled out of my mouth with a pop followed by a whimper as I didn't like him that far away from me.

"Finley, I want to finish in your ass. You up for that?" Lane asked, gently wiping my face clear of tears as I nuzzled into his touch, nodding.

Still buried inside me, Colt pulled me up and stepped off the bed. My legs wrapped around his waist, keeping us as close together as possible. The feeling of being one with him made me wonder if I could really follow through when the signal came to leave them. Lane came up behind me, kissing down my back, distracting me from my worry. With every touch, he reassured me, made me more comfortable with what was about to happen.

I'd never been the biggest fan of anal, but the last time we did it while I was in heat had blown my mind, making me rethink my position on it. Lane worked my asshole with two fingers, making sure I was lubed and ready to take him. A major perk of being an omega—prep time was a thing of the past. I felt the blunt head push against me, and I relaxed into the pressure as he filled me up, sandwiching me between two of my mates. I was beginning to believe that all other sex before this paled in comparison to what our connection brought to me in the here and now.

After taking a moment to make sure I was secure between them, they started to move. I pulled Colt into a kiss as Lane wrapped himself around my back, his face in the crook of my neck as he thrust. Moaning and grunting filled the air in a beautiful symphony of love and lust, our bodies practically reverberating with the strength of their purrs. Peering over Colt's shoulder, I found Elias leaning against the door jamb, cock in hand. He was matching their pace, heated eyes locking with mine. I grinned at him and watched greedily as he worked himself, making me wish I could have him here with us, but I knew he would refuse. My protector wouldn't feel as free to share me so unabashedly as my alphas did amongst themselves. No, he would want me all to himself for the first time. After that, I would work on him sharing me with another... or more than one other.

Lane started to suck on his mate mark as he sped up, letting me know he was getting close as he started to swell. Colt also latched on to his mark on my neck as he grunted, expanding inside my channel until they both locked in at the same time, tossing me off the edge that I was riding.

"Oh my fucking god, yes!" I screamed as they pushed me to my limit, keeping up their short thrusts. Spiraling from one climax to another, I didn't even notice we'd fallen back onto the bed, my mates wrapped around me like a pretzel. Grunting in my ear as they thrust, covering me in kisses, I melted into a blissful euphoria where all I could do was feel the love my mates had to give me. Eventually, they stopped their efforts to kill me with orgasms, and we laid there, listening to each other's heartbeats until they softened enough to pull out of me.

"Come here, little dove, let me clean you up," Zander's voice whispered over my hot skin, lifting me from the bed.

He cradled me against his chest and carried me to the bathroom where I found a filled tub. Stepping into it, we slipped into the hot water filled with lavender bubble bath, and he proceeded to wash me. I must have dozed off because the next thing I knew, I was being welcomed back to bed. Surrounded by my men, well fucked and cared for, I slipped into complete unconsciousness, forgetting about the note I had found in my pocket.

The sound of a siren going off jolted me out of sleep, and I abruptly sat up in the middle of a circle of mates who were also now on high alert and moving. Bleary-eyed, everyone was tossing around clothes as they got dressed and headed downstairs. Fuck, it was too early for this. Grabbing a shirt off the floor and slipping it on, I followed them into the kitchen.

"What's going on?" I asked. Colt was on the phone with someone while Zander was already opening up a laptop on the counter.

"Someone has breached pack lands; one of the wolves on patrol sounded the alarm," Lane explained just before a naked man banged on the sliding glass door.

Elias was there in a flash, pulling it open to let him in. "Alphas, there's a fire on the back service road; they set the supply shed up in flames. There were two more sightings of people dressed in black entering at other points as well. There's no way to know how many intruders we're dealing with."

"Alright, go to the greenhouse, get the watering truck filled, and head out with a group to get that fire put out. The last thing we need is the forest going up in flames. Colt and I will head to the pack house. He's calling all able-bodied men there to start our search. Elias, get all the women and children into the tunnels and take Finley with you," Lane barked out.

I looked around at my mates, ready to deal with whatever this crisis was going to bring us, but I knew what it really was. This was the diversion I needed to get out of here, but I didn't know what direction to go once I left the house.

"Finley!" Lane snapped. My body reacted to his command, instinctively spinning on my heel to face him, eyes wide. "You need to go with

Elias to the tunnels with the other woman and children. You have to stay out of sight. Do you hear me?"

I nodded, knowing that what he'd just asked of me was exactly what I could use to my own needs. Lane caught my arm as I moved to follow Elias, kissing me like it might be the last time he was going to. My wolf whined as we could feel Lane's warring emotions through his kiss, wanting to keep us close but needing us safe at the same time. She didn't want to leave him either, knowing we were safer together, but she didn't want to disobey his direct command.

"Be safe, mate of mine. We can't lose you," he whispered, his forehead touching mine. "Now go."

Giving a glance at my other two mates, both busily dealing with other matters, my heart tugged. If I made a big deal out of saying goodbye, I would tip them off. As soon as I was outside, I pulled my shirt off and shifted, taking off after Elias and our packmate to do as we'd been instructed. Once back in the pack village, it was utter chaos, with women holding crying children as men yelled and tried to lead them to the pack house. On the side of the house was a pair of open cellar doors, with children already being handed down to someone below. Elias shifted back and paused, waiting for me to do the same before he caught my hand and dragged me to the cellar.

"Finley, I need you to help the women and children stay calm in the tunnels. If anything goes wrong or they get breached, follow the stars. They'll lead you out to the border of our lands and into the mountains. Hide there. We'll come find you. Don't try to be a hero. I know you're strong, but you aren't prepared. Believe me, after this, you'll be getting some training. I swear on my life I will make it happen." A quick kiss, then he was off to help get the rest of the women from the houses.

The guilt of what I had to do ate at me as I slipped into the tunnels and shifted back into my wolf. No one knew what I looked like in this form, so it would be easier to sneak by and follow the path into the mountains. The thing about the Organization was that they were always prepared with overwhelming amounts of information about their targets; they had the resources to find out the pack's escape routes. At the moment, I wasn't sure what those resources were, but I didn't doubt that they'd know this star-marked path existed.

As I passed in the blackness, unnoticed, I studied those around me. Women huddled in the dark, clutching each other and keeping their little ones close. Thanks to my wolf, I was easily able to see in the dark, spotting the etching of a simple star on the wall, just past the crowd of worried women. *So that's what he meant.*

Clear of the hustle and bustle, I quickly ran through the tunnels, needing to put more distance between us as fast as I could before I changed my mind. Would I ever be back? Had Margaret changed her mind and decided to let me rejoin the Organization? Did I *want* to go back after I handled this? Too many questions, too many emotions clouding my thinking. This was the reason we didn't get emotionally involved in anything; it fucked with our ability to be objective. I was making the right call. I would not doom this pack because of the shadow that I'd brought with me. The Dark Ring was a danger to all supernaturals and needed to be stopped by any means necessary.

As expected, the exit was sealed with a thick metal door that was bolted from the inside. Seeing as I needed hands to deal with this, I shifted back. I kept my wolf close like Zander had explained, allowing me to use her night vision as I grasped the rusted pin set in the lock. Putting my body weight into it, I worked at the door, and the pin shifted... barely. Looking around, I spotted a rock and used that to knock the thick pin from its place, sending echoes down the tunnel. I prayed that I was far enough away that no one would hear it; the last thing I needed was for them to think we were being ambushed from behind. The pin finally shot free, and I was able to slide the locking beam out of the way and shove open the door, exposing the night air. Quickly closing the steel door with a deafening *clang,* I shifted and raced off into the mountains, knowing I would pick up on whatever scent I was meant to find soon enough.

THIRTY-TWO

FINLEY

As I ran through the foothills of the Great Smoky Mountains, I caught a familiar scent that made me pause. I knew it was someone from the pack, and while it wasn't a scent I knew well enough to match to a specific person, the hint of soil that I'd become all too well-acquainted with gave me a clue. Using all the tricks I knew and had learned from our game of hide and seek, I gave them a wide berth as I followed the trail.

When it became strong enough for me to know I was near where this person was waiting, I shifted back so I could climb up a tree and get a better look at my surroundings. It only took a moment to find one that towered above the rest. Out of curiosity, I focused on my hand, willing my nails to change into claws; amazingly, it happened, allowing me a better grip as I climbed. Reaching as high up as I could go, I looked over the scene. There were three people in the clearing, all dressed in black, along with another woman dressed in simple pajamas sitting on a rock.

I was right about whose scent it was—Peggy—but that made me question everything that I was thinking. Had she sold me out, or was she helping the Organization in order to get me out of the picture? Peggy might be spiteful, but I didn't think she was enough of a mastermind to manage this all on her own. Whoever was working with her knew me well enough to understand how I would react to the message and what the pack would do in the event of an emergency. It would seem Peggy had been the resource that provided the inside information on the pack, but who was the one giving them information on *me*?

Dropping out of the tree, I shifted at the last moment, easing my landing and muffling the sound of my descent. My wolf wasn't pleased with me at all at that moment, but it would seem being free from my alphas gave me enough control to tamp down her urge to run. Slinking through the underbrush, my wolf and I worked in tandem to keep hidden. It was easy to persuade her to keep us from being seen. The trick would be what happened once I revealed myself to those waiting for me.

"You said they would have the women and children in the tunnels by now. What's taking her so long?" a female voice demanded in a harsh whisper.

Peggy glared at the person. "You people are supposed to be the experts on her seeing as you're trained just like her. She's an assassin. What makes you think she would just fall into this plan so easily?"

"She's an omega now. Isn't she supposed to follow orders like a good little puppet?" another voice asked, this one male.

"That's the thing, isn't it? She's an omega, but she isn't acting like a real omega. She has far more spirit, and the fact that she has more than one mate—there's no way that's all she is," Peggy snapped. "I want her permanently gone. Do you hear me? This pack doesn't want her, so you better be serious when you say the Senate has work for her."

The Senate?! Why on earth would the Senate be looking for me like this? All they'd have to do is ask to meet with me. As a super, I'm under their jurisdiction anyway.

"You leave that to us. We just need her to get here," the man snapped.

"She's here already, has been for a little while," a silky woman's voice cut in, one that I knew right away.

Tabitha was the one person I might have been able to call a friend if we hadn't been separated right after our training. We'd been brought together for a joint mission that went off without a hitch, receiving better results than anyone had expected. Tabitha was just as lethal as I was, cold as the arctic when it came to doing her job, and one of the only people I respected as much as Miranda. If she was here to pick me up, then this was a serious matter indeed, so I took a deep breath, stepping out of the shadows and into the open.

"Foxtrot-seven-nine-five, report," Tabitha ordered.

I was pleased to see that my wolf was not at all fazed by her order, cautiously taking in everything that was going on around us. My plan was to fulfill what they believed about omegas until I was able to ascertain why I was getting called out.

"Following orders that I received via a note and awaiting further orders, Tango-eight-one-three," I responded, bowing my head to avoid meeting her gaze.

"Blakely, give her something to wear. I can't have you gawking at her the whole time," Tabitha directed as she turned to Peggy. "You are no longer needed. Remember, we'll know if you speak a word of what has happened here tonight. Do you understand?"

Peggy nodded and headed off into the woods without a word. Blakley begrudgingly shrugged off his jacket and tossed it to me. I easily caught it and slipped the jacket on, zipping it up to my chin so as to not cause the man more problems. It also made my wolf feel better; she was *not* happy that a man who wasn't pack or our mates was seeing us so vulnerable.

"Foxtrot-seven-nine-five, you are hereby reinstated into the Organization on authority of Mike-zero-zero- five. The Senate has requested that you continue the mission you failed by giving you another target and a team," Tabitha informed me. "I will be overseeing this so that there will be no further mistakes. If you fail this one as well, then you will forfeit your life, mate to a senator's son or not."

"I understand the situation," I said, nodding my agreement. "Who is my target?"

"Not here. You will come with us to the safe house where I will give you all that information; we can't risk anyone finding us here," Tabitha explained before she turned on her heel and marched into the woods.

The other two looked at each other and followed, leaving me one last chance to decide if I was going through with this or not. If I went back to my mates and explained everything, would it make any difference? Tabitha had already told me that Zander's mother would have no say in the matter, meaning Zander would have even less power despite being my mate. What would they do if they found out I was an elf? No, better to save that card for the last resort because I didn't plan on letting this next target get away.

Tabitha led us to a blacked-out Hummer, and I climbed into the back where I found a backpack filled with everything I would need. My favorite bodysuit, knives, guns, and my go-to poisons, stored in syringes and ready for use. That showed me that Miranda and Tabitha had no doubts of my loyalty to the Organization or my ability to complete this assignment. Tabitha drove us to a small airstrip that looked like it was used for the forest rangers, and a twin jet plane big enough to fit the four of us was waiting. Well, that explained why Blakely was here, considering he was a pilot, but I still couldn't decide what the other woman was up to. She didn't sound at all pleased to be working with a super. Or maybe it had just been Peggy; she did seem to have that effect on people.

Knowing that it would be go-time as soon as we landed, I leaned against the window and tried to get as much sleep as I could. I took this time to drown out all the noise and emotions my conscience and wolf were throwing at me. There was nothing I could do at this point. I'd made my choice, so I needed to see it through to the end, putting this all behind me for good. Images of my mates' faces appeared, but I gathered them all up and locked them away in my mind so that I wouldn't be distracted by them. All the lessons and meditation work that we did through training came to the forefront of my mind. I was no longer Finley the omega. No, I needed to be Foxtrot-seven-en-nine-five, one of the Organization's top assassins. By the time we landed, the dawn light starting to peek over the horizon, I knew that I was ready for whatever was going to come my way.

Shouldering my backpack, I noticed the sign on the airport said we were in the lower part of Florida. An SUV was waiting for us, and Tabitha climbed into the driver's seat, taking us to our next destination. We pulled up to a small house in the middle of swamp lands away from prying eyes. I say house, but really it was a shack that looked like it was falling apart from the outside. The inside was a whole different story. It was stocked with canned and dried rations, a secure satellite hookup for us to work from, and enough cots for six people. I could tell right away that this was not an Organization safe house; this must be something the Senate had provided for us. The Organization wouldn't have a safe house this high-tech or large since we never worked in a team larger than two people.

"Take a seat. We have a lot to cover before we make our hit tonight," Tabitha stated as she set up her laptop.

As I sat, I was able to take in the two other people I was being forced to work with. Blakely was a mature man in his late forties, early fifties, with salt and pepper hair, dark brown eyes, and a muscular frame. By the crew-cut and his posture, my guess was that he was ex-military. The woman was harder to gauge, but she was roughly around my age, probably older by the wrinkles around her eyes and the weathering of the skin on the back of her hands. Her thick black hair was in a tight bun at the back of her head, and she wore black fatigues like Blakely did, making me think military, but I could be wrong. The air that she had around her implied intelligence, like CIA or FBI, trained but not one to be out in the field.

"Vicky, inform Finley who her target is," Tabitha ordered as she continued to set things up.

Vicky frowned at the order, but when Tabitha all but ignored her, she turned to me. "Your job is to take out Rupert Sutton, the billionaire who owns one of the largest pharmaceutical companies in the States. Mr. Sutton is also a member of the Dark Ring, a much more substantial member than Delilah was. He'll be leaving tomorrow night to host an auction for kidnapped supers of all kinds. The plan is for you to persuade Mr. Sutton into telling us where they are being kept so we might free them before ending his miserable life."

"Easy enough," I answered, turning to Tabitha. "Why the extra people?"

"As I said, you've lost the trust of the Senate and the Organization with your failure," Tabitha answered bluntly. "They're here to ensure that things go according to plan... or to bring back your head if it doesn't."

How comforting.

"Where is the target located?" I asked, moving on.

"Mr. Sutton has a home in Palm Beach. It's a large estate with lots of space to hide supers. Blakely is going to get you close by boat, but you'll have to swim the rest of the way." Tabitha turned to Vicky next. "What's the status with security?"

Vicky grabbed the laptop and quickly pulled up the blueprints of the house. "We strongly believe that the supers might be in his own home with how advanced his security is. I'm sure it's nothing that you can't handle, but it will be a lot of perfectly timed movements since I can only bring down certain parts at a time. There was already a planted notice stating that the security company was doing upgrades. That way, we can account for any potential bugs in the security features throughout the night. According to information from the city permits office, Mr. Sutton paid off one of them to get an addition put on his house under the pool. He was *persuaded* to give me the plans, and it would be the perfect spot to keep supers locked up. It's reinforced steel with three feet of concrete, making it impossible to dig into or out of the space. It also helps keep any noise to a minimum."

"Alright, do you have the steps laid out for me?" I inquired as I studied the floor plan intently.

"You'll have an earpiece that will allow me to keep you on track, but here's the rough outline of what you're going to do," Vicky shared, flipping to a new tab with a detailed outline of the event.

We all worked on perfecting this for the rest of the day. I tried to stay as focused as I could, but in the back of my brain my wolf gnawed at me with worry. Why would they seek me out specifically? I mean, I knew the first job was botched, but the Senate was fully aware that I was an omega and no longer with the Organization—so why me? What was even stranger was that the Senate had sent their own people on top of

Tabitha being in charge. This whole thing didn't sit right with me, but I knew I didn't have the option to say no. That choice had disappeared once I left the pack lands.

Tabitha was a harsh taskmaster, so my only break was for a quick meal before I was put through the paces again and again until I could do it with my eyes closed. I understood why this was such a major play for the Senate because if I fucked this up again, it would show their hand in going after the Dark Ring. Two members in a matter of a week... Supers freed to tell their story to others... It would be their worst nightmare, forcing the Dark Ring out of the shadows.

I was too tense to eat dinner, and I could almost feel Mason glaring at me for not eating enough. He'd been the one to personally take on getting some extra meat on my bones. That simple lapse in judgment, thinking about my mates, almost undid all the work I'd put into locking them away for the time being. Once this job was done, I could prove myself and return to my budding family to grovel at their feet for leaving them like I did. There was no way they weren't freaking out or fighting over the situation, especially after finding out the whole thing had been a false alarm. Taking a deep breath, I looked out the foggy window of our shack and locked them away once more. I had a job to do.

THIRTY-THREE

ELIAS

I hated to send Finley into the tunnels without me, but I needed to help all the others. My pack was important, but I was finding out firsthand how clearly Finley was my priority. I started with the houses further away from the pack house, making sure everyone was out and accounted for. As a team, the five of us had developed this protocol for moments such as this when chaos reigned and no one knew who the enemy might be.

"Abby! Abby, where are you?" a frantic voice called out.

Rounding the house I'd just finished searching, I spotted Candice looking around wildly, calling for her daughter. "Candice!" I snapped.

Hearing me, she spun around and sagged with relief, grabbing my arm in desperation. "Beta Elias, I can't find Abby. She ran after her father before I could stop her."

"Go to the pack house! We're herding everyone to the tunnels. If she got lost in the mix, that's where she'll be. I still have more houses to check, and if I find her, I'll bring her right over," I promised as I guided her in the direction she needed to go.

"What if she's not there?!"

"Candice, we will do everything we can to get your daughter back to you. For now, I need you to do your part and be there to greet her," I explained, frustrated that she wasn't doing as I'd asked.

Begrudgingly, she let go of me. "Please find her."

"If she's missing, we will," I answered, cutting her off to send her on her way.

The pack thought me cold and heartless, and to be honest, I encouraged that. The farther removed I could be from the situation, the more rationally I could act. It was odd, or at least some sign of fate, that the woman I was meant to mate understood this on a level that no one else ever had.

The distant snap of a twig caught my attention. There was no way that whoever was attacking us was a super; we didn't make noise. No, the ones sent after such a large established pack would have been those that went bump in the night. The people in the woods were human, plain and simple, but the real question was what or who were they after?

"HELP!"

Before I could even think, I had shifted into my wolf and charged into the forest, knowing it was the voice of a child. Sure enough, there was little Abby, with her mess of blonde curls and wide blue eyes that matched her mother's. She was dangling from the arm of a vampire, of all creatures, throwing off my whole understanding of what was happening. The man stood in the waning moonlight, skin so pale it all but glowed. His red eyes watched me approach, and he flashed a fanged smile at me.

Shifting back to two legs, I leveled the vampire with a look that would make most cower in fear. The rage that burned inside me was always simmering just under the surface, waiting for the chance to come out and play. Now was a time that I didn't have to hold back that anger. "Put the girl down."

"Beta, you are barking up the wrong tree if you think I'll give her up for nothing," the vampire replied, lips twisted in an ugly sneer. "Make it worth my time. Hand over the omega you have hidden, and I'll relinquish the child."

I snarled at his request, and a new level of rage overtook me at the thought of this filthy bloodsucker laying one finger on my future mate. Thankfully, I knew that Finley was safe in the tunnels with the whole pack between her and this vampire. "I don't do deals with your kind."

"Oh, come now, don't tell me you're going to play into that whole farce about vampires and werewolves being mortal enemies. It's hardly fitting since everyone knows a dog isn't much of a challenge. It's an insult to my race if I do say so myself," the vampire sighed. "Now, go be a good boy and fetch the omega so I can be on my way."

The cocky bastard waved the child about as if she was just a doll in his hands, not a living person. Vampires might be toward the top of the food chain when it came to supers, but werewolves were right there next to them, ready to bite them in the ass when they faltered. Darting forward, I leaped and shifted midair, aiming for the arm that was holding Abby. One of the only advantages bloodsuckers had on us was speed, but this idiot wasn't ready for me to launch myself at him, giving me the chance to latch on to him. I flailed like an alligator dragging its prey under the water, biting off the arm from the elbow joint. The vampire screamed, blood pouring from the wound thanks to the werewolf saliva that prohibited their healing abilities.

"You mangy mutt, I'll rip you limb from limb before I take your heart and eat it!" the vampire bellowed.

Before he could act on his threat, I grabbed the back of Abby's shirt and sped out of the forest, handing her off to the first pack member I could find, which happened to be Noah. Tossing the girl to him, I spun back around with a howl echoing into the night sky. I had a vampire to hunt.

When I reached the spot, I found the arm but not the vampire; good thing the bastard was still bleeding. Nose to the ground, I picked up his trail, the path leading me away from the pack and into the mountains. The amount of ground the vampire could cover in his state was slightly impressive, but it just made the hunt all that more enjoyable to have a worthy trophy to bring back. Now in the foothills past our lands, I hesitated. I didn't want to abandon the pack when there might be more vampires hiding, but I couldn't chance this one getting away. He was here for Finley, and I couldn't let any threat to her live while there was still breath in my body, or I didn't deserve to claim the role of her Sentinel.

The blood stopped, the scent along with it, leaving me with nothing to follow but my own instincts. The night breeze picked up, and I caught a new scent that had nothing to do with the vampire. It set my blood boiling all the same. If what I smelled was right, this would be a bigger danger to my mate than the fucking vamp would be. Charging in the direction the scent led me, I found its source and tackled them to the ground, pinning her into the dirt until she submitted.

Shifting back with my hand around her neck, I growled a warning when she didn't shift back as well. Begrudgingly, she took her human form, eyes wide with panic and body shivering beneath the dominant energy I was sending her way. "What the fuck are you doing out here, Peggy?"

"I couldn't sleep, so I came out for a run," she stammered.

"This isn't pack land."

"I wanted to be closer to the stars."

A growl rumbled in my chest at her lies and the scent of fear pouring off of her. "You know better than to lie to me, Peggy. It makes me think that you had something to do with the attack going on back at the pack village."

"What?!" she gasped. "The village is under attack?"

"Seems whoever is behind it sent a lone vampire as a distraction that I was hunting before I caught your scent." Peggy started to wriggle under my hold as I spoke, only to freeze when I asked the next question. "Do you know what the vampire was looking for?"

"Why would I know that?" she challenged.

I narrowed my eyes as I searched her face. This bitch knew more than she was letting on, and I would bet my life on it. "Let's see if the walk back to the village will jog your memory, so when I ask you again, in front of your alphas, you might remember." Her face paled at that, letting me know I'd been right not to trust her. "Know that if you try to run from me, I'll drag you back by your tail if I have to."

She nodded slowly, letting me know I'd made myself clear, before we both shifted and headed back to the pack village. I made her lead so it would be easier to react if I needed to; thankfully, she did as she was told and returned without any problems.

"Shift" I ordered.

We had a few cells to hold werewolves that were awaiting punishment or couldn't be trusted in their wolf form around others. After I locked her away, I made for the pack house, only to find the whole pack gathered. They were all standing there, looking up at our alphas, along with Zander, Noah, and Mason. All of them were pissed, and the energy they were giving off told me that someone was most likely going to die tonight. Frowning, I headed right for the porch, knowing someone would fill me in. Colt spotted me first and locked his gaze with mine before he said three words that would ruin me far more than watching my pack get slaughtered before my eyes as a pup.

"Finley is missing."

THIRTY-FOUR

FINLEY

Blakely drove the black inflatable military speedboat as I hunkered down at the front, the ocean breeze whipping the loose strands of my hair into my face. He slowed as we neared the stretch of Ocean Avenue where Mr. Sutton lived. Blakely kept far enough from the coast that the soft sound of the engine didn't draw attention to us. He flashed me the *go* signal. Nodding, I adjusted my flippers and snorkel one last time before I tumbled out of the boat and into the shockingly cold water. My wetsuit helped to buffer most of it, thank god. Gathering myself, I headed toward the shore, feeling the drag of my waterproof backpack.

The border of Mr. Sutton's property was edged with a row of bushes to give some privacy to the pool. This gave me the cover I needed to creep onto the shore, ditch my water gear, and equip myself for the second half of this job. The first thing I did was open the small case with the earpiece that connected me to Vicky, giving it two taps to let her know that I was ready. I strapped on my knives and gun, placing my poisons in the small pouch on my lower back where they would be safe.

"You are a go to enter the grounds. Outdoor motion sensors are off-line for two minutes," Vicky alerted.

This was what we'd been training for all day; she couldn't keep the security down for longer than five minutes without alerting the company. Darting across the open section of the backyard where the pool was, I reached the bordering plant life that served as a privacy block.

I crouched as low as I could, hugging tight to the planters as I moved toward the house. Once I made it to the back door, I pulled out my lock picks and waited for the go signal.

"Grounds live, outside doors and living room sensors down. Target is asleep in his room upstairs, alone. Make sure to wait at the stairs for my go."

This was the trickiest part of the whole thing. I couldn't practice how long it would take me to get past the lock then to the stairs. On average, I could get a standard lock open in under a minute, but you stayed alive longer if you planned for the worst. I had three minutes to get in and over to the stairs before the motion sensor would catch me. The trick was making sure the stairs' sensor would turn off right away since they overlapped. Holding my breath, I worked on the lock, and just as I feared, it was created to deter being picked—at least by the average person. I'd mastered how to get around it with a modified tool; it just took the right movements. If I fucked this up, it would seal the whole door handle, then there would be nothing I could do but use another access point, and I didn't have the luxury of that as an option.

When the tell-tale *snick* of the lock sounded, I let out a breath and bolted for the stairs, dodging around the furniture that was hidden in the darkness. I didn't know that I could have pulled this job off as smoothly if I wasn't a super. Having sharp night-vision and faster reflexes to help deal with the tight time table was making all the difference.

"Well done, now count to five and head up the stairs. His room is the fourth door on the left hand side. He has a canopy bed, and the curtains are closed by the looks of it," Vicky informed me.

Closing my eyes, I took a deep breath, extending my senses to take in all the sounds and smells around me. There was something odd in the air, almost a metallic tang, and I couldn't place what it was coming from. Something about it seemed so familiar, but with my heightened sense of smell, it wasn't connecting to my memory the right way. This deeper access to the nuances of the scent were helpful, but at the same time, they made the familiar into something *un*familiar. Swiftly, I moved up the steps, thankful that I had five minutes to get into his room. His door was locked; however, this one was easy to pick. He likely thought his downstairs security would keep people from reaching him.

The moment I opened the door, I was hit with the musky scent of sex and what I could now tell was blood. With the curtains closed, I couldn't figure out if he'd just taken matters into his own hand and cut himself shaving or something. Otherwise, it could mean that someone had beaten me to the punch and lured him to bed, fucked him, and killed him, but Vicky had sworn he was alone. This was why working with a team needed a whole other level of trust because if I opened that curtain and he wasn't alone, this night was going down *very* differently than we'd imagined.

Silent as a ghost, I crept closer to the bed, peeking into the pitch black darkness while sniffing the air in an effort to get more information. I couldn't hear another heartbeat, but that wasn't a guarantee of anything in a world where supers were involved. What I *was* able to determine was that my target was alive and sleeping on the left side of the bed. The blood was coming from him, but the pace of his pulse, strong and even, told me that he was alive. Slinking to the head of the bed, I pulled back the curtain, and the soft light of the digital clock on the bedside gave me just enough light to make out the naked woman sprawled on top of him, blood smeared over them both.

Fuck! Dealing with a vampire was not something I was prepared for, but I would just have to make do. I could use a vial of the paralytic on both of them. It would only last for seconds with the woman, maybe a minute or so. Would that be enough time for me to cut off her head? It would have to be. I was far stronger than I'd been the last time I'd dealt with a vampire. In this moment, she was the greater threat, so she was getting dealt with first, then I would manage the pudgy billionaire.

I unclasped the knife on my hip, making it easier for me to grab it post-injection. Then I grabbed one of the syringes and readied it. Before I could doubt myself, I jammed the needle into her neck, causing her blood red eyes to snap open. They locked on mine, holding my gaze as I pushed the plunger down to shove the drug into her system. A sharp gasp left her lips, but I leaped onto the bed, grabbing her long, thick red hair to pull her away from my target and give me a better angle. My knife sliced across her throat, hitting her spine, but it didn't cut through it. Unable to think of anything else to do, I gripped her head with both hands and twisted, snapping her neck and ripping it off the rest of the way before I chucked it out of the bed.

"What the bloody hell is going on here!" My target spluttered as he woke up.

He hit a switch and screamed at the sight of the woman he'd fucked, now headless and bleeding out into his bed. My face was covered in a mask, adding to the fear permeating the air as he tried to scramble away, but I jammed the second dose into his leg, stopping his efforts. With a garbled cry, he flopped out of the bed, landing on the floor with a *thud*, his naked body wearing nothing but blood.

"Finley, did I just see you toss a head out of the bed?" Vicky asked once I pushed back the curtains and turned on all the lights. "Oh my god! You ripped that woman's head off!"

I looked up at the camera in the room and nodded, not having the time or interest to explain. Gripping my prey under his armpits, I dragged him over to the wooden rolling chair he had near a small writing desk. It wasn't ideal, but it would have to do. Once situated, I pulled out the zip-ties from my pack. These made it so simple to bind him to the chair by his wrists, ankles, and neck, giving me plenty of room to work with. His eyes were wide as he watched me manhandle him, unable to fight back or do anything about it. He broke out in a cold sweat, his body shaking when he tried to move and found he couldn't.

Peeling off the mask, I tucked it away, leveling him with a look of disgust. "Was she one of the supers you kidnapped, or was she just after your money?" He stared at me, unable to do so much as twitch.

Fuck me, duh. Sighing, I pulled out another needle and gave him a small amount of the antidote to free up his muscles enough that he could speak.

"Do you have any idea who I am?!" he demanded.

"Tell me where the supers are being kept for the Dark Ring, and I'll make sure you die quickly," I offered, ignoring his outburst.

He gaped at me, shocked. "You know I'm with the Dark Ring, yet you still attack me in my own home?"

"You get one more chance to tell me before things start to get worse for you, Mr. Sutton. Where are the supers you have hidden away for tomorrow's auction?"

Like all men who had money and power, he did the stupid thing and spat at me. I snarled at him in response, letting my wolf shine through my eyes even though she wanted nothing to do with what was going on. She'd much prefer to be cowering in the corner, but something else was combating her fear, allowing me to hold the reins.

I stabbed my knife into his thigh and got right up in his face, reveling in his screams. "I just ripped the head off of a vampire, and you think it's a good idea to piss me off?"

"You—you're a super?" he stuttered, trying to put on a brave face.

"Hmm, seems money can't buy intelligence," I mused as I twisted the knife in his thigh. "Might be why you can't seem to remember where the stolen supers are being kept."

"They won't let this stand, and even if you free them, you can't stop the Dark Ring. We are far larger than anyone realizes, and we have friends in high places," Sutton spat through clenched teeth.

"See, the thing is, you're the second member I've gotten my hands on. Granted, the other one got lucky and escaped, but I don't make the same mistake twice," I shared, ripping the knife out of his leg. "Let's see how many fingers it's going to take before you crack..."

I had to hand it to the man, he managed to hold out for four fingers. In the meantime, I got some useful information—through the choked back tears, of course. Especially helpful was the information about disabling the house's security system.

"They're here on my property in a secure room I had made under the pool, but you'll never get in," he sneered, his laughter borderline deranged. "The security down there is far superior to what I have in the rest of the house."

Wiping my knife on my leg, I slid it back into its sheath and headed for the control panel that ran the house's security system. Disarming it from the inside was easy, and now I was able to move freely about the house since Vicky had the access to cover our tracks. Jogging back to the main floor, I looked for the hidden entrance to the underground lair he'd made. In his office, there was a gigantic framed painting on one wall that just screamed for me to look behind it. I found hidden hinges on one side, and the catch was a magnetic lock. Following the worst security protocol ever, he kept a key for the lock in his desk. *Idiot.* Behind the painting was a thick steel door with a hand and retinal scanner followed by a keyed-in passcode. Seemed it wouldn't be all that hard to get into his secret area.

Back in the master bedroom, I promptly chopped off his right hand—I'd left all those fingers intact just in case—and then used my knife to pluck out his eye. "I'll be back if I need anything else." His screams would have echoed through the house, but I'd made sure to gag him. Better safe than sorry, especially after Delilah.

The hand and eye worked, which left only the passcode to figure out. For this, I counted on the fact that no one liked to memorize more than one set of long numbers at a time. I grinned when the same code for the home security worked for this as well. Lights flickered on as I headed down the concrete steps, leading me lower and lower just as Vicky had described. There was another door, but this one was just a handprint scanner with a wheel I needed to turn to undo the seal. Pulling the heavy door would have been impossible for me as a human since it took everything I had to manage it as a werewolf. Once the door was open and I entered the vault, I was frozen in shock by the sight of hundreds of cages made out of some kind of thick clear material. All those in my sight were occupied. Some were in their shifted forms, but the majority were human, cowering in the corner of their small square space.

Walking down the last few steps, I came face to face with the most stunning man I'd ever seen. His hair was so blond it was practically white, with highlights of gold intermixed. His eyes were a soft seafoam green color and had an almond shape to them that tipped slightly upward. He watched me with wide-eyed horror that didn't make any sense until the world went dark.

THIRTY-FIVE

FINLEY

When I came to, I found myself tied to a chair with thick chains wrapped around my shoulders, waist, and legs. I shifted around as subtly as I could, but I quickly realized I wasn't going anywhere. *Who could have knocked me out?* Then my attacker walked into the open, and I came face to face with Delilah's gorilla shifter bodyguard.

Does this mean that his owner is here as well? Was this whole thing a set-up? Did Tabitha defect and join the Dark Ring? Question after question flitted through my brain as I tried to figure out what the hell was going on.

"Seems the rat was caught in her own trap this time," the man commented, his voice deep and rough as if he didn't use it often. "My mistress will be pleased to find out that you're a surprise addition to this lot. Did you know she was trying to find you tucked away in that new pack of yours?"

I kept my face blank as he talked. The note I'd gotten said the Dark Ring was looking for me; I just hadn't known it was her directly. It would make sense if she'd seen me on TV and put two and two together.

"Imagine her surprise when she found out the pet you picked wasn't just any werewolf, but an omega. Our plant in the United Senate told us that one was being claimed by the largest pack in Tennessee at the same time the son of Senator Vaughn called off the marshals we sent," he rambled as he paced in front of me. "I knew Cory was an omega, but my mistress didn't understand what that truly meant at the time or that more could be created with a bite. Just think what perfect slaves they will be once we create more with your help."

Thankfully, they didn't know the other part of my nature that had made the bite take. For them to believe this meant I would be kept alive and most likely not sold in a normal auction—if it got to that. This gave me at least a fighting chance to get out of this, but I needed to get out of the chains first. *One step at a time, Finley,* I reminded myself.

"Seems I should go check on our host since you made it in here. I was told that would be nearly impossible," he muttered, frowning at me. "Don't go anywhere. There are big plans for you."

Once the big man left, it gave me the chance I needed to get a better look at what I was tied down with. The chair I was tied to was metal, but it had to be reinforced for super-level strength since I couldn't break out. Peering down at my feet, I noticed a padlock that secured the chains to the floor and me along with it. Taking a deep breath, I pulled on the chains with every ounce of strength I had; they creaked and groaned but didn't budge an inch no matter how hard I pulled or flexed. Panting, I relaxed back into the chair, leaning my head back to look up at the ceiling.

Tap, tap, tap.

Whipping my head around, I spotted the man I'd seen when I first walked into the place. He was smashing his chains on the clear barrier, his face a mask of rage as he threw his whole body behind the action. Finally, when I was sure he might give up, I saw a slight crack start to grow. He paused in surprise, and then our eyes met. I gasped as a connection of sorts slammed into me, coursing through my body and tossing off whatever invisible chains I had on my other nature that had been hidden for so long. My skin started to glow and pulse with power, causing the chains to burn against my skin. A scream burst from my lips at the pain, and a sensation unlike anything I'd ever felt registered in my brain. It was almost as if someone was pouring acid onto my skin where the chains touched.

In an effort to get away from it, I fought against their grip, thrashing until they snapped, and I tumbled out of the chair. My skin began to glow even brighter now that it was free from the metal, light shooting out of my fingertips and toes as if the power inside me couldn't be contained by my feeble body any longer. I screamed again, but this time it felt like when I shifted for the first time.

My body was reforming into something new, and once the power had done what it set out to do, I crumpled to my knees on the concrete floor, trying to comprehend what had happened. My hair fell loose around me, ten times longer and richer in color than it had been before. Reaching out to touch it, I noticed my skin had a shimmer to it, almost as if light danced in my veins. I felt stronger, powerful, ready to take on the world, and in the center of my chest there was a warm, soft glow of cool blue light, ready to do my bidding.

Brushing my hair out of my face, I looked around. Every cage now stood open, but none of the supers within them moved. All of them were transfixed by me, eyes wide in shock, and I couldn't blame them. If I were in their shoes, I'd be skeptical too. Taking my time, I stood, balancing on shaky legs as I took in everything around me. If I thought my eyes and ears were better after my first shift, then this was that on steroids. It was like getting glasses or hearing aids when you'd been living in a foggy world your whole life.

"It's all right. I've been sent by the Senate to free you from the Dark Ring. We need to get you all out of here before they come back to sell you off in the auction," I called out in a clear voice that sounded a tad bit more musical... if that was even a thing.

"She's *edhel*," a female vampire whispered to the super standing next to her.

"How can that be? They've been gone for centuries!" a wolf shifter protested once they returned to their human form. "You heard the gorilla; she's an omega. Only werewolves can be omegas."

This is bad. The one thing all my mates agreed on was me keeping my elf heritage a secret.

"I'm a werewolf and an omega, but before I was either of those things, I was an assassin hired to take down part of the Dark Ring. The Senate tasked me with that job, knowing you were all here and about to be sold off. Please, you need to leave," I begged.

Sensing movement behind me, I whirled and crouched, ready to attack if it was a super who didn't believe what I was saying. Instead, I found the blond-haired man kneeling before me, his head bowed and hand over his heart.

"*Nin emel, nin faer, i er meant na complete nin im am at cin service,*" he said in the most beautiful language I'd ever heard.

"I'm sorry. I don't know what you're saying," I explained, standing up from my crouch.

He looked up at me with a frown and cocked his head to the side. "*Cin don't heni- i lamb -o mín núr?*"

Shaking my head, I turned away and walked to the door, hoping there was a way for us to get out. There was a control panel that required a hand and retinal scan along with the passcode. Looking around, I found the objects in question, lying where I had been knocked unconscious. When I turned to head back to the scanner, the man blocked my way, his arms crossed as he looked down on me. Now that he was at his full height, I noticed just how ridiculously tall he was. I didn't know that I'd ever seen someone as tall as he was.

I sighed. "I already told you I don't understand you."

"How can you not understand your own language?" he bit out.

Blinking at him, I tried to figure out what he was asking. "That isn't my language. I was raised here in the States. Granted, it was through the foster system, but I believe my English is perfectly understandable."

"You were *what*?!" he snarled. "My mate was raised by humans?"

My brain came to a screeching halt at that. "I'm sorry. Did you just say *mate?*"

"Yes, did you not feel the connection between us when our eyes met? It's clear that you're my mate although I didn't expect to find you in the lair of the Dark Ring," he mused.

"I don't even know your name, and you're claiming to be my mate?" I growled in frustration.

My wolf tried to reach out and soothe me, feeling my volatile emotions bubbling up inside, but the powers that had been lurking deep inside me were now out and pissed about being locked away for so long. As much as I'd been struggling to manage my new submissive nature, this raw power was just as overwhelming to contend with.

The frown on my supposed mate's face grew deeper as he watched my reaction. "What have they done to you that you don't recognize the one who matches your soul? I am Rathal Zintris, offspring of Feno, the only surviving mate to Sarya of the Light Elves."

"There's no time to deal with this right now! I need to get this door open and make sure everyone gets out. Then I need to make sure my target is dead and try to kill the gorilla shifter that knocked me out," I stated, moving around him.

Jogging up to the door, I slapped down the hand, scanned the eye-ball—which I had to clean off—and entered the code. The door hissed open as I thanked whoever was listening that the gorilla man hadn't sealed the door completely. This time, as I shoved open the door, I didn't have nearly as much trouble thanks to my newly enhanced strength.

"Alright, everyone up and out. The security is off through the whole house, so get out wherever you can," I yelled before I charged up the stairs first.

I didn't have to look back to know that Rathal was right on my heels as I headed back into the study. My first priority was to make sure Sutton was dead so the Senate didn't have anything to hold over me. Entering the bedroom, I found him slumped forward, a large puddle of blood pooling under the chair. I couldn't hear his heartbeat or any blood flowing through his body—he was dead.

Hands grabbed my shoulders, and I acted. Ducking low under the arms, I stepped to the side, sweeping a leg out as I grabbed an arm and yanked the person forward. Rathal went flying across the room, though he rolled into the toss, then popped up onto his feet, quickly and smoothly, before he stalked over to me.

"Why did you do that?" he demanded.

"You shouldn't have surprised me like that when I'm in the middle of a job," I growled, baring my teeth in irritation.

He narrowed his eyes at me, seeming to look at me critically for the first time. "You're not just an elf..."

"No, I'm an omega werewolf who's also an assassin," I shared.

Stepping right into my personal space, he cupped my face and moved my head to the side so he could see it better. "You have a mate already?"

"Six, actually, but only three have been claimed. My elf nature hadn't shown itself until tonight when I met you."

I had no idea why I was telling him this, but with his touch on my skin, I could feel that connection he talked about humming through my body. Without realizing it, I was nuzzling into his hands, sighing at the contact just like I would if it was one of my wolf mates holding me.

"So your body does recognize me even if your brain hasn't quite caught up," Rathal said as his thumb stroked my cheek. "To be so young and still call so many to you before your powers had manifested is astounding. You, my mate, are something special indeed."

Tilting my face up, he dropped his head, and as our lips fused together, I moaned at how perfect it was. It felt like I was returning home to someone I'd been away from for years and had missed dearly.

Everything was new and exciting as much as it was familiar, such was the duality of connection. The sound of a shotgun being loaded had me shoving Rathal away from me before ducking and charging in the direction of the sound. My nails extended into claws as I whipped my hand out, slicing into the soft skin of the belly, making our attacker curse as the shotgun went off. Apparently, the Senate wasn't happy with the job, seeing as Blakely was trying to put a shotgun shell in my brain.

"Didn't anyone tell you it's bad business to double cross an assassin?" I snarled down at the man sprawled out on the floor. "Was this the plan all along?"

"You weren't supposed to be able to finish the job," he croaked. "They were supposed to catch you and sell you off with the rest of them."

"The Senate is working *with* the Dark Ring?" I demanded, confused.

"You'll have to find that out for yourself," Blakely said with a grin right before foam started to froth out of his mouth.

Fucking hell, the bastard killed himself! Tossing him away from me, I looked over my shoulder to see Rathal sitting up with a huge bloody spot growing on his chest. Terror hit me at the thought of losing him, and I scrambled over to his side, catching him when he started to fall back to the floor.

"What do I do? Please tell me there is something I can do about this," I pleaded, the panic I was feeling not at all matching up to the fact that I'd just met him.

Rathal started to cough, causing blood to spill from his mouth as he looked up at me. "I can't heal myself, but you could... Trust your power...it will guide you."

"No—no, no, no. You can't just tell me something like that. That's not how I work! I train, and I practice. I don't do things off of instinct. Ask my wolves," I countered, but Rathal wasn't going to argue with me seeing as he'd passed out.

Laying him on the ground, I pulled up his shirt and saw where the pellets had entered him, all centered in his chest so that they hit both lungs. There was no chance I could save him... right? That was just crazy talk! Magic like he was talking about didn't exist. No matter how crazy this world got, it just didn't happen.

Taking in the sight of his beautiful face pinched with pain as he gasped and struggled to breathe, blood leaking out of the side of his mouth, nearly broke my heart. He was going to die if I didn't do something, so what did it matter if I fucked up?

Closing my eyes, I centered myself just like they'd taught us day after day, letting my lungs fill all the way up, then empty, pushing out every ounce of air that I could. Feeling slightly calmer, I placed my hands on his chest, one hand over each lung, and did the breathing exercise again while willing Rathal's chest to do the same. I visualized the pellets lifting from this body, leaving the same way they'd entered, and the damaged tissue being repaired as they were removed. Breath after breath, I poured my will into my actions, having no idea if what I was doing would work, but the coughing lessened, so I didn't stop. Then, at the end of another breath, hands covered mine, and my eyes snapped open to see Rathal's seafoam green eyes looking back at me, clear of pain.

"You did it, heart of my heart. You healed me," he whispered.

Then he pulled me down into a kiss that took the air right out of my lungs, but I would gladly give it to him if it meant he didn't leave me. Breaking the kiss, I looked down at him, running my hands over his chest where a strange mark had bloomed, a mass of swirling lines that made the shape of a heart.

"Seems you claimed me, mate of mine. My heart now beats for you. My soul is tied to yours forever, and after a hundred years, my life is just beginning—as your Guide."

His words echoed through me, and I knew that they had power to them, but as he'd said, we had the rest of our lives to learn what that meant.

If we survived long enough now that both the Dark Ring and people within the Senate were coming after me. Not to mention that the world was going to know that elves weren't as extinct as they'd thought...

The end!

To be continued in book 2: *Hidden Nature*

About Author

Elizabeth is an International Best Seller, originally from Illinois but now living in sunny Phoenix, AZ. Elizabeth has been writing for nine years and started out in YA Fiction but recently found herself loving the Reverse Harem genre. Like her favorite books, Elizabeth loves to write about strong women of all varieties. Not all strength is flashy or apparent at first glance—some lies just under the surface.

Don't Miss Out!

Be the first to know what is coming next by following Elizabeth's social media! You never know when or what will be coming next!

Website: ElizabethKnightBooks.com

Facebook: Elizabeth Knight's Unicorn Queens

Instagram: elizabethknightauthor

TikTok: elizabethknightauthor

Newsletter: sign up here

ALSO BY

Book 1 - Two Tricks

Book 2 - Three Tricks

Book 3 - Four Tricks

Book 4 - More Tricks

Book 5 - Our Tricks

<u>Hidden Empire Novel</u>

Harper's Renegades

<u>Omega Assassin - Complete series</u>

Book 1 - Dual Nature

Book 2 - Hidden Nature

Book 3 - Perfect Nature

www.ingramcontent.com/pod-product-compliance
Lightning Source LLC
Chambersburg PA
CBHW060301310726
48976CB00007B/2161